1
Strike the Blood
The Right Arm of the Saint
Gakuto Mikumo
Illustration by Manyako
W9-DHN-849

Kojou Akatsuki
The Fourth Primogenitor
The world's mightiest,
laziest vampire

Yukina Himeragi
Sword Shaman
The Lion King Agency's
pretty watcher

Aiba Asagi
Cyber Empress
Gorgeous, selfish
high school cyber genius

Yaze Motoki
A friend...?
Cheerful classmate,
or two-faced jester?

Nagisa Akatsuki
Sister of the Primogenitor
Innocent, hyperactive,
and wise little sister

Rudolf Eustach
Armed Apostle
Weaponized exorcist
in a strange land
Astarte
Homunculus
The pure doll in which
a Beast Vassal resides

Contents

Intro		1
Chapter One	Demon Sanctuary	17
Chapter Two	Here Comes the Watchdog	71
Chapter Three	She's Crying	113
Chapter Four	The Right Arm of the Saint	155
Outro		203
Afterword		217

Design / Hirokazu Watanabe (2725, Inc.)

STRIKE THE BLOOD

THE RIGHT ARM OF THE SAINT

1

GAKUTO MIKUMO

ILLUSTRATION BY

MANYAKO

NEW YORK

STRIKE THE BLOOD, Volume 1
GAKUTO MIKUMO

Translation by Jeremiah Bourque

Edited by ASCII MEDIA WORKS
First published in Japan in 2011 by
KADOKAWA CORPORATION, Tokyo.
English translation rights arranged with
KADOKAWA CORPORATION, Tokyo,
through Tuttle-Mori Agency, Inc., Tokyo.

Yen On
Hachette Book Group
1290 Avenue of the Americas
New York, NY 10104
www.hachettebookgroup.com
www.yenpress.com

Yen On is an imprint of Hachette Book Group, Inc.
The Yen On name and logo are trademarks of Hachette Book Group, Inc.

The publisher is not responsible for websites (or their content) that are not owned by the publisher.

First Yen On edition: September 2015

ISBN: 978-0-316-34547-7

10 9 8 7 6 5 4 3 2 1

RRD-C

Printed in the United States of America

INTRO

A midsummer city—

The place was called Itogami Island, a small outcropping floating atop the Pacific Ocean. It was entirely artificial, constructed with carbon fiber, resin, metal, and sorcery.

A white moon floated high in the sky, but the sea that enveloped the city reflected a cold light.

It was close to midnight: almost time to shift to the new date.

Glass windows of buildings with the lights turned off reflected the illumination of lampposts, making them look much like cracked magic mirrors. The bustling city in front of the station was a dazzling sea of neon: family restaurants operating late at night, karaoke joints, convenience stores. The streets were still full of young people.

As they laughed in innocent clamor, they sometimes argued about silly rumors.

These were meaningless subjects, pure distractions from boredom. A common urban legend: that a vampire known as the Fourth Primogenitor was somewhere in this city.

The man spoke with a serious tone. The Fourth Primogenitor was immortal and indestructible. Rejecting his vampiric brethren, he did not desire domination, but only the service of the twelve Beast Vassals that were disaster incarnate, the sipping of blood, carnage, and destruction. The vampire was said to be ruthless and heartless, completely beyond the doctrines of the world—a monster who had laid waste to many cities in the past.

A bored-looking woman said...

—*Oh yeah? What else?*

This was the Demon Sanctuary called Itogami Island. In this city, monsters were not a rarity.

Up to and including the world's mightiest vampire.

The Fourth Primogenitor, subject of those rumors, continued walking down a sidewalk toward the residential district.

He had the appearance of a young man wearing a white parka hood over his head, swinging a convenience-store shopping bag.

He appeared to be fifteen or sixteen years of age. He looked like an ordinary high school student, which he actually was. His forelocks had a rather thin tint to them, like the fur of a wolf, but even including that, nothing about him stood out. Any way you sliced it, he looked like a completely ordinary teenage boy.

His steps were listless, but not because he was tired. He had the air of a high school student forced to carry the contents of the shopping bag, bought at the nearest convenience store, all the way back home.

There were other people on the streets besides the boy.

There was a pair of young women wearing vibrantly colored *yukata*.

The women were surely only slightly older than the boy was. They seemed like students, still, but they had a charm beyond that of a high schooler's. From time to time he saw the sides of their faces; their makeup was thick, but they were both quite beautiful.

The young man was walking apart from the pair. However, perhaps out of unfamiliarity with the wooden *geta* sandals they wore, the women's pace was slow. The distance between them narrowed bit by bit. Carried on the night breeze, the scent of the women's perfume drifted over.

A small shriek arose before the young man.

One of the women tripped over an irregularity on the street, lost her balance, and fell over. The *yukata*'s hem rode up quite heavily, exposing even the woman's thighs as she fell onto her rear.

The young man unwittingly stopped in place and stared.

However, what attracted the young man's gaze was not the risen hem of the *yukata*, but rather the backs of the girls' necks. He peered at the gaps between the collars and the raised hair, and at the slender, bare, white napes of their necks.

Even under the dim streetlights, he could easily make out the locations of the pale blood vessels showing through.

He cleared his throat a bit, once only, as if assaulted by a powerful thirst. He covered his eyes with his right hand, perhaps to hide his red-dyed irises.

His entire body gave off an unearthly aura. The girls raised their voices in laughter, not having noticed that yet.

"...!"

The next moment, the young man made a low sigh as he pressed on the tip of his own nose.

He began walking off once more as if nothing had happened.

Crimson liquid spilled from his fingertips. A lukewarm sensation spread within his mouth cavity. A nosebleed.

His blood smelled sweet and metallic.

As he furiously wiped away the blood that gushed from his nose, the young man left the place as fast as his feet could take him. Behind him, the women's laughing voices continued on.

The midsummer moon was above him. A lukewarm, humid sea breeze blew through the city.

"...Gimme a break."

The young man muttered to no one in particular. The nosebleed hadn't stopped yet.

A midsummer forest—

Late at night, the brightly burning fire illuminated the temple grounds.

Pale moonlight illuminated the hall of worship. A chill over the air, enough to make one forget the season, was surely due to the barrier that surrounded the Shinto shrine.

Even the noisy cries of the insects could barely be heard now.

The girl knelt in the center of the hall of worship without a word.

Some childish features remained, but the girl had a very pretty face.

Her slender body was delicate, but it gave no impression of being fragile. To the contrary, the girl gave off a sense of supple tenacity, like a finely crafted blade. Perhaps it was her seriousness that conveyed it: how her lips pressed together, the strong light that shone in the girl's eyes.

The girl wore the uniform of a private junior high school in the Kansai region.

Though a famed alma mater for Shinto traditionalists, few knew it was a subordinate branch of the Lion King Agency.

Three people preceded her in the hall of worship.

A bamboo blind obstructed her view of them. However, the girl had been informed of their true nature beforehand.

They were the elders of the Lion King Agency, known as "The Three Saints."

Though each was a medium or magician of the highest rank, they were enveloped by an aura of tranquility, as if there were nothing coercive about them at all. The very lack of it was frightening.

Subconsciously, the girl tightly gripped the cuffs of her uniform. Then—

"State your name."

She heard a voice from beyond the bamboo blind. The tone was solemn, but she felt no frigidity. The voice was younger than she had expected. It was a woman's voice that, somewhere in it, held the trace of a smile.

"Himeragi. Yukina Himeragi."

She answered a moment too slowly. There was a faint shudder in her voice from tension. However, the woman on the other side of the bamboo blind paid no heed and continued her questions.

"Your age?"

"In four months I will turn fifteen."

"I see… Yukina Himeragi. You began your training seven years ago, yes? Right around your seventh birthday…on a cold, snowy night, you were brought to the agency, alone. Do you remember that day?"

The woman behind the bamboo blind suddenly spoke in a monologue-like tone. A chill went down Yukina's spine. Surely she hadn't looked into that in advance. She'd read Yukina's memories. She'd shrugged aside Yukina's mental defenses with an overwhelming level of ESP.

"No… I have only vague memories of it."

Yukina shook her head slightly. Surely the woman had noticed that her words were not truthful. However, the woman said nothing of it, continuing her questions instead.

"Your grades seem good. Endo praises you highly."

"Thank you very much."

"It seems you have worked together with Endo a number of times. She was an Attack Mage of rare excellence. Your mental defense technique shares the same quirks as hers. Did Endo teach you anything else?"

"All ritual techniques, as well as shaman techniques, illusion techniques, and exorcism."

"And magical techniques? That should be Endo's area of expertise…"

"A general understanding of continental Chinese technique. Only basic theory of Western magical techniques."

"Any combat experience against demons?"

"I have undergone intensive training twice in training school, involving mock battles. No actual combat experience."

"Martial arts?"

"I am somewhat capable in them."

"Yes? *I certainly hope so.*"

She sensed a small laugh from the woman behind the bamboo screen.

"—?!"

That instant, Yukina leaped, sensing an explosive level of bloodlust welling up.

She kicked off the wooden floor, landing with a backward roll. This wasn't an action of conscious thought. Her body, sensing danger, moved subconsciously.

A blade rent the atmosphere, slicing through the space in which Yukina had been sitting a moment before.

If Yukina had moved even an instant slower, she would no doubt have lost her life. It was a serious cutting attack with a real blade.

Two large, armored samurai appeared, seemingly melting in from out of the darkness itself.

One faceless warrior gripped a large, unrefined blade. The other, a four-armed warrior, wielded bows to its left and right.

They were beings without physical form, *shikigami* produced via ritual techniques. No doubt the work of one of the Three Saints behind the bamboo screen. But before she could process that, Yukina had shifted to a counterattack.

"Distort!"

Chanting the short spell within her mouth, she focused ritual energy into her palms, slamming them past the attacking war god's armor, directly into its innards.

The armored samurai instantly vanished. All that remained were the large blades it had gripped.

Yukina grabbed the long sword that had been used as a catalyst for creating the *shikigami*. She used the weapon to defend against the second armored samurai's attacks, fending them off. And, the moment after her opponent finished firing its arrows, she sliced it in half with a horizontal slash of the long sword. The second armored samurai vanished without a trace.

"What's...the meaning of this?"

As she panted lightly, Yukina turned the long sword toward the bamboo screen.

She was not inclined to face any more *shikigami*. Inferior in physical strength, Yukina had no chance of victory in prolonged combat. Even if her opponents were the elders of the Lion King Agency, if they intended to continue this farce, she'd have to strike down the casters directly. Such was her judgment.

"Ha-ha-ha-ha-ha. Excellent judgment, Yukina Himeragi. Well done."

She heard hearty laughter from a man with a low, throaty voice.

Next, in a voice she couldn't distinguish by age or gender...

"Rituals and divinations might not be her forte, but she excels at spiritual detection and swordsmanship… Just as the report said, a classical Sword Shaman. I suppose I must first say you have passed."

"Passed…?"

As she heard the voices of the elders beyond the bamboo screen, Yukina knit her eyebrows with a sound of annoyance.

"Yes. Ordinarily, you would need to complete a four-month course to become qualified as a Sword Shaman. However, circumstances have changed. Please sit, Yukina Himeragi."

So said the first woman. Reluctantly obeying her words, Yukina returned to her kneeling position. She made a sigh and put down the long sword.

"Now, let us get down to business."

"All right."

"Good answer. First, look at this."

Along with those words, something appeared through a gap in the bamboo screen. It was a single butterfly.

Flapping without a sound, the butterfly landed in front of Yukina and transformed into a single photograph.

The person shown was a single male student wearing a high school uniform. Someone seemed to have secretly taken the photo while he was having a friendly chat with a friend. He had a defenseless, wide-open expression.

"What's this photograph of?"

"His name is Kojou Akatsuki. Do you know him?"

"No."

Yukina firmly shook her head. She'd never seen him in her life. Surely they'd expected that answer from the beginning. The woman pressed on with a tone lacking any deep feeling.

"What do you think of him?"

"Huh?"

The sudden question threw Yukina off.

"I cannot give a precise answer from a mere photograph, but he is likely either a complete amateur concerning the martial arts, or in beginner territory. He does not particularly appear to have any kind of dangerous fetish on him, after all, and shows no sign of sensing the presence of the photographer."

"No, I do not mean that, I am asking what you think about *him*. In other words, do you like him?"

"E-excuse me? What do you…?"

"For instance, if he has a good or bad face, if you like or dislike how he looks, and so forth. What do you think?"

"Um… Are you playing a prank on me, by any chance?" Yukina asked back with a sullen tone. She didn't know what the elders really intended, but she detected bad faith in their inappropriate questions. She unintentionally stretched her hand toward the long sword sitting on the floor.

The woman on the other side of the bamboo screen made a dejected sigh at Yukina's reaction.

"Well then, Yukina Himeragi, have you heard of the Fourth Primogenitor?"

Yukina sucked in her breath a little at the even more abrupt question. Most upstanding Attack Mages went silent for a while at the mere mention of that name.

"You mean the Kaleid Blood? The Fourth of the Primogenitors, said to be served by the Twelve Beast Vassals—"

"Correct. A vampire split off from all vampiric brethren, alone, aloof, and the mightiest of all."

The calm woman's voice reverberated throughout the hall of worship.

The Fourth Primogenitor, Kaleid Blood—

It was impossible for anyone even remotely related to demons to be ignorant of the name.

After all, it was the title of *the world's mightiest vampire.*

Not that it was a self-declared title, but at the very least the world had recognized that it was true. And at the very least, the enemies thereof made no argument to the contrary. That was what kind of being the Fourth Primogenitor was.

"However, I have heard that the Fourth Primogenitor does not actually exist. That it is merely an urban legend."

Yukina felt as if the woman shook her head at the words.

Primogenitors were emperors who ruled over the clans of darkness.

They were the oldest, equipped with the vastest magical energy, the "first vampires." Each commanded an army of thousands or tens of thousands of their brethren, constructing sovereign Dominions on three separate continents.

"Certainly, there are only three Primogenitors publicly acknowledged to exist: 'Lost Warlord,' who rules Europe; 'Fallgazer,' who dominates western Asia; and 'Chaos Bride,' who rules South America—in comparison, the Fourth Primogenitor possesses neither his own clan nor his own territory."

"Indeed. However, this is insufficient to disprove the existence of the Fourth Primogenitor," the man with the rough voice related to her, following the woman's words. In turn, the voice of the other elder followed his.

"Do you remember the explosions that occurred in Tokyo in spring of this year?"

"...Eh?"

"There was the train incident in Rome four years ago, and the disappearance of a city in China. There was also an explosion in Manhattan's seafloor tunnel. Also, a great fire in the old section of Sydney."

"You don't mean...this is all the work of the Fourth Primogenitor?"

Yukina's expression twitched. The incidents the elders were so casually referring to were vile, large-scale terrorist incidents with enormous loss of life. In each case, the culprit remained unidentified. However, if these incidents were the work of a Primogenitor, one could only call it fortunate the damage had been no worse than that.

"Though all circumstantial evidence, this indicates the existence of a Fourth Primogenitor," the first woman related as Yukina paled.

"They always appear at turning points in world history, bringing with them slaughter and great destruction to the world. However, that is not the only concern. The very existence of the Fourth Primogenitor disturbs the order and stability of this world. Do you understand the reason why?"

"Yes." Yukina nodded stiffly.

Vampires, a species possessing high intellect and vampiric characteristics, were by no means in constant conflict with humanity.

As many of them preferred to live their lives melted away into human society, they had been careful to avoid making an enemy of the entire human race until now.

Furthermore, every national government had signed treaties with the Primogenitors banning indiscriminate vampiric activity, bringing about what seemed like peaceful coexistence on the surface. However, that was the result of the exceedingly precarious balance of power among the three Dominions.

"In the decades since the Primogenitors signed the Holy Ground Treaty, the Primogenitors have remained in a three-sided stalemate with one another. Constantly concerned about the other Primogenitors, they have had no strength to spare to make enemies of humanity."

"Yes."

"However, should a fourth Primogenitor arise bearing strength equal to theirs, this equilibrium would surely shatter with ease. In the worst case, humanity would be dragged into a large-scale war."

"Do you know where the Fourth Primogenitor is located?"

Yukina asked with tension in her voice. She had a bad feeling about this, for some reason.

"Yes. Though not yet unconfirmed, there is likely no mistake."

"Where is he?"

"Tokyo district, Itogami City—the Gigafloat's Demon Sanctuary."

The woman's words struck Yukina speechless for a while.

"The Fourth Primogenitor is in Japan…?!"

"This is why we have called you here today, Yukina Himeragi. In the name of the Three Saints of the Lion King Agency, we hereby assign you watch the Fourth Primogenitor."

Though calm, the woman informed her of this in a tone that left no room for dissent.

"I am to…watch the Fourth Primogenitor?"

"Yes. And, should you determine that the target of your observation is a dangerous being, you are to eliminate him with extreme prejudice."

"Eliminate…?!"

Yukina was shaken and at a loss for words.

She was afraid of the Fourth Primogenitor. She was also anxious about being entrusted with such an important duty. Her training had not been shoddy, but in the end, Yukina was only an apprentice. She was not conceited enough to seriously think she could defeat a Primogenitor. In the first place, a Primogenitor was said to possess the combat power of an entire national army; they were monsters of the first rank.

But, unless someone did it, calamity would strike, and a great many people would lose their lives.

"Take this, Yukina Himeragi."

The woman presented something through the gap under the raised bamboo screen. The bonfire made the object, a single spear, shine as it floated up in the darkness. Yukina knew its name.

"This is…"

"Mechanical Demon-Purging Assault Spear Mark Seven, also known as 'Schneewalzer.' Its name is 'Snowdrift Wolf.' "

When the woman asked, "So you know of it, do you?" Yukina nodded vaguely.

Schneewalzers were weapons with special powers developed by the Lion King Agency for confronting demons. The spearhead, crafted with refined metalworking techniques, had an elegant silhouette resembling a state-of-the-art fighter aircraft. Truly, *mechanical spear* was an appropriate name for it.

However, since the weapon employed a priceless ancient spear as its core, it could not be mass-produced; it was said that only three existed in the entire world. Either way, it was safe to say that they were the mightiest of the secret weapons at the Lion King Agency's disposal.

"You're giving this…to me?"

As she accepted the spear offered to her, Yukina asked with an expression of disbelief.

However, the woman exhaled with a heavy heart.

"Against a Primogenitor, I would prefer a more powerful weapon to grant you, but this is the mightiest of arms we can provide you in the present circumstance. Please take it."

"Yes, of course…but…"

As Yukina spoke, a perplexed expression came over her.

The spear had not been all that had been presented through the gap in the bamboo screen. Wrapped in vinyl, there was also a brand-new school uniform ensemble, neatly folded and hand-delivered. Its base colors were white and blue, with a sailor-collared blouse and a pleated skirt. It seemed to be a girls' summer uniform for junior high school.

"Er, what's this?"

"A school uniform. It was procured to match with your height."

"Er… What I mean is, why a school uniform?"

"Your target for observation is a student at a school with this uniform."

"Wha?"

Yukina was a bit confused, unable to comprehend what she was being told.

"…The target for observation…the Fourth Primogenitor, is a student? Huh?"

"Saikai Private Academy High School, first year, class B, seat number one. That is the present social status for the Fourth Primogenitor, Kojou Akatsuki. So as you see, we do not have anyone available who can approach him peaceably, save one exception: you, Yukina Himeragi."

"Kojou Akatsuki… The person in this picture is the Fourth Primogenitor…? What?!"

Yukina's eyes widened as she looked down at the picture that had been tossed onto the floor.

She somehow felt the strained smiles of the Three Saints through the bamboo screen. Only now did Yukina finally understand why an inexperienced Sword Shaman such as her had been selected for such an important mission.

"Let us amend our orders, Yukina Himeragi. From today forward, *you are to make every effort to contact and then observe him*. The formalities for your transfer to Saikai Academy have already been taken care of. You are dismissed."

Leaving no room for any response to their words, the auras of the elders behind the bamboo screen vanished.

Yukina, now the only person remaining in the hall of worship, forgot even to breathe, simply continuing to stare blankly at the spear in her hands.

Fourth Primogenitor. Transfer. Contact. Watch. Eliminate. She wondered if she'd become involved in a terrible disaster. With such thoughts, Yukina let out a small sigh, still beside herself.

Though divination was not her forte, she would not know her intuition had been correct until a little later…

CHAPTER ONE
DEMON
SANCTUARY

1

Powerful sun rays poured down mercilessly from the red-dyed western sky.

"So hot… I'm gonna burn. To a crisp. I'm gonna be ash…"

A family restaurant, in the afternoon. Kojou Akatsuki muttered weakly as he lay facedown on the window-side table, utterly exhausted.

He was a high school student, complete with uniform. Aside from the hooded white parka, there was nothing you could really say stood out; just another male student. Thanks to the languid expression he made with his face and his narrowed, sleepy eyes, it felt like he was sulking.

It was the last Monday of August. The weather was clear. The external temperature had already surpassed the internal temperature of the human body, and even here on the verge of sunset, there was no sense that it was dropping whatsoever. Even with the air conditioner on full blast, the cold air didn't seem to have enough margin to reach all the way to Kojou's seat inside the shop.

As murderous levels of ultraviolet rays penetrated the paper-thin blinds, a listless Kojou glared questioningly across the table.

"What time is it?"

What escaped from Kojou's lips was a murmur, as if speaking to himself. One of his friends, sitting in a seat across the table mixed a laugh with his tone of voice as he replied.

"It'll be four thirty soon, in…three minutes and twenty-two seconds."

"...Geez, already? Tomorrow's make-up exam is nine a.m., right...?"

"If you don't sleep a wink tonight, that's still seventeen hours and three minutes. Gonna make it?"

The other person sitting at the table asked in a lighthearted, not-my-problem sort of voice. Kojou made no reply. He directed an expressionless gaze at the pile of textbooks for a while.

"Hey... I've been kinda thinking about this lately."

"Mm?"

"Why do I have to take this huge pile of make-up exams?"

Kojou muttered his question as if to himself, and his two friends looked up at him.

Kojou had been ordered to take a total of nine make-up exams, including two for both English and math, plus a phys ed half marathon on top of that. Certainly there weren't many souls who had to go through this on the last weekend of summer.

"...I mean, the range of questions asked in these make-up exams is too broad. I haven't even had classes in this stuff yet. And supplemental lessons seven days a week—what the hell? Do my teachers have some kind of grudge against me?!"

The two friends glanced at each other's face as the young man bitterly cried out. They wore a male and female uniform, respectively, from the same school. They shared a brief glance at each other, as if to say, *What's he going on about* now?

"Er... Yeah, they do have a grudge."

It was the male student who replied, twirling a mechanical pencil round and round, headphones hanging around his neck, hair short and combed spikily back. His name was Yaze Motoki.

"You just casually skipped out on their classes all that time, day after day. Of course they think you're dissing them. ...Plus you were absent without permission for the tests before summer, too."

Aiba Asagi smiled, gracefully touching up her nails as she spoke.

She had a gorgeous hairstyle and a uniform decorated right up to the limit of school regulations. Rather mysteriously, she still didn't come off as overly gaudy, perhaps because she had good taste. At any rate, she was a girl whose appearance stood out.

She'd be an undisputed beauty if she'd kept silent, but perhaps due to always having that smirk on her face, she wasn't very charming. Perhaps that's why being with her felt like being with one of the boys.

"...But that was an act of God. There were circumstances! For starters, I told that homeroom teacher over and over that my physical condition makes it hard for me to take tests first thing in the morning..."

Kojou made his excuses with an irritated tone. The thin lines of blood in his eyes were not out of anger, but from simple sleep deprivation.

"What do you mean, physical condition? Got hay fever or something, Kojou?"

Asagi inquired curiously. Kojou, realizing he'd made a verbal slip, halted his tongue.

"Ah no. I mean I'm a...night person. It's hard waking up in the morning."

"How's that a physical condition issue? It's not like you're a vampire."

"Y...yeah. Ha-ha."

Kojou smiled stiffly as he made a verbal parry. Vampires were not a rare sight in this city. The very fact that you were just as likely to bump into one as a hay fever patient was the real problem for Kojou.

"I love Natsuki-chan, though. She has wonderful taste. And she's letting the insufficient-attendance thing slide with the extra lessons, isn't she?" As Asagi spoke, she sipped her juice, making small slurping sounds.

"I guess," Kojou agreed.

"Plus, I'm taking pity on you and tutoring you, too."

"Don't apply for sainthood when you're eating whatever you like on someone else's dime."

Asagi glared vilely at Kojou across the top of the textbooks piled before her. There was no sign of where it all fit in her slender body, but Asagi was a huge eater beyond all bounds of common sense. He wished he'd remembered that when she'd told him *I'll teach you how to study, so treat me to lunch.*

"Just to say it, you're paying for Asagi's lunch with the money I lent you. You'd better pay up, Kojou."

Yaze pointed that out in a calm voice. Rich man's son or not, he was really uptight about this kind of thing.

"I get it. Dammit... And you call yourselves warm-blooded human beings?"

"No, no, any way you slice it, it's he who thinks he can shirk his debts who is the villain…and, besides, talking about hot blood vs. cold blood, that's discrimination. Better watch yourself."

"On this island, at least," Yaze said with a cynical laugh.

"What a bothersome world…not that *they* give a damn, though."

At the very least they don't give a damn about me, Kojou thought with a sigh.

"Aw, look at the time. Well, I'm off. Job and all."

Asagi gazed at her cell phone, and she gulped the last of her juice all at once as she got up. Kojou looked up at her.

"What was it, again? Part-time at the Gigafloat Management Corporation…?"

"Yep. Security division computer maintenance. Good stuff."

After acting like she was tapping a keyboard in midair, Asagi waved with a "Later!" and left the restaurant. Her carefree tone was like someone heading out to work at the cash register at a grocery store, but the Management Corp's security division was no place for an ordinary person to enter.

"I'm always thinking it, but it's totally unfair for a genius programmer to have those looks and that personality. It's still hard to believe, but… Yeah, her grades were way up there since she was a kid."

Yaze rested his chin on his hands as he gazed at Asagi as she departed.

Yaze and Asagi had known each other since before they'd been in primary school. They'd lived on this island for more than a decade, making them an older generation of Itogami City residents than Kojou's. It hadn't even been twenty years since this city, built atop the artificial island, had been completed.

"If it means getting tutored for the tests, anything's good."

Kojou spoke without raising his face. Yaze observed Kojou, his tone very casual.

"Actually, I didn't expect Asagi to tutor you. She hates that kind of thing."

"Hates it? Why?"

"She hates people thinking she's smart, she's a crammer, and so on. It doesn't look like it, but she had a tough time about it as a kid."

"Huh… I didn't know that."

Kojou spoke with a blunt tone while a complicated factorization problem was giving him fits.

It'd been four years since Kojou had moved to Itogami City. It was right after he'd entered junior high. Soon after, he got to know Yaze and Asagi; they'd hung out together every so often ever since. He didn't remember what brought it on, but his memory held that Asagi had spoken to him first.

"She didn't make one complaint about teaching me, though. She let me copy most of her homework this time, too."

"Oh ho. Quite mysterious. I wonder why you're a special case, Kojou. You ever think about that?"

Yaze made an exaggerated tilt of his neck, making what seemed to be a pointed cough.

However, Kojou only replied, "Not really," and shook his head. "I mean, I'm paying her back in every way she asked. Treating her to lunch, daily expenses, pushing her cleaning chores onto me… I've had it pretty tough here, too."

Yaze dropped his shoulders in resignation, his eyes saying, *They're both hopeless*. Kojou raised his face at his friend's odd behavior.

"Something wrong?"

"No, it's nothing. Guess I'll head out, too."

"Huh?"

"No, just I'm done copying the homework, and Asagi isn't here, so studying like this is meaningless. I'm only taking an extra test in one subject, so I should manage with just tonight to study. Anyway, hang in there."

Kojou gazed up with an absentminded look as his friend put his things in order and rose up with a "Later!"

Apparently, while Kojou had been adrift in turmoil Yaze had finished shrewdly copying his own slice of the homework. On the other hand, Kojou was largely unable to grasp his own homework whatsoever. Since this went well beyond simple preparations for a make-up exam, that was only natural, but the visible, overwhelming disparity was sufficient to smash Kojou's fragile heart to pieces.

"I don't even feel like trying…"

Now left all alone in the family restaurant, Kojou slumped over the table once more.

He realized he was actually quite hungry. But Kojou's wallet had no margin left for another order at the moment. The ability of all-you-can-drink soda to fool his empty stomach had finally hit its limit.

The popular image was that at least vampires could get by on drinking wine or tomato juice alone, but in actual fact, they got hungry and ate solid food like anyone else; he felt let down somehow. At any rate, sleepiness during daylight aside, being able to go have a normal life was a blessing.

Kojou, still ghastly pale, gazed vaguely at the pile of study problems.

Suddenly, he remembered something he'd heard during class. Among the various life-forms that evolved, those with the highest probability of survival were the species *best adapted to their environment*, and accordingly, the present survivors are the children of those best adapted—according to theory, anyway.

The logic of survival through adaptation was known as natural selection.

Some thought it was too simple, but the theory was widely accepted.

To put it another way, the species that had been naturally weeded out were those that had not adapted to their environment.

The same logic could be applied to the heroes of old, with power rivaling the gods in their hands, and similar species with supernatural powers that had not survived.

They had not adapted to their environment.

Kojou Akatsuki understood that very well.

No matter how much power you possess, no matter how resilient your flesh, even if you were called *the mightiest vampire on Earth*, such powers counted for nothing in modern society.

It couldn't even help him finish a single sheet of problems covered by the make-up exam—

"Guess I'll go home… Hope Nagisa didn't forget to make something to eat."

As Kojou muttered to himself, he stuffed his textbooks and problem sheets into his satchel, picking up the check as he stood up. He paid up at the cash register. His wallet, which always left him feeling dismayed, contained only a little small change now. At this rate he wouldn't even have money to pay for breakfast tomorrow.

What kind of excuse should he make to borrow money from his little sister? …As Kojou thought seriously about it, he made his way to the restaurant's exit. Then he suddenly halted. His eyes narrowed from the dazzling, setting sun.

Right in front of the family restaurant. Toward the intersection.

A lone girl stood amid the lighting.

A female student, in uniform, carrying a black guitar case over her shoulder.

She stood without a word with the sun at her back.

The girl continued to stand, not moving an inch, as if she'd been waiting there for Kojou.

2

Itogami Island was an artificial island floating in the middle of the Pacific, some three hundred and thirty kilometers south of Tokyo. It was a completely man-made city, built from a linked series of giant floating constructs known as Gigafloats.

Its total area was approximately a hundred and eighty square kilometers. Total population was about five hundred and sixty thousand. Administratively, it was known as Itogami City, and was part of the greater Tokyo metropolis, but in reality it was a special administrative district with an independent political structure.

Thanks to the influence of a warm current, the climate was gentle, with temperatures averaging above twenty degrees Celsius even in the middle of winter. It was located in the tropics: an island of everlasting summer.

However, the island's main industry was not tourism.

In the first place, there were rigorous inspections of all those entering and exiting the island. No mere tourist would ever visit.

Itogami City was an academic city. Representatives from major Japanese industries, such as pharmaceuticals, precision machinery, high-tech materials manufacturing, and so forth, along with research organizations from famous universities, all tripped over each other on this island.

That was because of one field of research permitted only on an artificial island, far from the Japanese mainland.

"Demon Sanctuary."

That was the other name that Itogami City had been given.

Beastmen, spirits, half demons, artificial life-forms, and vampires—on this island, these demonic races, their numbers depleted to the verge of extinction by the effects of environmental devastation and battling the human race, were officially recognized and protected. And their physical makeup and special powers were analyzed and used in science and development in several fields of industry.

Itogami City was an artificial city built precisely for this purpose.

The majority of the island's residents were either those very demons, researchers, or those with special powers recognized by the city.

The demons that were the object of research were of course included as well. The demonic races cooperating with the management of the special district were in turn accorded residential rights, the same as human beings, and were permitted to study, work, and live their lives.

Itogami City was a model city of communal existence between demonic races and mankind—

Or, perhaps, a giant, caged laboratory.

"—Crap, wish they'd at least do something about the heat."

Kojou cursed as he wore the hood of his parka low over his eyes, resisting the rays of the sun with all his might.

On this hot, humid island, the body felt the heat more than the thermometer level indicated. In a certain sense, the wind heated by the midsummer ocean's surface was harder to deal with than hot desert winds. Never mind vampires being weak in the sun—this was a pretty harsh environment even for regular humans.

Kojou's home was about fifteen minutes away from the family restaurant by monorail. However, the small change in Kojou's wallet meant he had no choice but to hoof it. Bathed in the setting sun, feeling like his skin was going to burn to a crisp, he walked along the seaside shopping mall.

And, checking behind him with a casual motion, he made an unamused snort.

"I'm being followed...aren't I?"

A lone girl was walking about fifty meters behind Kojou. It was the girl with the bass guitar case over her shoulder that he'd seen when he left the family restaurant.

The girl was wearing, as Asagi did, a Saiga Academy girl's uniform. That she had a ribbon around her neck instead of a necktie marked her as a junior high school student.

He couldn't place the face. While she was pretty, she gave off an aura like that of a stray cat unused to having people around her. Perhaps she wasn't used to the short skirt, but her movements threatened to leave her dangerously unguarded from time to time.

The girl was maintaining a constant distance from Kojou, walking at a pace that matched his own. When Kojou stopped, she stopped, too, hiding behind a roadside tree. All the same, she showed no sign of coming to speak to him.

She was clearly tailing him. Furthermore, she had apparently not meant for Kojou to notice.

"...A friend of Nagisa's maybe?"

Kojou weighed various possibilities and came up with a conclusion.

Akatsuki Nagisa, Kojou's younger sister by one year, was a Saiga Academy student as well. A junior high school student he'd never seen before taking an interest in him was likeliest to have some relation to his little sister.

But he had no idea why she didn't just talk to him if that was the case. Tailing someone under this burning sun couldn't be a fun thing to do.

No, to be frank, there was indeed *one* other reason why someone Kojou didn't know might be following him around. He just didn't want to think about the possibility.

"Guess I'd better check, at least..."

This said, Kojou entered a shopping mall he'd noticed. His destination was a video game arcade near the entrance to the mall. He didn't know why the girl with the guitar case was following him, but Kojou was wondering what she'd do if he went into a store.

And as it turned out, the girl was clearly thrown off. She forgot about hiding herself and stopped right outside the store, seemingly having lost her way.

She didn't want to lose Kojou, but if she did go into the shop herself, the odds of coming face-to-face with him were fairly high. That was no good, either. She was caught between two conflicting interests.

No, more accurately, it was simpler than that; this strange and unfamiliar place called an "arcade" had her on her guard. That's what it looked like.

The sight of the girl standing all alone in front of a beat-up shopping mall at sunset gave Kojou a vaguely miserable feeling. As he observed her from the other side of a crane game cabinet, Kojou was assaulted by guilt, as if he'd horribly wronged her.

"..."

Making a long sigh, Kojou reluctantly went back out on the street. It wasn't like he could remain in hiding forever, so he figured he'd try talking to her instead.

But, unfortunately, it seemed that the guitar case girl had thought of the same thing herself.

The instant Kojou tried to go outside, the girl entered the shop with a determined look on her face, encountering him right at the entrance.

For a few moments, their gazes met without a word between them. Somehow the guitar case girl was the one to react first.

"F...Fourth Primogenitor!"

As the girl shouted in a nervous voice, she adopted a stance with a lower center of gravity.

Up close she still looked like a pretty girl, but that only made Kojou feel even more dejected.

With that one utterance just now, he knew very well the reason why she'd been following him. She was searching for the vampire known as the Fourth Primogenitor. She didn't seem to be a demon after the life of a Primogenitor, or some kind of bounty hunter, but there was no doubt she was a troublesome opponent. No one sane was part of a group that would address Kojou as "Fourth Primogenitor."

For only a moment, Kojou silently pondered what in the world to do.

"Oh! Mi dispiace! Auguri!"

And suddenly he spread both his arms in an exaggerated gesture.

As Kojou recited foreign words he barely remembered, the guitar case girl looked up at him, dumbfounded.

"Huh?"

"I am…an Italian passing through. I do not…know Japanese very well. *Ciao! Arrivederci! Grazie! Grazie!*"

Yelling such things rapid-fire, Kojou quickly made his escape. He slipped past the side of the dumbstruck girl and left the store. A moment later…

"Wha…?! Wait, Kojou Akatsuki!"

Suddenly regaining her senses, the girl called out Kojou's name loud and clear.

Annoyed, Kojou looked over his shoulder with a grimace. He'd inherited the title of *the world's mightiest vampire* a mere three months prior. Since he'd worked hard to conceal it, only a very small number of people knew of the fact.

At the very least, here in Itogami City, only a single person besides Kojou himself should have known that Kojou Akatsuki was the Fourth Primogenitor.

"Who the hell are you?"

Kojou glared at the girl to display his wariness.

The girl returned Kojou's gaze with serious eyes, replying with a hard, somewhat grown-up voice.

"I'm a Sword Shaman of the Lion King Agency. By the command of the Three Saints of the Lion King Agency, I have come on assignment to watch over the Fourth Primogenitor."

Ha, thought Kojou, listening to the girl's words with a stale face. He had no idea what the girl was saying. Lion King Agency. Sword Shaman. He'd never heard of those terms before.

The only thing conveyed was that his premonition that this was trouble had been exceedingly prescient.

Utterly perplexed as to how to deal with this, Kojou finally decided to act like he hadn't heard any of it.

"Ah… Sorry. You've got the wrong guy. Go try someone else."

"Eh? Wrong guy? Eh…?"

The girl's gaze wandered about, looking confused. Kojou had just made up the wrong-guy thing on the fly, but she seemed to have actually bought it.

Perhaps she just had an unusually frank personality.

As Kojou seized the opportunity, turning his back to her and running off, the girl hurriedly called out to him.

"W-wait, please! I don't really have the wrong guy, do I?!"

"No, keeping watch and stuff, that's got nothing to do with me. I'm busy, so…!"

Kojou made a sloppy wave as he left the place in a rush.

The girl with the guitar case on her back stood in place where she was, a dumbfounded, bewildered expression still on her face. Whether his assertion of mistaken identity had done the trick or not, she seemed to have given up on tailing him. Even so, he still had no idea what she really was, so the matter remained fundamentally unresolved, but that was still better than being sucked into something troublesome on the day before a make-up exam.

Arriving around the entrance to the shopping mall, he looked back one more time to make sure the girl wasn't following him. The scene that greeted his eyes startled him.

Two guys he didn't know were standing together in front of the guitar case girl from earlier, obstructing her path.

They looked twenty years old, give or take. They had long, extravagantly dyed hair and gigolo-style black suits that didn't suit them all that well. They seemed to be frivolous, easy-to-understand men.

"…Hey, you there, baby. What's wrong? Guy-hunting didn't work out?"

"If you're bored, how 'bout you come play with us? We just got paid, so we're loaded…"

He heard bits and pieces of the men's voices over the wind. They seemed to be hitting on the girl he'd distanced himself from.

The girl brushed the men off with a cold attitude, but that only seemed to make the atmosphere stormier. One of the men yelled at her in a rough voice; Kojou saw the girl talk back with a sharp expression.

"...Little old to be layin' a finger on a junior high schooler, aren't you, geezers?"

Color faded from Kojou's face. He knew he should let things be, but the girl knew of the existence of the Fourth Primogenitor and had been following him around. If by some chance this got out of hand and became a law enforcement matter, there was no guarantee it wouldn't lead straight to Kojou.

And Kojou had another reason for concern: the metal bracelets around both men's wrists. Those were Demon IDs, with biosensors, magic sensors, and transmitters, etc., inside them. Those who wore them were not human. They were special registered citizens of the Demon Sanctuary. In other words, inhuman. "Freaks"—that's what they were sometimes called.

It wasn't often that bracelet-wearing registered demons caused harm to human beings. If they did, the Island Guard's Counter-Demon Agents came after them in force. Therefore, the girl was in no immediate danger.

The problem was, it was possible the fact that he was the Fourth Primogenitor might slip from the girl's lips.

If that happened, the name Kojou Akatsuki would be on every demon's lips in no time. And naturally, there would no doubt be those who wanted to make an ally out of Kojou, those who'd want to use him as a guinea pig, and perhaps even those who wanted to kill him to raise their notoriety. Any way you sliced it, it'd herald the end of Kojou's days of peaceful living. He had to smooth things over here somehow before that happened.

With a deep sigh, Kojou began to run back toward the guitar case girl.

The next moment, the skirt of the girl's uniform fluttered up.

One of the men, having flipped the girl's skirt, spit out a reckless remark that sounded like, "Well, ain't you all high and mighty." Kojou unwittingly stiffened, the checkered pastel colors that had appeared filling his field of vision. Then...

"Young Thunder!"

The girl's beautiful eyebrows raised high, she chanted a spell; the next moment, the body of the man who'd laid his hand on her skirt was blown away with enough force to flip a truck.

3

Probably an open palm strike, he thought.

But whatever had actually occurred, there was no way Kojou had an accurate understanding of it. What he *did* understand was that with a single blow, the small girl's thrusting arms had blown a grown man away.

He hadn't felt any flow of magic. He had not sensed the work of spirits. Of the remaining possibilities, some kind of qigong or arcane art perhaps. At any rate, there was no question the girl had considerable skill.

Kojou surmised that the girl might be much older than she appeared to be, but he immediately corrected himself: No, couldn't be. There wasn't—*couldn't be*—any long-lived species that would wear cute panties like that.

The man who'd been blown away seemed to be some kind of anthropomorph; in other words, a werewolf or close cousin thereof. Though he didn't seem all that powerful, his physical strength and toughness still far surpassed that of a human being. Yet receiving a single blow from a delicate girl had sent him smashing into a wall, from which he did not move.

"This brat's an Attack Mage—?!"

The other man had been in shock, and finally shouted once he regained his senses.

Counter-Demon Attack Mage was a catchall term for human beings who possessed various skills, such as sorcery and spiritual power, to oppose demonkind. Be they employed by armies, police S.W.A.T. units, private security corporations, or yet other organizations, they belonged to many groups, and the skills they used came in numerous varieties, but whatever the case, there was no doubt they were the worst enemies of demonkind. No small number of Attack Mages made a living exclusively as demon hunters, much like assassins.

Of course, in the Demon Sanctuary of Itogami City, the activities of Attack Mages were as strictly regulated as those of demons. At the very least, one didn't get attacked just for talking to a girl on the side of the road.

But, the man was surely unnerved because it had happened so suddenly.

His expression twisted by fear and anger, his true, demonic nature asserted itself. Crimson eyes. And…fangs.

"A D-type—!"

The girl's expression turned grim. Among the various types of vampires, D-type referred to those who claimed the "Lost Warlord" as their Primogenitor, chiefly seen in Europe. They were the vampires that best fit human beings' common perceptions about vampires.

What'll you do? Kojou asked himself, bewildered.

By normal thinking, you should go rescue a girl being attacked by a vampire, but it seemed that this girl was no ordinary middle schooler.

The girl had been following Kojou around, to begin with. Worst case, she was Kojou's enemy. The chances of an Attack Mage targeting Kojou were certainly not zero.

But even so, he couldn't just let her be.

Her opponent was no ordinary demon. He was a vampire. No matter how skilled an Attack Mage she was, he didn't think she could defeat a vampire all by herself.

Even if this was before sunset, vampires had physical powers far surpassing common sense, and resisted magic as well. And they had incredible regenerative abilities. Moreover, they had one other, overwhelming trump card to play, suited to those called Lords of Demonkind.

"—Shakti! Take her out!" the vampire man yelled out; a moment later, something spewed forth from his left leg.

It resembled fresh blood, but it wasn't blood at all. This was black fire, shimmering like yin and yang.

From that black fire finally emerged the distorted shape of a horse.

Its high-pitched neigh made the air shudder; the flames that enveloped it scorched the asphalt.

"To employ a Beast Vassal in the middle of a city—!" the girl shouted with an angry expression.

The bracelet the man wore on his left hand, having detected offensive magic, emitted a noisy alarm. A siren blared, urging those at the shopping mall to evacuate.

A Beast Vassal. Yes, the monster that the man had summoned was a familiar called a Beast Vassal.

The existence of Beast Vassals was the very reason Attack Mages feared vampires.

There were numerous demon races that matched vampires in brute strength, agility, and innate special powers. In spite of that, why were vampires alone feared as the Lords of Demonkind…?

The answer was Beast Vassals.

Beast Vassals came with a variety of forms and abilities. However, even the least powerful among them surpassed the combat strength of an attack helicopter or a state-of-the-art main battle tank. It was said that the Beast Vassals employed by the "Elders" were capable of blowing away entire villages.

Naturally, the Beast Vassal of the young man was not quite that capable. However, no doubt the incandescent ghost horse could do enough damage merely running around to take out an entire shopping mall.

He'd turned and set loose a dangerous summoned beast like that against a single girl.

Surely the man who was its lord had never turned a Beast Vassal on a human in the flesh outside of a laboratory setting. His expression was gripped by fear, the strain of magical feedback apparently heavy.

The Beast Vassal he'd let off the leash was in a quasi-berserk state, mowing down trees along the street and melting down metal streetlights. It was literally a mass of destructive energy with a mind of its own. Surely a single graze would turn a human being's body to ash in an instant.

In spite of that, the girl's face showed no sign of fear whatsoever.

"Snowdrift Wolf—!"

The girl drew something out of the guitar case still on her back.

It was no musical instrument, but a silver spear with an icy sparkle.

In an instant, the spear's shaft slid longer, and at the same time, the main blade stored within thrust out as a spear tip. Side blades extended to the left and right of the main blade like the wings of a variable-geometry fighter plane. Its appearance was that of a weapon refined for modern times.

But there was no doubt this was a primeval thrusting weapon. He didn't think it could oppose the Beast Vassal scattering tremendous flames all about. Indeed, he had his doubts a girl of such small size could even swing the thing around. However, the girl's alert eyes glared coldly at the Beast Vassal as it pressed near.

Whew. A quiet exhale escaped the girl's lips.

The girl easily controlled the beautiful spear's nearly two-meter length, thrusting it toward the flaming ghost horse running amok. However, the ghost horse did not halt its charge.

A vampire's Beast Vassal was a sentient mass of magical power so ultra-dense as to take physical form. In other words, it was magic itself. Once released, there was no way to stop a Beast Vassal except by smashing it with an even more powerful magical force.

For the girl to attack it would be like turning a single spear against an overflow of lava.

The man laughed because he knew as much. It was not a laugh confident of victory. It was a straightforward laugh of relief. He was simply afraid of her. Afraid of the unknown Attack Mage girl who'd blown away his pal with a single blow—

But, in a single instant, the man's laugh of relief was drenched in fear.

"Wha…?!"

For he saw his Beast Vassal had stopped, impaled by the silver spear.

The girl had wordlessly thrust her spear in a flash. The ghost horse's giant body warped, ripped apart, and vanished without a trace.

It had been as quick as snuffing out the flame of a candle. The form of the Beast Vassal had completely vanished. All that remained was the scorched asphalt.

"N…no way! Wiping out my Beast Vassal in one shot?!"

The man gave a much-delayed shudder at the loss of his familiar. However, the girl's expression remained a grimace.

She glared at the man with anger-filled eyes, poised her spear, and charged his frozen, unmoving form. And, just as the silver spear was about to impale the man's heart—

"Whoa there!"

The spear's tip suddenly veered up, changing course.

"Huh?!"

The girl's eyes, brimming with cold rage, widened in surprise.

It was Kojou who stood there.

Kojou leaped in from parts unseen, deflecting the spear just in the nick of time, halting the girl's attack. He hadn't wanted to get involved in a fight between a vampire and an Attack Mage, but he couldn't just stand back as a life was taken. Surely the vampire didn't want to die by impaling just because he'd made an unsuccessful pass at a junior high schooler.

"Kojou Akatsuki?! Stopping Snowdrift Wolf with your bare hand…!"

The Attack Mage girl leaped back with a shocked expression. As she put some distance between them, wary of the suddenly appearing Kojou, she landed on the roof of a station wagon parked nearby.

"Hey, you. Grab your pal and get out of here," Kojou yelled in an agitated tone to the man, still rooted in place behind his back. "And learn your lesson already. Don't pick up junior high schoolers. And don't use Beast Vassals irresponsibly, either!"

"Y…yeah… S-sorry… I owe you one!"

The man nodded, his face pale, then carried off his pal's unconscious body. The girl glared at their backs with hostile eyes. Kojou made an exasperated sigh.

"You, too… I don't know what you meant to do, but it's too much. Just let it go."

When she heard the seemingly tired Kojou's words, the girl's shoulders shook with surprise. Alertly keeping her spear's guard up, she gave Kojou a sullen glare. She spoke with a scolding tone.

"Why did you interfere?"

Kojou's expression became even more languid.

"'Interfere,' huh? I think it's normal to stop a fight that's happening right in front of you. Why do you know my name, anyway?"

"…To turn demon in a public place, and furthermore, use a Beast Vassal in an urban area, are flagrant violations of the Holy Ground Treaty. Surely no one would question it even if they were killed."

"Since you're gonna put it like that, weren't you the one who struck first?"

"That's not—"

The girl went silent midway as if calmly reflecting on the matter. She seemed to be recalling how the dispute with the men had began. *See?* thought Kojou, giving the girl a strong stare.

"I don't know who you are, but waving that thing around and trying to kill people over having your panties seen a little is a bit much. Just because demons are concerned..."

As he spoke to that point, Kojou realized he'd slipped up. The girl poised with the silver spear glared at Kojou with a disgusted look.

"Did *you* see them, by any chance?"

"Ah, er, that's..."

Kojou's lips fumbled for an excuse. Surely she thought he was a guy who'd not only abandoned a girl getting hit on, he'd arbitrarily saved demons running wild in an urban area. And as that was in fact the case, all he could do was try to explain it away.

"Hey, now, it's not anything to get that worked up over. It's not like I'm interested in a junior high schooler's underwear, and they were kinda cute and all, so it's not like having them seen should get you all bent out of shape. I th..."

"..."

As she gazed at Kojou making excuse after excuse, the girl made a deep sigh. However, the scornful look she made toward Kojou remained. And that instant, as if he'd chosen it that way, the strong wind characteristic of isolated islands blew across the seaside shopping mall.

As she stood on top of the station wagon's roof, the girl's skirt casually soared upward, leaving her defenseless.

Kojou's posture stopped moving then and there. His gaze was unconsciously sucked in, leaving him unable to move.

An oppressive silence fell.

"Why are you looking at them again?"

The girl asked, keeping her spear poised with both hands.

Her voice finally caused the completely frozen Kojou to regain his senses.

"Er, wait. You can't blame me for that just now. It's because you're standing in a place like that—"

"...It's fine."

The girl said that in a sobered voice, gazing down icily at the flustered Kojou.

She released her posture, sheathed the extended blade, and returned the spear to the size of a guitar once more. The girl replaced it inside the guitar case, dropping down to the ground without a sound.

"Ah, wait a—..." As she withdrew without a word, Kojou somehow managed to call out to her.

"Pervert."

The girl glanced at Kojou, leaving that word behind, and this time she was the one to turn her back on Kojou, running off.

"..."

Whew. Having been left alone, Kojou thrust his hands into his parka's pockets and leaned against a nearby wall, exhaling.

He felt he'd been arbitrarily and severely slighted, but for some reason, he just didn't feel angry with the girl.

That was probably because the girl's face had been beet red just before she'd run off.

However calm she pretended to be, she was still just a kid, he thought.

Having detected the magic power of a Beast Vassal, the Island Guard would surely be here in no time. They were armed Counter-Demon Agents charged with maintaining law and order on the island. Even if he felt a bit guilty, staying here any longer would bring nothing but trouble.

"Hmm...?"

His eyebrows rose as he belatedly noticed something that had fallen onto the street.

It was a simple wallet, with a red border around a white background.

It was split into two parts, one for bills and one for small change. The part for bills held several one-thousand-yen bills, and one ten-thousand-yen bill. It was a large enough amount of money to make Kojou jealous, but not enough to make anyone's eyes dizzy.

The card holder had a single credit card and a student ID inserted into it.

The student ID had a photo of an awkwardly smiling girl's face, and a name inscribed—Yukina Himeragi.

4

Finally, the sun set, and the night grew late. And morning approached.

The bell continued to ring. The bell that he seemed to hear from far away in the past.

The Fourth Primogenitor dreamed.

The moon peering from the broken sky was crimson. The sky illuminated by the moon, as well. The flames of the ground that enveloped the old castle shone crimson as well. A small shadow stood against that crimson sky.

The shadow bore hair as scarlet as the surging flames, and blazing red eyes.

Victory is yours, the shadow announced. White fangs drenched in blood peeked out from her lips.

I shall fulfill my promise, the shadow announced. *I shall grant thy wish.*

Now it is your turn, the shadow announced. Her eyes were wet. Her shining crimson eyes were wet with tears.

It was a nightmare seen many times over.

Kojou Akatsuki had a dream.

He passed the night in shallow sleep. And morning came.

The bell continued ringing in his ears.

The time-honored bell of an anachronistic alarm clock.

With an anguished sigh, Kojou Akatsuki fumbled around, silencing the clock.

And as he tossed back into bed, just about to return to tranquil sleep once more…

"Kojou, wake up. It's morning. You set your alarm because you have another make-up exam, right? I made breakfast, so eat it quickly! And laundry's not done. Your futon's all sweaty, so move already."

The rapid-fire babble was punctuated by the theft of his bedsheet, and Kojou, at his wits' end, rolled right off the narrow bed. As he looked up with unfocused eyes, there stood the familiar form of his little sister.

She was an expressive girl with impressively large eyes.

The way she wore her hair up made it look like her long hair suddenly came to a halt, giving her what looked like a short-cut style at a glance.

Though her looks and physique gave her a somewhat childlike impression, she surely wasn't that far off from average for a junior high schooler.

This morning she was in casual attire—short pants and a tank top—with an orange apron on top of that.

Looking down at her older brother, who had not moved since falling on the floor, Nagisa put her hands on her hips in exasperation.

"Hey now, wake up. Still sleep-deprived? Did you study for your test till dawn? You mustn't make so much trouble for Ms. Minamiya. Don't slack off on extra lessons. If I see your name posted on the staff room billboard again, it's going to be so embarrassing! Ah, geez, and I *told* you to get those uniform trousers off and put them on a hanger!"

As Kojou listened to his little sister's ceaseless complaints, he rose sluggishly.

Perhaps he was biased in his thinking, but Nagisa was a capable little sister. Her looks were quite adorable, and her grades were up there, too. She was skilled at all varieties of housework.

But there were flaws of course. One was that she was a clean freak to the point of illness, a demon of disposal. The other was the avalanche of words.

Anyway, Nagisa spoke a lot. It wasn't that she did it to *everyone*, but against family with forgiving hearts, she showed no mercy. He didn't feel like he could win a verbal spat with her, ever.

The one saving grace was because of Nagisa's guileless personality, she rarely had an ill word to speak about others, but when she *was* angry it was quite terrifying. Back in junior high school, when Yaze had inadvertently let her see he had a porn video on him when coming over to play, Nagisa gave him enough of a tongue-lashing in her fit of rage to turn him gynophobic for a while.

As Kojou was remembering that, absentmindedly gazing out of the window…

"—Hey, Kojou-kun, are you listening?!"

Nagisa switched to rapid-fire yelling. Kojou hurriedly corrected his posture.

"Yeah, sorry. What'd you say?"

"Geez…! I said, a transfer student."

Nagisa pursed her lips, perhaps out of annoyance that her older brother hadn't heard her story.

"…Transfer student?"

"Yeah. Our class had a transfer student come since the start of summer break. A girl. Yesterday, Ms. Sasasaki introduced her when I went to school for club activities. She came for formalities before transferring, Ms. Sasasaki said. She's this really cute girl. There'll definitely be rumors about her even in the high school, really soon, I think."

"Huhhh..."

Kojou ignored that with a cold shoulder. However cute she was, she was a middle schooler. And his little sister's classmate. Totally outside of Kojou's field of interest. However...

"Hey, Kojou. Did you do something to this transfer student?"

"Huh? What the heck?"

Kojou asked back incredulously at Nagisa's sudden question.

What could he have done to a transfer student before she'd even transferred? However, Nagisa seemed displeased somehow, looking back at her older brother with a serious expression...

"I mean, she asked about you. Once I introduced myself, she asked me if I had an older brother. What kind of person he's like, and stuff."

"...Why?"

"That's what I wanna know. I was sure she must've met you somewhere before..."

"No, I don't think I have any younger acquaintances, but..."

Kojou crossed his arms and sunk into thought. He had a vaguely unpleasant premonition.

"So, what'd you tell her?"

"Well, I did kind of properly explain things, some true and some not."

"What?!"

"Kidding, I spoke only the truth. Like about the city we lived in before moving here, your school grades, what foods you like, the gravure idols you're into, about Yazecchi and Asagi-chan, and then about your big heartbreak story from middle school..."

"Geez... Why'd you have tell all that to someone you'd just met?"

"Er, well, she's cute?"

Nagisa said it with an unapologetic tone. It was the answer he'd expected. Even under normal circumstances Nagisa was tempted to speak to anyone at all, which made the protection of secrets a nearly impossible undertaking.

Her habit of saying exactly what it was she wanted to say, and her difficulty in not doing so was her personality, too.

"Well, a girl having an interest in Kojou-kun's such a rare opportunity. I thought I'd be as helpful as I could."

"Liar...you just wanted to talk, didn't you?"

Kojou exhaled at her fire-and-forget attitude. That moment, an ominous thought floated up into a corner of his sleep-deprived, slowly operating head. Though he wouldn't call her an acquaintance even by mistake, there was one, and only one, name that came to mind: that of a certain junior high schooler who might be checking into Kojou.

"Wait a sec. What's the transfer student's name?"

"Mm, her last name's a bit odd. Err... Right, it had a flutter to it, like the name of a queen."

"'Flutter'? Himeragi, by any chance?"

Kojou bitterly asked back, his ominous premonition swelling larger and larger. Nagisa's expression brightened.

"Ah yes, that's it! Yukina Himeragi-chan."

"...She's...the transfer student...?!"

"That's right. So you really *do* know her? Hey, hey, how do you know her? Explain it to me! Hey, Kojou...!"

Nagisa continued shouting something, but Kojou wasn't listening.

All he could think of was the spear-using girl who'd tailed him all over the place and finally annihilated a vampire's Beast Vassal with a single blow.

So she'd transferred to the same class as Kojou's little sister. But why? For what purpose? Such tortured thoughts made an unpleasant sweat break out, drenching Kojou's entire body.

Somewhere along the way, Kojou's sleepiness had entirely vanished.

5

Natsuki Minamiya was Saikai Academy's English teacher.

She claimed her age was twenty-six, but she actually looked considerably younger than that, enough that, the terms *beautiful girl* and *lovely child* suited her better than *beautiful woman*.

The line of her face and shape of her body were both on the small side, almost doll-like.

On the other hand, maybe she'd inherited noble blood from somewhere; she was oddly dignified and charismatic. Thanks to that, she was a highly capable teacher, with high regard among students as well.

"Er… Aren't you hot there, Natsuki?" Kojou asked, his loose uniform disheveled amid the oppressive, sweltering heat. Kojou was the only student in the classroom for the make-up exam. Of course they didn't permit the use of a civilized invention like air-conditioning.

Against the hellish backdrop of the pouring midday rays of the sun, an incessant hot wind blowing in through the window, Kojou was translating the suspicious English text "Researching the Shape of Mythology in Post-Primitive Man" under the supervision of a teacher who looked younger than he was. This was no longer an exam; a better term for it might be *discipline*, or perhaps *torture.*

"I've told you before. Don't address your teacher by her first name."

He heard Natsuki's haughty voice from the center of the platform as she sat atop the luxurious, velvet-covered chair she'd brought in from somewhere on her own, drinking hot black tea.

She wore a lace-heavy, black, one-piece dress. Except for the frills from the cuffs and the front of the neck, her hip proportions were being flaunted by a laced-up corset. For so-called goth loli, it was rather high-end, but that didn't make it seem any less stifling in this heat. However, as Natsuki elegantly fanned herself with a black lace folding fan…

"This level of heat is nothing compared to the start of summer."

"Er… It looks hot from where I'm sitting, though."

I just don't get it, thought Kojou, resting his chin on his palms.

It was this charismatic teacher, Natsuki Minamiya's, greatest shortcoming. Her fashion sense had an absolute lack of consideration of time and place. Natsuki's wearing of a stifling dress in *this* heat, on an artificial island in the tropics, was violence to his eyes in and of itself. Not that it didn't look good on her…

"And what are you drinking there, all by yourself?"

"Ah yes. I tried adding some light flavor based on candy from Ceylon using herbs; also, just the right amount of brandy to bring out the taste of black tea."

"Not sure you should be waving the smell of alcohol in front of a student taking supplemental lessons, but… May I go now?"

"As if I could supervise tests during summer break without a drink. I'm grading, so wait a minute."

As the smell of Western liquor hung in the air, Natsuki picked up the supplemental test's answer sheet, which Kojou had somehow managed to finish writing, with her fingers. She crossed out several errors with a red pen.

"Hmph. Well, fine. Make sure you pass the rest of the make-up exams."

"Sure thing."

As Kojou said so with an unenthused voice, he began putting his things on top of the table in order. Natsuki silently watched that for a while, tilting her teacup, but…

"Ah, Akatsuki. Apparently some idiot vampire let a Beast Vassal loose at a shopping mall in Island West yesterday. Do you know anything about that?"

"Huh?"

His homeroom teacher's abrupt question brought Kojou's motions to a spontaneous halt.

The shopping mall in West. Beast Vassal. Vampire. Of course he knew, but there was no way he could talk to Natsuki about that. After all, Yukina Himeragi was intertwined with the incident the day before.

If by some chance she *was* questioned as a witness to the incident, it would be very awkward for Kojou. After all, no vampire such as the Fourth Primogenitor existed here in Itogami City. In other words, Kojou was an unregistered demon. It would be exceptionally troublesome if his true nature was exposed to the Island Guard.

Kojou shook his head as if his neck were a rusted gear. Natsuki made a *hmm*, exhaling.

"I see. Fine, then. I was worried some Attack Mage who knows your true nature had encountered and come into conflict with a stray vampire while following you around."

She said it like she'd seen the whole thing. At Natsuki's all-too-accurate inference, a twitchy smile came over Kojou.

"Ha-ha-ha… There's no way…"

"Surely not. That's fine. Let me know if you do notice anything."

So saying, Natsuki pulled back surprisingly easily. Kojou made a sigh of relief. Though her arrogant tone made her difficult to understand, her saying she was worried about Kojou was probably the truth.

Natsuki Minamiya, English teacher, also bore the title of Counter-Demon Attack Mage.

The Demon Sanctuary's educational institutions were obligated by treaty to employ a certain percentage of teachers bearing National Counter-Demon Agent licenses; Natsuki was one among these. Furthermore, she was a combat veteran. She was very much an active professional Attack Mage, also serving as an instructor with the Island Guard.

And she was one of the extremely few people who knew Kojou was the Fourth Primogenitor. Kojou's being able to go to school like an ordinary person, in spite of having the physical makeup of the so-called world's mightiest vampire, was due to Natsuki's machinations.

That was why Kojou couldn't look Natsuki in the eye. From time to time, Natsuki had Kojou assist her in her private work, but he could only accept that as fate and move on.

"Ah, come to think of it, there is something I wanted to ask you."

Suddenly remembering, Kojou raised his head. Natsuki gloomily looked back at him.

"What is it?"

"The Lion King Agency… Know of it?"

Natsuki was silent at Kojou's question, a clear expression of displeasure coming over her.

"How do you know that name?"

"Er, it's not that I *know* it, it just slipped past my ears a little."

"Oh ho. That really makes me want to prod you for details. Slipped past *these* ears?"

As Natsuki spoke, she pulled on Kojou's ears without restraint. As Kojou yelled out, "Ow, ow…"

"…Are you, uh, angry about something?"

"I'm just a tad annoyed at hearing an unpleasant name. They're the competition, after all."

Kojou exhaled roughly as Natsuki let him go. As Kojou pressed on his stretched earlobes…

"Competition…to National CDAs, you mean?"

Natsuki gave Kojou a frosty warning as she looked him over.

"They'll come to kill in earnest, even against a Primogenitor. That's what they were made for, after all. Do take care not to approach anyone related to the Lion King Agency."

"...Made for?"

Kojou asked with a dubious look, but Natsuki clicked her tongue as if she'd said too much and did not say another word about it.

It seemed that in the end, Natsuki's answer was: *Don't go near the Lion King Agency.*

"Ah, right. Natsuki, there's a staff meeting for the middle school today, isn't there?"

As Natsuki moved to leave the classroom, Kojou stopped her with another question. Natsuki dubiously raised an eyebrow.

"And what business do you have with the middle school, Akatsuki?"

"Ah, er. Just had something to ask Ms. Sasasaki, my little sister's homeroom teacher."

"Misaki?"

Natsuki's face grimaced unpleasantly. Now that he thought about it, she and the junior high school teacher Misaki Sasasaki shared the same alma mater, and for some reason, got along famously poorly. Sure enough, Natsuki made a blunt, sharp expression.

"As if I'd know anything about the people in junior high. Go see for yourself."

"...I'll do that."

Kojou meekly went along with Natsuki's words. He instinctively determined that this wasn't a subject he wanted to get dragged into.

However, that was hardly enough to restore Natsuki's humor after being bent out of shape.

"Incidentally, Kojou..."

"Yes?"

Natsuki's black lace fan lashed out. He didn't know she'd done it, but Kojou's forehead was struck with enough force to cave a normal person's skull. Kojou fell right on his back.

"Why do you call her *Ms.* Sasasaki and me *Natsuki*?! I told you, don't you *Natsuki* me!"

Her skirt in a flutter, Natsuki left those words behind as she violently took her leave.

"Shit… Corporal punishment's…not cool," Kojou murmured weakly, looking up at the ceiling as he held his forehead.

6

Saikai Academy was a coed institution with middle and high school integrated. Itogami City had a large, youthful population, and the large-scale, mundane school was a reflection of it.

But, fated to share the critical lack of land as all construction on Itogami Island, the school site was difficult to call *spacious*. The gym, pool, cafeteria, and many other facilities were shared between the middle and high school sections; for that reason, there was an unusually large number of chances for high school students to see junior high school students on school grounds.

On the other hand, it was rare for a student of the high school section to visit the junior high school section; it just wasn't necessary.

As Kojou thus felt a mix of vague familiarity and vague unease, he found himself standing absentmindedly before the junior high school section's staff room, somewhere he hadn't visited in quite some time.

Kojou held in his hand the white wallet he'd picked up at the shopping mall the day before.

The one dropped by Yukina Himeragi.

If the story he'd heard from Nagisa was true, that spear-wielding girl had apparently transferred into the Saikai Academy junior high school section. The student ID in the wallet also backed up Nagisa's testimony.

That being the case, it'd be faster to get it back to Yukina Himeragi by handing it to her homeroom teacher than to the police. That thought was why he'd come out of his way here to the junior high school section.

"Sorry, Akatsuki. Ms. Sasasaki doesn't seem to have come in today."

So said an elderly teacher who Kojou didn't recognize, suddenly bringing his plan to a halt.

"Ah, that so…"

"Something to give her? How about you leave it with me?"

"Er, well… I do, but I'll just try again tomorrow. Bit of a troublesome thing."

Kojou thanked the elderly teacher, making his way out of the staff room. With only two days until summer break ended, Misaki Sasasaki seemed to be making the most of what was left of her vacation.

This is becoming a real bother, Kojou thought.

If he could, he wanted to put the wallet into the owner's hands ASAP. If not, he'd have a misunderstanding with that short-tempered junior high schooler, and *that* might get him suddenly impaled to death from her spear.

Natsuki's words, *Don't get close to the Lion King Agency*, tugged at him, but trusting a nonhomeroom teacher to return a wallet with actual money in it seemed rather irresponsible, and Kojou wasn't of a mind to request it.

Leaning on a pillar of an adjoining corridor, Kojou absentmindedly gazed at the campus.

Here in broad daylight in the middle of summer, there weren't all that many students doing club activities. Even so, he could see athletics club members doing solo training here and there on the grounds.

Cheerleaders were practicing a dance in the shadow of the school building. On the tennis court, club members seemed to be having practice matches against each other. As he watched the flutter and sway of the female members' skirts, they made him remember Yukina Himeragi the day before.

She had such a bizarre level of combat power she'd faced down a demon-race male and utterly crushed him, and her silver spear had annihilated a vampire's Beast Vassal in a single instant. And the flushed look of her face when she held down her skirt over her pastel-colored panties. It was such an impactful scene, even if he thought of forgetting, it wasn't something easy to forget at all. There may have been suspicious parts about her, but she really *was* a pretty girl.

Those legs were pretty, too… Kojou clicked his tongue a little as he casually thought about that.

At the same time a light dizziness assaulted him, his throat felt extremely parched. It was an unusually bad sign.

"If she'd at least put a contact number or something in here..."

To break his train of thought, Kojou hurriedly averted his eyes from the campus and opened up the wallet he'd picked up. It didn't seem to be a luxury brand, but it was a nice wallet that he could tell had been well cared for.

It had a faint, pleasant smell to it.

The wallet itself was made of common, readily available textiles; in other words, this smell was no doubt the lingering scent of its owner. It was not the strong scent of perfume, but a gentle, comfortable, pleasant scent. Well, the point being, this must be what a girl smelled like—

The instant he subconsciously thought about that, this time Kojou's whole body was assaulted with a strange thirst.

"Ugh..."

Not good, thought Kojou as he covered his own mouth.

With a pale face, he locked his knees together as his shoulders shuddered a little. *Not now!* he thought as his lips twisted. Sharp, tapered canine teeth poked through the gap between his lips.

However, it wasn't that Kojou was in bad physical shape. What was causing him distress was a simple physiological reaction. However, this was an abominable, troublesome condition specific to vampires: the urge to drink blood.

—Not good not good not good not good...

Kojou desperately wanted to fight the desire to drink human blood that gripped his entire body. He knew all too well the crimson-dyed hallucination filling his field of vision.

There were still many things misunderstood by the world at large, but the species known as vampires did not drink the blood of others to satisfy hunger. Food and drink were sufficient to address simple hunger and thirst.

Certainly vampires could replenish their magical energy through the act of drinking blood. Magic also existed that used blood as a catalyst.

However, these were nothing more than by-products.

A vampire's urge to drink blood was triggered mainly by sexual arousal. In other words, by *lust*.

A fierce impatience. Oppression that felt like it was tearing your body apart. Thinking of someone, you felt like you couldn't just stand still any longer. Then, suddenly, you attacked without warning.

To escape from that suffering, many vampires in the past, unable to control themselves, attacked whoever was nearest them, sometimes even their own loved ones.

But conversely, one could still say that it was merely sexual arousal.

"Shit… Gimme a break."

Kojou groaned as he felt a dull pain inside his nose. The taste of metallic blood spread within his mouth. The urge to drink would not continue for long. A little surprise or fear could be enough to make it vanish; once it did, even he wouldn't understand why he'd suffered so much.

In Kojou's case, the solution was bleeding from the nose.

In other words, as he'd simply come to love the taste of blood, there was no problem if it was his own blood he tasted. When he was aroused, his nose bled—perhaps because happened to have that predisposition, it always returned Kojou to his senses when assailed by the urge to drink blood.

As Kojou wiped away the trickling blood flowing out of his nose, he made a tedious sigh.

It was good it'd passed without causing trouble for anyone else, but the problem with this predisposition was that it looked *very* uncool. A human being unaware of his circumstances watching Kojou just now would have simply seen a boy who sniffed the scent of a girl from her wallet and suddenly had blood spurt out of his nose. Most would think him a simple pervert.

The form of a female student wearing a uniform entered the corner of his warped field of vision. Kojou became intensely nervous.

Here in the junior high school section corridor, there was no place to hide, and his nosebleed had not yet stopped.

The approaching female student came, stopped, and stood behind Kojou, who still had his knees locked. The girl exhaled calmly.

"To think, aroused by sniffing the scent of a girl from her wallet. You are a dangerous individual indeed."

So said the familiar-sounding voice.

"…Wha?!"

The girl standing behind Kojou bore a guitar case on her back over her schoolgirl uniform. She was a female junior high schooler with somewhat adult looks, but she looked over Kojou with scornful eyes.

"Yukina… Himeragi?"

In shock, Kojou called her by name. He wondered for a moment if this was a hallucination caused by the urge to drink blood. However, Yukina asked back in a cold tone, her expression never changing:

"Yes, what is it?"

Kojou made an even more relieved expression.

He'd suddenly realized the urge to drink blood had completely vanished. Perhaps it was due to his heavy surprise. His nosebleed had stopped, too. Confirming that his extended canine teeth had subsided to their normal length, Kojou lowered the hand he'd covered his mouth with.

"What are you doing here?"

"I think I should be asking that, Akatsuki-senpai. This is the middle school section of campus, isn't it?"

"Er…"

When the younger girl calmly pointed it out, Kojou had no rebuttal.

Yukina made an exasperated sigh and pointed to what Kojou held in his hand.

"That's *my* wallet, isn't it?"

"Y-yeah. Right, I came to get this back to you. They said Ms. Sasasaki was off for the day, though."

When Yukina held a pocket tissue out to him, Kojou wiped his nosebleed with it, nodding in grateful acceptance. Yukina fell silent as if determining the truth or falsehood of Kojou's explanation.

"Did sniffing that scent arouse you enough to make your nose bleed?"

"It's not like I was turned on by the scent of the wallet. Just, I remembered about you from yesterday—"

Kojou's words made Yukina's voice slip in a bewildered-sounding "Huh?" For a moment, she stiffened as if she were a doll.

"…?!"

Far too late, she subconsciously held down the skirt of her uniform. She bit her lower lip with a flushed face.

No doubt she was recalling the incident that had taken place when she'd encountered Kojou the day before. And realizing that she herself was the cause of the sexual arousal Kojou had felt.

"P-please forget about yesterday." Yukina spoke with a tone containing all the calm she could muster.

"Er, even if you tell me to forget it..."

"Please forget it."

"..."

As Yukina glared at him, Kojou silently slumped his shoulders. He realized that if he got her overly upset here, she might break that lance out and go on a rampage just as she had the day before.

"Also, please return my wallet. That's what you came here for, isn't it?"

Yukina made her legitimate request in a gentle tone. However, Kojou did not fulfill that request. He raised the wallet up high, beyond where Yukina's hands could reach.

"I want to ask you a few things first. Who the heck are you? And why are you looking into me?"

"...Understood. So I may take you to mean that I will have to take my wallet back by force."

Yukina gave Kojou a long stare as she made her declaration. As if drawing a katana from its sheath, her hand reached toward the guitar case on her back.

So this is how it's gonna be, Kojou thought, halfheartedly giving up as he lowered his center of gravity. As though playing defense in basketball, he adopted a posture from which he could deal with any attack. Yukina's eyes grew guarded.

Grrrrrr. ...The next moment, a low sound reverberated across the corridor.

Kojou's eyebrows rose without a word.

When Kojou realized what that low growl was, a somewhat awkward expression came over him. It was a grumble from Yukina's stomach.

"Err... Himeragi, are you hungry, by any chance?" Kojou asked Yukina as she remained frozen stiff.

Yukina was silent. That *was* her answer.

"Haven't you eaten since yesterday? Ah, because you didn't have your wallet? Himeragi, you actually live alone, don't you?"

"Wh-what of it?!"

Yukina tried to keep her voice calm, but of course it came out a bit flustered.

Somehow he'd felt like that was the case, but apparently Yukina had come to live here on Itogami Island apart from her family. Since she'd just transferred, she didn't have any friends yet, and having dropped her wallet, she had no money. That had to be why she hadn't had a bite to eat since the day before.

With a somewhat flustered look, Kojou tilted his head and gently presented the wallet in front of Yukina.

Even as Yukina became agitated, as if wondering, *Wh-what are you doing?* her guarded expression never faltered.

"So, uh, treat me to lunch. The guy who picked up your wallet has a right to ask that much, right?"

Kojou spoke with a voice drained of tension.

Yukina blinked over and over, looking at Kojou as if trying to weigh his true intentions.

Like a plaintive, hungry puppy, her stomach made a low growl once more.

7

Yukina Himeragi ordered a retro-version Classic Teriyaki Burger, onion rings, and grapefruit juice combo. They were a five-minute walk from Saikai Academy at a big burger chain franchise on Island South.

With refined etiquette, Yukina, sitting up straight in her seat, gripped her teriyaki burger with both hands, a happy look on her face. Kojou watched her absentmindedly.

"What are you looking at?" Yukina asked dubiously, noticing Kojou's gaze.

"Ahh, er… I was thinking, so you eat hamburgers like normal people, too, Himeragi."

"What do you mean?"

Yukina's eyebrows flattened in a scowl.

Kojou sipped on an iced coffee that was heavy on the ice and thin on the coffee.

"Err, somehow I had the impression you hadn't been to this kind of place, like you'd be asking where the knives and forks were, and stuff…"

"I am not entirely sure, but might you be making fun of me?" Yukina made a sigh, as if a little wounded. "Certainly, the town High God Forest is in is no city, but it does sell hamburgers at least."

"…High God Forest? Is that the school you were at before?"

"Yes. On the surface, it's a girls' school for Shinto adherents."

Yukina's explanation was oddly roundabout. Kojou made an *mm* sound and lifted his face.

"On the surface—meaning there's something behind it?"

"…It's a training ground for the Lion King Agency. You know what the Lion King Agency is, right?"

"No, not a clue."

As Yukina saw Kojou shake his head, she blinked.

"Why don't you know of it?"

"You say it like of course I'd know about it, but…this is the first time I've heard the name."

Kojou spoke with a conflicted expression. Yukina murmured, "Huh?" with a perplexed look.

"The Lion King Agency is a special agency established by the National Public Safety Commission."

"Special agency? So you're civil servants?"

A pretty extravagant name for a government institution, Kojou thought. He wondered if that name carried some kind of special meaning.

"Yes. The agency conducts information gathering and strategic sabotage to stop large-scale magical terrorism and catastrophes. As its roots go back to the Takiguchi Musha, the guards who protected the Inner Palace from evil spirits and apparitions during the Heian period, it is an organization older than the present government of Japan."

"I don't know about the roots thing, but…the gist is, it's like a police force?"

Kojou could understand it in those terms.

If regular police forces had special squads for dealing with organized crime and terrorist organizations, it was no surprise that there was a government agency besides Counter-Demon Agents that dealt with magical terrorism and catastrophes. That'd explain why Natsuki referred to the Lion King Agency as "the competition."

No doubt the vague-sounding "special agency" bit was because demons were its opponents. After all, a lot of people with counter-demonic abilities, like psychic mediums and sorcerers, didn't like dealing directly with the government.

"So, Himeragi, since you came from their training ground, you're part of the Lion King Agency, too?"

"Yes. Though as an apprentice," added Yukina frankly after a humble nod.

Figures, thought Kojou as he nodded once more. She was still just a junior high schooler, after all.

Thanks to her explanation, he somehow understood the true nature of that spear Yukina carried. It had to be some kind of special antidemon weapon developed by the Lion King Agency.

"So why were you tailing me around, then, Himeragi? That special agency thing's job is dealing with magical terrorism and catastrophes, right? What does that have to do with me?" Kojou asked in a blunt tone.

Yukina's eyes bulged a bit. "Huh?"

"Yesterday. You were tailing me, right?"

"Don't tell me you noticed...?!"

"Wha? Er, did you think I wouldn't notice *that*...?"

It was the fact *she* was surprised that surprised *him*. Yukina made a faint *ugh* sound.

"That being the case...er, Akatsuki...senpai...? Perhaps you really don't know?"

"Know what?"

He felt like he wasn't going to get used to Yukina calling him *senpai*.

"Senpai, your very existence is treated identically to war or terrorism."

"Huh?"

"The Primogenitors who rule the Dominions each possess, by themselves, the might of a national army. The Fourth Primogenitor is treated the same way, of course. If you were to cause trouble within Japan's national borders, Senpai, it would be seen not as a criminal act, but an act of war. I think that is why it is the Lion King Agency, and not the

Police Administration's Counter-Demon Section, that is acting," Yukina explained to Kojou with a tone of concern.

"Treated the same as an army… What the heck…? Who the hell decided that…"

As might be expected, Kojou couldn't hide his agitation. He was being treated on the same level as a war or a terrorist strike; or rather, his very existence was being treated as a national crisis. Even though he was suffering through his vampiric condition, now he wasn't even being treated as a life-form, let alone a human being.

"So you really didn't know, *Senpai*…"

Yukina made an exasperated sigh. The pitying look that came over her face rubbed Kojou's nerves the wrong way somehow. To calm himself down, Kojou thrust some hard-fried potato into his own mouth.

"I dunno about the other Primogenitors, but I don't remember bein' treated like *that.* I haven't done anything, and I don't rule any kind of empire, anyway."

"That's true."

Yukina quietly nodded. She shot Kojou a cold, antagonistic look.

"I was already planning to ask about that. Senpai, what do you intend to do in this place?"

"To do… Er, what?"

"Yesterday, I asked your little sister about you."

"Yeah… I heard."

Kojou unintentionally scowled at Yukina's words. He remembered the fact that Nagisa had already spilled to her all the secrets of his past.

However, Yukina's expression remained completely serious.

"You're hiding the fact you're a vampire from your little sister, aren't you?"

"Well, I am, but…"

"Don't you have some kind of objective, infiltrating the Demon Sanctuary, hiding your true nature from even your family? For instance, ruling Itogami Island from the shadows, adding the registered Demons to your own army and the like? Or perhaps you've come to commit slaughter for your own pleasure…you monster!" Yukina muttered in a tone that could be taken either as brooding or fantasizing.

Kojou groaned in a low voice, "Why does it have to be like this?"

"Now, just hold on a minute, here. Himeragi, aren't you misunderstanding something?"

"Misunderstanding?"

"I'm not *infiltrating* anything; I lived in this city since before I became a vampire."

"...Before you became a...vampire, you say?"

"Yeah. Check the records or anything you like. I've had this condition only since spring of this year.

"I moved to this island when I was in this junior high school so, that's almost four years ago," Kojou explained in an unpleasant tone.

That's right. Kojou Akatsuki had not been born a vampire. Until a mere three months prior, he'd lived as a normal human being with no relation to demons whatsoever. However, during spring of that year, an incident Kojou had become wrapped up in changed his destiny. Kojou had encountered the one called the Fourth Primogenitor and had taken her powers as well as her life.

However, Yukina shook her head, as if to say, *I can't believe that.*

"The Fourth Primogenitor was a human being? That cannot be so."

"Huh? Uh, say that all you want, but it's the truth."

"Normal humans cannot change into vampires midway. Even if one is infected from drinking vampire blood, the person would be a mere 'Blood Servant'—an imitation vampire."

"Yeah. Seems that way."

"So why make up an easily exposed lie like this?"

"It's not like I'm lying to you, geez."

Kojou made a tired sigh. He was bad at explaining things to overserious types like this.

Yukina adopted the tone of a private tutor addressing a slacker of a student.

"Now listen, Senpai. Primogenitors are the oldest and first vampires who received the curse of immortality from now-dead gods."

"I am kind of aware of that, but..."

"The only way for a normal human to become a Primogenitor would be to become undead by using a secret curse from the lost gods on oneself. Are you saying you are capable of that, Senpai?"

"Uh, no. I don't have any gods for BFFs, sorry."

"So how did you become a vampire, then? There's only one other way to become a Primogenitor, and that's..."

Having said that much, Yukina suddenly cut off her words as if she'd realized something. The color of her face turned faintly pale. Aside from being cursed by the gods, there was but one other method by which a human being could become a Primogenitor. She'd just remembered what it was.

"Senpai... You don't mean, you...consumed a Primogenitor and took his power into you...?! But that's not..."

The softness that had been in Yukina's expression a short time before had vanished. In its place, a look of fright came over her.

If you couldn't become a Primogenitor yourself, there was but one way that existed to obtain a Primogenitor's power. That was to consume the Primogenitor's existence and to take the power, and the curse, into one's own body.

However, there shouldn't have been any way for someone inferior in magical power to take the quasi-godlike power wielded by a Primogenitor into oneself. Clumsily laying a hand on a Primogenitor would only result in one's own existence being consumed and annihilated.

All the more so where an ordinary human was concerned: consuming a vampire simply wasn't possible.

And yet, in point of fact, Kojou Akatsuki was saying he'd obtained the power of the Fourth Primogenitor.

"'Consumed a Primogenitor'... Uh, please don't put it like that. It makes me sound like a ravenous beast."

Kojou sluggishly rested his chin on his hands as he sipped on his iced coffee. Yukina's expression remained sharp and impregnable.

"Are you saying you obtained a Primogenitor's power by some other method, then?"

"Sorry, but even I can't explain the details. I just had that idiot push this troublesome condition onto me, and that's it."

"Pushed onto you...?"

Yukina blinked in what seemed like surprise.

"Senpai, you didn't become a vampire of your own will?"

"Who the heck would *want* to be like this?"

Kojou spoke in an offhand tone. Yukina glared at Kojou with a dubious look.

"And who is this idiot?"

"The Fourth Primogenitor. The previous one."

"The previous Fourth Primogenitor…?!"

Yukina sucked in her breath in shock.

"You're talking about the real Kaleid Blood?! You're saying you inherited *those* powers? Why did the Fourth Primogenitor choose you as his successor? How did you even encounter the Fourth Primogenitor in the first place?"

"Er, that's…"

As Kojou tried to speak, his face suddenly grimaced, as if assaulted by a fierce headache.

The coffee cup he'd been drinking from fell over, spilling the melting ice and thin liquid that had been within.

Without noticing that at all, Kojou lowered his face onto the table, clutching his head. He let out what seemed to be anguished pants from having bitten his tongue. Like a curse, Kojou's lost memories brought torment to his entire body.

"S-Senpai?"

Yukina spoke in a flustered voice at Kojou's completely unexpected reaction.

"Sorry, Himeragi…"

But Kojou did not raise his face. He suppressed the fierce pain in his heart, as if impaled by an invisible stake, and simply panted painfully. The only thing that came into the back of his mind was a lone girl whose face he could no longer remember, smiling amid the flames.

"I'm gonna have to leave it at that."

Kojou spoke in a frail tone. Yukina tilted her head a bit.

"Eh?"

"I don't have any memory of it. When I try and force myself, this is what I get."

"Is…that so? I understand… In that case, it cannot be helped."

An expression that seemed relieved came over Yukina as she watched Kojou finally lift his face. It seemed she'd believed without any doubt what Kojou had said about having no memory. She must have had a fundamentally straitlaced personality.

Kojou was actually a bit disappointed in Yukina's all-too-quick reaction.

"You believe me?"

"Yes. I believe I understand you at least well enough to know you are not lying, Senpai."

Yukina spoke matter-of-factly. A conflicted expression came over Kojou. He wondered if that was a roundabout way of saying he was a simpleton.

Yukina got up and wiped up the coffee spilled on the table with a napkin.

After that, she came beside Kojou and leaned over him, pulling out a handkerchief.

"Turn toward me. I'll wipe your pants clean."

"Er, ah. That's okay, I..."

"They'll get stained. See?"

Yukina spoke as much as she reached toward Kojou's pants. Kojou couldn't breathe or move a muscle. Yukina didn't seem to be aware of it, but if anyone they knew saw them, they'd get a really big misunderstanding from this posture, to the point that Kojou wanted to suspect that she was trying to trigger his vampiric impulses on purpose.

Yukina leaned over between Kojou's legs, her pale, white neck defenseless before him.

"Senpai, I have been ordered by the Lion King Agency to watch you, but...also, to eliminate you if I determine you to be a dangerous being, Senpai."

"E...eliminate?!"

Kojou's whole body stiffened in an entirely *different* sense at Yukina's calmly delivered, matter-of-fact words.

However, Yukina spoke in a gentle tone. "I think I understand the reason why. You lack a certain self-awareness, Senpai. I sense great danger in you."

"Er, I think you're pretty dangerous yourself, Himeragi..."

As Kojou unwittingly added in a mumble, "Plus, you dropped your wallet," Yukina glared at him.

"Anyway, as I shall be observing you from this day forward, do take care not to try anything strange. After all, I do not completely trust you yet, Senpai."

"Watch... Huh."

Well, fine, thought Kojou as his shoulders eased. Some parts made him uneasy, but Yukina didn't seem to be a bad person. He didn't foresee that being watched would have any serious drawbacks, and if he was going to have someone keeping tabs on him, he was a little glad it was a girl and not some stiff-necked male Attack Mage doing it.

"Oh, right, Himeragi. About Nagisa..."

Kojou suddenly shot Yukina a concerned look. With a bit of a mischievous smile, Yukina nodded.

Rare for her, it was a youthful, smiling face that matched her age.

"I understand. I shall keep the fact you are a vampire secret from her, Senpai. So please do the same for me."

"Yeah. I just need to treat you as a normal transfer student, right?"

Kojou shrugged his shoulders as he replied. Either way, even if he told people a junior high schooler like her was a watcher from a secret organization, it wasn't like anyone would *believe* him.

"Thank you very much."

With those words, Yukina stood erect. She already had the usual serious look back on her face.

"Well then, Senpai, what do you plan to do after this?"

"Oh yeah... I kinda meant to go to the library and do my summer break homework, but..."

As he spoke, Kojou had an unpleasant premonition.

"Himeragi, you don't mean to go with me, do you?"

"Yes. Is that a problem?"

"Er, it's not a *problem*, but...is this, like, um, full-time?"

"Of course it is. It's my duty to watch you."

Speaking without any special change in expression, Yukina pulled the guitar case containing her spear over her back and began cleaning up after dinner.

8

One of the four Gigafloats that composed Itogami Island, Island West, was a city that never slept. In this district, where many restaurants and business establishments were gathered, many stores continued operating until daybreak.

Much of demonkind loved the night. In addition to that, many demonic residents flocked to this city because of the wealth of services geared toward them. In one sense, this dazzling neon nighttime display was emblematic of Itogami City and the peaceful coexistence of humans and demons within.

However, no matter how much light shone through, it did not completely banish darkness from the city at night.

"—Would you come play with us?"

It was night at the park, emptied of signs of human life. As the drunken men passed along the scenic street that overlooked the sea, they suddenly heard a voice calling them to a stop.

A lone woman stood below a faintly glowing streetlight.

She was small with long indigo hair.

Her eyes were a lighter shade of blue. She wore a one-piece cape coat over her body, but she didn't seem to be wearing anything under it whatsoever. She was barefoot.

"Hey, whoa? Fishin' for men in a place like this?"

"Tch…another kid, ain't it?"

As the faces of the two men met, they spoke loosely with lewd expressions. As the girl seemed to beckon them, they staggered closer because of her oddly beautiful appearance.

She had almost transparent white skin and big eyes. Her face was perfectly symmetrical.

Somehow, her presence was faint for a living being. The girl seemed fairylike.

"You sayin' that knowin' we're Freaks, little girl?"

"You ain't gettin' off with a few laughs for gettin' our attention in a place like this. We're in a real bad mood today, especially toward little girls."

The men spoke as they approached, seemingly hemming the girl in from the left and right. They were both around twenty years of age. They both had brown hair and wore black gigolo-style suits, with an air of roughness floating around them.

One of the men bared his fangs, revealing his true nature as a demon. He was a D-type vampire. Surely he was being assaulted by vampiric impulses from a series of sexual arousal.

The other individual violently ripped off an armband from his own right arm.

Now there was nothing to restrain his demonic powers. As he pulled off and tossed away his upper garments, his musculature swelled up as a brown-colored mane rose over his spine. It was a beast man's transformation.

"This might get just a bit scary for ya, but don't take it personally."

"If yer gonna hate, hate the brat who picked a fight with us yesterday!"

The men glared at the girl with angry, excited looks. However, the girl's expression did not change. She somehow seemed sad as she looked up at the two men, as if her eyes swayed from pity. Then—

"—A district without night where demons strut about in plain sight... Truly this island is a cursed, forsaken city."

A gentle voice spoke sadly from behind the two demons.

In surprise, they turned around to face the odd presence that had appeared without any warning.

Standing in the shade below one of the trees along the roadside was a man dressed in what seemed to be the robes of a priest.

He was a blond foreigner with a short-cropped military-style haircut.

He had a metal monocle buried in his left eye socket like an eyepatch.

He had to be over a hundred and ninety centimeters tall. His age was forty years, give or take, but based on his broad, powerful shoulders, it did not seem he had weakened any with age.

In addition to his imposing physique, he was wearing some kind of metal armor under his vestment. It was some kind of armored augmentation suit used by heavy infantry in the military. It gave off an overbearing feeling.

The man's right hand gripped a metal bardiche, a battle-axe with a giant blade. It had to be rather heavy, but the man easily carried it with one hand.

"Who the hell are you, an Attack Mage?"

The vampire man asked with bloodlust in his tone.

"If you were watchin', you get it, then. Just now, she invited us. You got no right to butt in on this. So stay out of it and get lost!"

The beast man also spoke, his voice husky and hard to understand.

The man in the vestment looked over both demons without emotion.

"I am well aware. However, did she not ask you to play with us?"

As he spoke, he turned the blade of his axe toward the two demons.

And then he tossed the baggage he had been carrying in his left hand at the two demons. The weapons piled within easily thrust through the long narrow sports bag. There was a sword, a katana, a javelin, and an axe. The bare katana blade thrust straight through the bag, piercing the ground. These weren't replicas; these were real weapons.

"If you would claim you cannot fight unarmed, please pick your fancy. What's wrong? Do not tell me you are afraid, pitiable demons."

"Don't look down on us, gramps… So the brat's in on this with you, huh?"

As the beast man exclaimed, he picked up the sword, which was nearest to him. He was a belligerent demon by nature. He growled as he bared his fangs, unable to contain his murderous impulses.

"I'll kill ya just like ya want—!"

The beast man kicked from the ground, his body accelerating with explosive force. He charged the defenselessly standing man from the front, moving to beat him down with the sword by brute force. However, midway through the sword's attack, the vestment-wearing man's axe easily knocked it aside. The beast man's expression twisted in shock, and he redoubled his attack. However, the outcome was the same.

"A lycanthrope, is it? As fast as I'd expect. Yet all too simple."

"What?!"

"Indeed, no comparison to the beast men who serve in Dominion regular forces. Pathetic…"

The augmented suit beneath the vestment emitted a revving sound like the roar of a beast. With his strength increased to its absolute limit, his lunging step split the asphalt covering the street and cracked the air. His battle-axe flashed, leaving a blur trailing behind it. It was a blow too swift for even a beast man to react.

"Gaha…!"

Slashed from its armpit down to its hip, the beast man's huge body was blown away. Fresh lukewarm blood splattered, filling the surrounding area with the scent of blood. The sound of bones breaking and flesh tearing came after the fact. A human being would have no doubt died instantly. Even for a beast man, with such a resilient life force, it was a grave, potentially fatal wound.

"Wh-why you—!"

Gazing dumbfounded at his wounded comrade, the vampire man howled. He picked up the javelin that had rolled onto the ground and hurled it at the man in the vestment.

The vampire's brute strength was even greater than that of the beast man's. The spear he'd thrown flew at bullet-like speed would have pierced the man's chest—had the latter not easily knocked it down a moment prior.

"Shit… What the hell are you?!"

The man in the vestment replied to the vampire's question with majesty.

"My name is Rudolf Eustach. An Armed Apostle of Lotharingia."

"Armed Apostle? What's a priest from the Western Church doin' out here—?!"

"I have no obligation to answer."

Tch. The vampire man clicked his tongue. Pitch-black flames welled up from his left leg.

"Kill 'im, Shakti!"

The flames took the shape of a distorted horse and assaulted the man in the vestment. The Beast Vassal burned at a thousand degrees Celsius. The air shimmered from the heat; the melting surface of the ground left a burning smell behind.

"Hmph. I had heard there was a fool using a Beast Vassal in urban areas; it appears that is true. So our search has borne fruit."

A smile came over the man's lips as if this is what he had been waiting for.

And then the man halted the charge of the flaming Beast Vassal with his own left hand.

"What…?!"

The vampire man's eyes bulged at the completely unexpected display. Something like an invisible wall had emerged in front of the man in the vestment, stopping the incandescent spirit horse's attack cold. The girl, standing beside the Armed Apostle, had extended a strange barrier to protect him.

The flaming Beast Vassal could not reach the man with the barrier holding it at bay.

However, it seemed that even the girl's defensive barrier did not possess the power to completely repel the Beast Vassal.

As the intense flames slammed against the wall, the very air creaked from the strain. Finally, as if unable to bear the strain of the clash, a frail sigh escaped from the girl's lips.

"Evidently even this degree of Beast Vassal cannot be completely neutralized. It seems there is indeed room left for improvement."

"Huh…?!"

Not knowing the meaning of the man's utterance, the vampire raised a cry of triumph. No doubt he'd judged that continuing to press on meant victory.

However, as an anguished expression came over the girl, the man in the vestment seemed to have lost interest as he called out.

"Tonight's experiment is over, Astarte."

"Yes, Armed Apostle."

The girl with the indigo-colored hair he'd called Astarte gently closed her eyes. As she stretched out her cape coat, she reported in an artificial, robotic voice.

"Accept. Execute 'Rhododactylos.'"

At the same time as the voice finished, something gushed out from the seams of her coat.

It was a transparent arm with a dim white glow to it. It was a giant arm larger than the girl's slender body. That arm, stretching from her abdomen as if thrusting right through it, lashed out like a living snake and impaled the vampire's Beast Vassal.

"—Shakti?! The hell?!" The vampire exclaimed at the unbelievable display.

The flaming Beast Vassal, its torso pierced, howled as if in anguish. Yet the transparent arm's attack did not relent. It mowed down the flaming Beast Vassal over and over, as if consuming it.

"What the hell have you done…?!"

Unable to maintain its physical form, the flaming Beast Vassal dissipated; the vampire man collapsed on the spot. Unable to move from the vast loss of magical energy, the man's lips quivered from terror.

The man in the vestment casually explained.

"A Beast Vassal can be defeated by striking it with a stronger Beast Vassal. 'Tis a simple thing."

"No way... That's a Beast Vassal...?!"

The vampire exclaimed as he gazed at the giant arm that stretched from the girl's body.

The man in the vestment coldly looked down at both fallen demons.

"Though you are not worth killing, you would perish along with this island soon enough. You can at least fill Rhododactylos's belly. Astarte, grant them mercy," he told the expressionless indigo-haired girl.

Realizing the meaning of those words, the vampire shrieked.

"S-stop...! Don't...!"

The girl looked at the man with her pale blue eyes. A great melancholy dwelled in her eyes; her lips trembled.

"—Accept."

The giant arm, glowing faintly white, wriggled like a malicious beast.

The man's screams reverberated.

Chapter Two
Here Comes the Watchdog

1

Island South, Itogami Island's southern district, contained Kojou Akatsuki's residence among many others. He lived on the seventh story of a nine-story apartment complex. On this Gigafloat, where building height was severely restricted, it was a comparatively tall building with a commanding view.

Though it was the last day of summer, the sun was already high when Kojou slipped out of bed. At this hour, he might barely make it in time for that day's make-up exam.

Kojou had been nocturnal to begin with, but his turning into a vampire had only ratcheted that up another notch. Rather than being stronger at night, it was simply that his head didn't really kick in before noon. Thanks to that, he'd been late time and time again this last semester; that was why he was buried in supplemental lessons and make-up exams, trampling flat his precious summer vacation.

"Ugh… So sleepy."

Kojou made a languid murmur, his expression gloomy. He had make-up tests for four subjects to go. He still had homework and a half marathon left, too. If he could, he'd just drop everything and flee the island altogether, but that'd mean the last semester would start without him, and he'd have to repeat the year for sure. More than that, he was terrified of the scolding Nagisa would give him.

Even so, it was somewhat better than the desperate situation it had been up until the day before.

That was because Yukina had helped him study until nightfall.

Somehow, at that Lion King Agency thing, she'd already gained a high school graduate–level education, and was better than Kojou at pretty much every subject he was taking. As she said things like *studying is something you need to do for yourself,* she answered questions for him one after another. He was grateful for how she taught from the basics on up, unlike Asagi, who was the genius type.

Kojou did feel rather pathetic to have to be taught all this by a junior high schooler younger than him, but with his back against the wall, he had no leeway for worrying about petty pride.

"Nagisa…is at club, huh?"

When Kojou finished changing and went out into the living room, he saw a single five-hundred-yen coin resting on a plate on top of the table. It seemed to mean, *Since I didn't make you breakfast, go buy something.* Kojou gratefully picked it up, pulled his parka on, and headed out.

Incidentally, Nagisa was in the Cheerleading Club. They were really busy every year, cheering on all the other clubs and practicing for their own tournament. *Nice to have a full plate,* Kojou thought wistfully.

"…Hot."

Kojou took the elevator, which received no benefit from air-conditioning, down to the ground level and headed toward the apartment complex's front entrance.

Floating on top of the Pacific Ocean as it was, Itogami was prone to have rainfall at all times of the year and had been struck by a number of typhoons, but it'd been unreasonably clear and sunny for the last several days. The relentless downpour of the sun's heat onto the artificial surface made the temperature considerable. Mirages rose up from the asphalt that covered the streets.

As Kojou noticed a familiar rear profile floating up among the mirages, he narrowed his eyes with a *hn* sound.

It was a girl wearing a Saikai Academy uniform with a guitar case on her back.

"Ah… Senpai."

Standing in front of the automatic door, Yukina noticed Kojou and slowly turned around. She said, "Good day," speaking her greeting in her usual, overly serious tone. Based on her refreshed expression, not a single drop of sweat on her face, she must had some sort of barrier deployed around her, but it scared him a bit to see someone further removed from humanity than Kojou, a demon.

"Himeragi, were you standing here the whole time? To keep a lookout for me…?" Kojou asked anxiously, sensing a stalker-like level of tenacity. Yukina looked back at Kojou with no expression.

"Yes, it's my duty to watch you, after all."

"Uh, seriously?!"

"I am joking."

As Yukina spoke, she made a small giggle. Kojou twisted his lips in silence. Due to the oddly calm tone she used, his inability to tell how serious she was made his heart skip a few beats.

"I was waiting for my things. I was told they'd arrive at this time."

"…Your things?"

Kojou was a bit perplexed at Yukina's unexpected words. Yukina nodded lightly.

"Yes. This was an urgent mission, so I didn't have time to prepare. Until yesterday I'd been loaned a hotel room, but as that is quite inconvenient—"

Before she could finish that sentence, a single small truck rolled over the sidewalk and entered the apartment grounds. It parked right in front of the entrance Kojou and Yukina were near.

Two deliverymen in shipping company uniforms got out of the truck. As they picked up freight and carried it over, she called out to the younger deliveryman in a strong voice.

"Excuse me, this way, please."

Yukina was pointing to the elevator Kojou had ridden on just earlier.

"Wait a minute. You can't seriously mean you're moving *here*…"

"Yes, to this apartment complex. And?"

"Why?!"

"I do believe that this is where you live, Senpai…?"

Yukina asked with a doubtful expression. Her attitude seemed to say, *Why are you asking me something that obvious?* It seemed she was hell-bent on observing even his private life. Kojou made a morose scowl.

"Did the Lion King Agency order this, too?"

"Yes."

Yukina got into the elevator along with the freight carried in from the truck. Kojou, somehow rather anxious, followed her right in. As if to validate Kojou's anxieties, Yukina pressed the elevator button for the seventh floor without hesitation, turning to the two deliverymen.

"Room seven-oh-five, please."

"Now hold on!" Kojou spontaneously yelled out, making the surprised deliverymen stare at him.

"What's wrong, *Senpai*? Why would you raise your voice in a narrow space like this?"

Yukina spoke with a tone of rebuke. Kojou hugged his head in irritation.

"Seven-oh-five is right next door to my place, isn't it? I was kinda starting to think so, but geez, you're really taking it that far?! Wait, did you make Yamada, who was in room seven-oh-five here, move out last week so that you could get in here today?!"

"It's not as if I intimidated him into leaving. I simply convinced him in a peaceful manner, and he left."

" 'Convinced'?"

"Yes. Convinced him that there was an evil aura filling the room, that the ghost of the man who killed himself previously remains here, how he would die in an unfortunate accident at this rate, that I know a very reliable spiritual medium..."

"In what world is that not intimidation?! Are you some kind of con artist?!"

"I'm joking."

Yukina ended with the same demure expression with which she'd begun, letting out an amused sigh. Kojou was simply and completely bewildered.

"...Huh?"

"The previous occupant of room seven-oh-five moved out after being properly paid to relocate. I heard he was provided with a nicer place than this to move into."

"Really?"

"Yes. Though we have our faults, we are a government agency, after all."

Ah yeah, they are, thought Kojou as he patted his chest down in relief.

Though he'd never even properly said hello, he still wouldn't sleep soundly if it'd been his fault someone who'd lived right next to him went through a hard time.

The shipping company deliverymen stared at Kojou and Yukina with expressions as if they wondered what in the world these two were talking about. Finally, the elevator reached the seventh floor, and the door opened.

The freight they carried in was only three corrugated cardboard boxes. After getting Yukina to sign for the delivery, the deliverymen gave modest waves and made their way out.

"Senpai, could I get you to bring these boxes inside?" Yukina asked without hesitation as she opened the exterior lock.

"Why do I have to..."

Grumbling under his breath, Kojou picked up one of the corrugated cardboard boxes. What was the point of a vampire's physical strength if you couldn't use it at a time like this?

Yukina's room 705, constructed just like room 704 next door, where Kojou and Nagisa lived, was a three-bedroom apartment with a living room, dining room, and a kitchen.

It was a bit cramped for family living but had an overabundance of space for a single person. The lack of a single piece of furniture made it seem especially desolate.

"Hey, uh, Himeragi, is this all you have?"

"Yes. It is, but..."

Yukina tilted her slender neck a bit as she looked back at Kojou.

"I didn't have much for personal belongings when I lived in a student dorm. Is there something wrong with that?"

"There's nothing wrong, but looks like you're hard up for stuff. I don't even see a futon here."

"I can sleep just about anywhere. Plus I have the cardboard boxes."

"Please, just...stop."

As Kojou spoke, he leaned against a wall with an exhausted look. He'd never get a good night's sleep while thinking about a female junior high school student watching over him, sleeping on cardboard the next room over.

"I did actually mean to go buy necessities later, but..."

Muttering as if making excuses, Yukina glanced over at Kojou's face. Seeing on Yukina's face there was something left unsaid, Kojou raised an eyebrow with an *mm* sound.

"Wait, you figure you can't take the time and go shopping because you have to watch me?"

"Well, yes. It is my duty, after all..."

Watching Yukina nod with a straight face, Kojou made an exasperated sigh. He thought it was easier to just cover it up with something convincing after the fact, but the thought didn't seem to occur to Yukina.

"If that's the case, I go shopping with you and it's fine, right, Himeragi?"

"Together with...you, Senpai?"

"That way you don't have to skip watch duty."

"That's true, but you're all right with that?"

"I have make-up exams till afternoon, but I'll go with you after that. I owe you one for helping me study for the exams anyway."

Kojou checked his watch as he spoke. He'd lost quite a bit of time due to unexpected events. If he didn't finally get to school, he really would be late for his make-up exams.

"Is that so? That being the case, I'll wait for you inside school grounds until you've finished your exams, Senpai."

Having said this, Yukina made a somewhat happy smile. Then she picked her guitar case back up and returned it to her back. It was the black case that contained the silver spear she'd called "Snowdrift Wolf."

"Hey, do you, ah...need that spear for shopping?"

Kojou's face grimaced as he asked. If possible, he didn't want to bring something that dangerous along when shopping for daily necessities, but—

"Of course. I'm on duty, after all."

As Yukina spoke in a composed tone, Kojou made an exhausted sigh.

2

Kojou brought Yukina to a nearby home and garden center that promised one-stop shopping for all your household needs. The moment they entered the store, Yukina's eyes widened and stayed that way.

There was nothing unusual about the store itself. Itogami Island, a research city far from the mainland, did have its share of disreputable shops selling suspicious devices and drugs, but compared to that, this was just a robust general store for daily needs.

However, it seemed Yukina had never been to one of the places known as a *home and garden center*. The girl was bewildered at seeing a store of this scale for the first time in her life. She gazed at the products that lined the shelves with open suspicion on her face.

"Is this a weapon? It appears to be some kind of mace."

"Uh, no, that's just a golf club. It's for a sport."

Kojou replied to Yuki's completely straight-faced question with a quizzical look. He didn't know how seriously she'd asked that question.

"Is that so? Then what of this heavy gear that looks like a flamethrower..."

"That's a pressure washer. They use it to wash cars."

"This is most definitely a weapon. I've seen it in movies."

"A chainsaw, huh? Well, I suppose that *is* a weapon..."

"Ah, I learned about this at the Lion King Agency. What a frightening store, to even sell this."

"Isn't that just liquid detergent...?"

"Yes. You can use this to create poison gas. By mixing an acidic compound with a chlorine compound—"

"No! You do NOT use it like that, EVER!"

After buying anything and everything Yukina needed, Kojou was completely and utterly exhausted. The damage from the morning make-up test and the half marathon had added up, too.

On the other hand, a rather cheerful expression had come over Yukina. It seemed that she was really fond of the home and garden center. She also looked happy just from going shopping with someone else like this.

"By the way, are you all right paying for all this, Himeragi? You bought quite a bit of stuff here."

They'd left the store and were on their way to the bus station when Kojou asked. Yukina nodded casually.

"Yes. I was paid an expense allowance in advance for things like this."

"Ahh, so that's it."

Kojou accepted this without any particular doubt. Even if she was an apprentice, it would've been odd to send an Attack Mage into unfamiliar territory without at least that level of support.

"Expense budget, huh? How much are we talking about here?"

"Err, ten million yen."

"Ten mil...?!" Kojou exclaimed, gawking at Yukina's calm reply. Any way you sliced it, that wasn't the kind of money you just handed over to a junior high schooler. Seeing Kojou standing still with a dumbfounded look, a mysterious expression came over Yukina's face.

"The Lion King Agency accountant lady said that against the Fourth Primogenitor, I could perish at any time, so I ought not leave behind any regrets, so...that's what the expense budget is for."

"It's my fault?! You're rich because of me?!"

No way, Kojou wanted to shout. He could understand the logic of an expense budget rising the more dangerous the mission, but the inconvenience of Yukina's arrival had mostly been his: dragging him into a fight with demons, watching his private life, threatening him with that crazy spear. So why was her piggy bank bigger than his?

But, if Kojou yelled out all his troubles, Yukina would take it the wrong way.

"I'm sorry, Senpai, making you carry all the baggage like this."

"Oh, that's no problem, really. You can't carry it all yourself, right?"

"Yes. Having you with me really helped, Senpai."

Yukina smiled as she spoke. Kojou silently shrugged his shoulders. Inside the bags swinging from Kojou's hands were the daily necessities Yukina had bought: bedroom curtains, bath mats, toilet slippers, cups and toothbrushes, mugs. Kojou thought, it's just like what a pair of students would get right after moving in together.

And, just as Kojou, carrying the bags, and Yukina arrived at the monorail boarding platform...

"—Kojou?"

There was a surprised voice right in front of them.

"Eh?"

Kojou reflexively lifted his face as someone called out his name. Standing there was an attractive—even gorgeous—female high school student. Her face was very familiar to Kojou.

"Er, Asagi? What are you doing here? Your place ain't this way, is it?"

"It's not. I was coming home from work… I thought I'd bring that World History report you asked me for over to your place, but…"

Though Kojou was speaking to her the same as usual, Asagi seemed to have her guard up for some reason as she replied. Her gaze flowed over the baggage filled with that daily-life feel.

And then Asagi's eyes turned toward Yukina, who stood beside Kojou.

"Who's the girl?"

"Oh, Himeragi? Err, she's a transfer student who's entering middle school right about now." Kojou introduced Yukina in a carefree tone.

Yukina lowered her head in a little nod. Asagi stared squarely at Yukina.

"And what are *you* doing with a transfer student going into middle school, Kojou?"

"Er, that is," Kojou mumbled. After all, he'd promised to keep secret the fact she was from a special national agency and had come to watch over Kojou.

Not that he thought Asagi would believe any of that even if he told her, but…

"R…right, she's Nagisa's classmate."

Kojou's voice sprang out as he finally remembered that. Asagi suspiciously raised an eyebrow.

"Nagisa's?"

"Yeah. Apparently she and Nagisa got to know each other when she did the formalities for transferring."

"…So, Kojou, you're saying Nagisa introduced this girl to you?"

"Yeah, that's it."

As that wasn't really wrong, Kojou deftly parried. As Yukina listened to the exchange between Kojou and Asagi, an expression came over her like she'd just realized something.

"Pretty girl, isn't she…"

Asagi turned her face to Kojou's, speaking in a soft voice. She had the usual leering smile on her face, but she didn't look like she was smiling when you looked at her eyes.

"Well, yeah."

Kojou honestly agreed without any special thought involved. When he saw Asagi's cheek twitch, he amended his words in a bit of a hurry.

"...Er, Nagisa said that, too."

"Hmm. I see."

Asagi distanced herself from Kojou, an artificial smile still on her face. From the way she looked, Kojou felt a dangerous aura about her.

"Ah, Asagi?"

"Well, the train's coming. I'm heading home."

Just as Asagi said, the train was just arriving at the monorail loading platform. She turned in the opposite direction of the stop toward Kojou and Yukina's apartment complex. Kojou hurriedly called out to her, "Huh? Weren't you gonna show me that World History report?"

"Yeah. I meant to, but apparently I forgot it somewhere."

Asagi spoke with a smiling face filled with quiet rage. Her eyes conveyed a silent message that he *would* be explaining this at school tomorrow.

"Huh? Hey, Asagi!"

"Bye-bye!"

The train doors shut right in front of the bewildered Kojou's eyes. For some reason, Asagi ignored Kojou, waved amiably to Yukina alone, and left.

"What's up with her?"

Kojou tilted his head as he muttered. Yukina had an expression on her face as though she felt responsible.

"I'm sorry, Senpai. It may be my fault there's some kind of misunderstanding..."

"Misunderstanding?"

Kojou glanced back with a mystified look at Yukina, who was dejected for some reason. Finally, he *ahh*ed as it clicked.

"Er, no way. There's no misunderstanding. She's just a friend, you see."

"Just...friends, is it?" Yukina asked back as if weighing whether that's what Kojou really thought. Kojou nodded without hesitation.

"Well, we go back a long way. It's like we're best buds."

"Senpai..."

For some reason, Yukina was looking up at Kojou with a scolding look over his indifferent reply.

"What?"

"No, it's nothing."

Her words were accompanied by a deep exhalation.

3

In the end, it was nearly evening by the time Kojou and Yukina arrived back at their apartment building.

The sun's rays were as strong as usual, but the breeze was just starting to have a bit of nighttime chill mixed in.

"—Huh, you and Kojou-kun are back only now? Pretty late, isn't it?"

As Kojou and Yukina dove past the apartment complex's entrance, as if fleeing from the setting sun, someone's voice was there to greet them. With the elevator door still open, a female junior high school student, in uniform, motioned with her hand for them to hurry over.

"Nagisa, huh. What's with the bags?"

As Kojou entered the elevator, he raised an eyebrow at his little sister's appearance. Nagisa's right hand had a sports bag packed with her baggage for club activities in it. And her left hand held a shopping bag filled with a large amount of cooking ingredients.

"What do you mean what? It's for our transfer girl's welcome party."

Looking at the surprised Kojou, Nagisa spoke in apparent amazement.

"Welcome party?"

"That's right. I mean, she only just moved here, so she can't prepare supper for today, right?"

"Well, you've got a point there."

Kojou nodded, remembering how Yukina's room had lacked cooking utensils and even basic tableware. Then a suspicious look came over him.

"Wait, Nagisa, did you know Himeragi was moving in next door…?"

"Yeah. I mean, she came over to say hi this morning. You were asleep, though."

Nagisa spoke in a tone that seemed to fault him for sleeping in late. She was more reserved with the amount of words out of her mouth than usual, though, and was no doubt being prudent in front of Yukina.

"That so?" Kojou asked Yukina in a low voice.

"Yes," Yukina replied, nodding.

"Er... But is it all right, having a welcome party?"

"Totally all right! I already bought meat for it anyway. Kojou and I can't eat it all by ourselves."

Nagisa had a warm, affable expression as she spoke. *That's for sure*, thought Kojou with a strained smile.

Thanks to their parents divorcing four years before, the Akatsuki household was currently a three-person family. Furthermore, their mother, working as head of research for a corporation based in the city, would be away from home for one or two weeks at a time depending on circumstances with her work.

Since her children could go meet her at any time, it didn't feel all that lonely, but Kojou and Nagisa substantially lived on their own together as brother and sister. Though not by a giant margin, they couldn't eat the 1.5 kilograms of on-sale, special-cut beef that Nagisa held in her arms.

"Thank you very much. As you prefer, then."

Yukina said that after a bit of thought. She was probably telling herself it was just another part of her duty to watch Kojou. Hearing those words, Nagisa made a happy-looking smile.

"I'm so glad. So come over after you've put your stuff away. Ah, are you all right with only a pot of stew? I hope there's nothing you can't eat in there, Yukina. It sure feels like a luxury having the air conditioner on full blast and eating stuff like this in the middle of summer. Which do you like the taste of better, miso or soy sauce? Yukina, is there anything you can't eat, or can you eat everything? It really does feel like a luxury, eating stew in the middle of the summer with the AC turned up. For the broth, I use bonito, kelp, chicken bones, and potatoes, but today I prepared some crab, too, so maybe I should use soy sauce. The crab's hair crab from Okhotsk. Today's just the right season—"

"Leave it at that, Nagisa. Himeragi's in shell-shock."

Kojou lightly tapped his little sister on the head to quiet her motor-mouth down. Nagisa went, "Ow," and glared at Kojou with tearful eyes.

A look of being completely overwhelmed came over Yukina, but even so:

"Er, how about I help you with it? If it's just preparing a stew, then..."

"No, no, today you're our guest, Yukina. You must be tired from having come a long way. Hey, Kojou, entertain Yukina, would you?"

"Don't say something you just came up with like you planned it. I'm goin' to my room to finish off my homework."

Kojou let out a small sigh as he gazed at the setting sun. Before he'd realized it, his remaining summer vacation time had become all too brief. He couldn't conceal his sense that he might already be too late.

"If that is the case, how about I help you with your homework, then, Senpai?"

Yukina spoke as she left the day-to-day goods she'd bought in the entryway to room 705.

Her unexpected offer threw Kojou off. He was truly grateful for the suggestion, but there were too many problems with his little sister's classmate helping him study, at least as far as his dignity as an older brother was concerned.

But, Nagisa cared nothing for Kojou's inner conflict.

"Sorry, Yukina-chan. Please take good care of Kojou-kun. He's not a very bright older brother."

As she made another monologue, she brought Yukina back with her to her own residence. Kojou followed the girls with a sullen face. Dignity as the older brother? No such thing. He was grateful that at least Yukina didn't act like Nagisa's pushy invitation bothered her at all.

Entering her own residence, Nagisa immediately tossed on an apron and began preparing the ingredients.

As she did so, Kojou led Yukina to his own room.

Since Nagisa was a clean freak and tidied up without asking, *May I?* whenever she saw an opening, Kojou could show her his room without any embarrassment, at least.

Even so, the room was dreary with little in the way of content to begin with. It wasn't quite at the level of Yukina's room, but aside from the bed, a desk, and a half-empty bookshelf with old magazines stuffed into it, it was bare.

"This is… Senpai, you're a basketball player?"

Yukina had noticed the album sitting on top of that bookshelf when she asked, apparently a bit surprised.

The album was a record of Kojou's time in Basketball Club in junior high school. He'd gotten rid of all his basketball equipment when he'd left the club, but this was the only thing not thrown away.

"So you know what basketball is, Himeragi? Even though you said a golf club was a type of mace?"

Kojou spoke in a joking tone. Yukina's lips twisted in a pout.

"A city championship is an impressive record."

"Well, that was a long time ago."

"Was obtaining the power of the Fourth Primogenitor why you gave up basketball, Senpai?"

Yukina said those words as she looked at him with a serious expression. Kojou shook his head like the issue was tiresome. It felt a bit odd that a whole year had passed since then, he thought.

"My condition's got nothin' to do with that. I quit basketball before then, you see."

Yeah, not like I could compete with this body anyway, Kojou thought, laughing at his own expense.

He had the ability to leap with monstrous strength and the agility to catch a bullet. Using demonic power was the antithesis of sportsmanship. As cheating went, doping scandals had nothing on this.

But Kojou had quit basketball over a year ago, before he'd become a vampire.

"Why did you, then?"

"Really, it's not that rare a story. I didn't understand club activity isn't something you can do by yourself.

"The point being, I was isolated on the team."

"Eh?"

Watching from the side, Yukina seemed surprised as Kojou talked about it as if it involved someone else. Kojou executed a languid flop onto the bed, making a strained smile as he looked up at the ceiling.

"Back then, I thought we'd win if I just played hard enough. And till midway, that's actually how it was. We were what people call a one-man team. Because I was a good player, I really got carried away with myself."

Like it was ever gonna work out like that, Kojou thought with a laugh.

The trigger was the final tournament in junior high. Kojou had been injured in the district qualifiers. He'd taken a hard foul from the opposing team and had been forced off the court midway against his will. Fortunately, they'd had a large lead; Kojou's injury wasn't all that severe, either. If they'd won he should've been able to play in the next round.

But the instant Kojou went off the court, the team's morale collapsed.

They let the opposing team roar back and build a huge lead, and lost just like that.

From start to finish, all Kojou could do was watch the process from the bench, dumbfounded, unable to do a thing.

"More than that, I was shocked at how calmly the other players accepted defeat."

Kojou made an offhanded shrug of his shoulders.

"That's when I finally realized *I* was the one who'd taken their willpower away. They figured, even if they didn't try hard, someone else would win it for them. I made them think I'd always come through, even though the truth was I couldn't do anything on my own. Not that understanding that means I can do anything about it now."

That was why Kojou quit the team, citing the need to recover from his injury. Some of his fellow players remained, but Kojou didn't continue to play basketball with them, for Kojou reasoned that so long as he was at their side, they'd never change. At any rate, Kojou himself had lost all desire to continue.

"I don't think… that it was all your fault, though, Senpai." Yukina, having silently listened to his story, spoke in an overly serious tone.

As Yukina did so, Kojou made what seemed like a teasing smile at her.

"Yeah, well that's all right. I just lost my motivation all on my own, after all. But…" Then Kojou bared his canine teeth. His eye color changed to red for just a moment. "When this ridiculous Fourth Primogenitor thing got pushed onto me, I did think about it a little. Like if I used these powers, I'd probably be able to solve a bunch of the problems of today's world. At the very least, I could kill off fiendish criminals and wipe out dirty politicians… Stuff like that."

"Senpai. That's—"

"I know. That's no good. Just 'cause a guy like me gets his hands on a bit more power than the next guy doesn't make fiddling with the world any which way a good thing. If I do something like that, there'll probably be a reaction coming from somewhere."

Yukina exhaled in what seemed like relief. And, as if suddenly realizing something, she raised an eyebrow.

"Senpai, is that why you hide the fact you're a vampire and live as an ordinary human being?"

Well that, too, thought Kojou as he made a vague nod.

"I don't need vampire powers anyway, and I don't want anything to do with 'em if I can avoid it. I'm not cut out to be some hero anyway. Besides, to be honest, these crazy powers I've been given are beyond me. I don't have any faith I can use 'em right."

"I see..."

It's not that I don't understand how you feel, thought Yukina as she watched Kojou with sober eyes. Then...

"But, Senpai... Isn't that just an excuse to do nothing?"

"Eh? Er... Is that what you think?"

An expression came over Kojou like he was hurt.

"I kinda meant to say something profound there, but, ah..."

"Hee-hee, I suppose you did. I have a somewhat better opinion of you now, really."

"O-okay."

"Quite."

Yukina made a small giggle.

"Now then, right now there's something you have to do, so shall we begin, Senpai? Let's stop memorizing answers for now. After all, if you can take care of basic formulas you'll be all right."

As Yukina opened one of Kojou's textbooks, she spoke with the tone of a private tutor older than he was. With a *geh,* Kojou's face grimaced, but for some reason, Yukina seemed somewhat amused.

4

The supper Nagisa had prepared should have been enough for light servings for seven or eight people, but the three of them exhibited ravenous hunger as they devoured the whole thing. They even managed to finish off the last of the rice gruel broth.

"Ahh—we sure ate. I can't move anymore."

Nagisa, wearing a thin camisole, flopped onto the living room sofa. When Yukina tried to help clean up after, Nagisa went, "It's okay, it's okay," and coerced her back to her own room; by the time the kitchen was spotless, she seemed to have used up all her strength.

"Hey, Nagisa. Don't fall asleep in a place like that. You'll catch cold."

As his little sister happily clutched her tummy, Kojou watched with an incredulous expression as he spoke bluntly. Nagisa waved him off with an annoyed look.

"Just for a little bit—I'm tired from today's club practice, too—ah, Kojou?"

"Where are you going?"

"Convenience store. Gonna go drink somethin' so I can stay awake," Kojou replied while putting on his parka over his loungewear.

Nagisa, still facedown, raised her face, sounding like it took significant effort.

"Ahh, buy some ice cream while you're at it, then. Same one as last time."

"You can still eat? ...You'll get fat, right around the gut."

"Oh, shut up. I hate it when you say that, Kojou." Nagisa's cheeks puffed up as she objected.

"Yeah, yeah."

As Kojou thought, *She's angry 'cause she knows I'm right*, he tied his shoes and opened the front door. Yukina was standing right in front of him.

"—Where do you think you're going at a time like this, Senpai?"

"Whoa!" Kojou unwittingly cried out. Yukina's eyes were narrowed, seemingly on guard as she gave Kojou an icy glare.

"H-Himeragi?!"

"Yes. What is it?"

Seeing Yukina tilt her head a bit as she asked, Kojou felt just a little relieved.

Yukina's hair was still wet, with water droplets dripping from the tips. Furthermore, the only thing she'd thrown over her bare upper body was her blouse, looking quite defenseless. She didn't have that guitar case on her back. He wondered if she'd been waiting outside the residence, watching guard the whole time, but apparently that had not been the case.

She'd probably been in the middle of taking a bath when she'd felt

Kojou heading out. No doubt she'd rushed out in a big hurry. That kind of stupidly blind dedication to her work was just the thing the all-too-serious Yukina would do.

"You don't actually plan on coming with me? Dressed like that?" Kojou asked as he felt a light headache.

"It's my duty to watch you," Yukina replied with her usual deadpan tone, but even she exhibited a bit of timidity and anxiety.

Circumstances being what they were, she probably wasn't even wearing panties under her skirt.

Kojou shook his head in dismay.

"Hey, it's okay. Go…dry your hair and whatever. I'll wait here till you're done."

"Really?"

Yukina blinked, looking a bit surprised. Kojou's face continued to grimace.

"As if I can take a junior high schooler around looking like that?! I'll get arrested!!"

"I—I suppose you're right. Please come in and wait, then."

"No, that's all right. I'll wait here. Not like I'm gonna run away."

Kojou hid the dejection on his face as he spoke. Any way you sliced it, being alone with a girl coming out of the bath was *bad*. It cranked the difficulty level too high for Kojou.

Yukina left him with a "Well, then," seeming to flee as she returned to her own room.

Kojou looked up at the sky from the apartment hallway. He innocently counted the stars. After all, he had a feeling that he'd be assaulted by vampiric impulses if he visualized Yukina changing clothes instead.

Finally, the door to Yukina's room opened once again, and Yukina came out, fully dressed this time around. She indeed had that guitar case over her back.

Maybe she doesn't have any clothes aside from school uniforms, Kojou suddenly thought. *I'm gonna have to take her shopping sometime soon.* While having that entirely natural thought, Kojou realized something and sank lower.

He felt like he'd brought a small, high-maintenance pet home.

"So, where are we going, Senpai?" Yukina asked, ignorant of Kojou's inner conflict.

Kojou got in the elevator as he replied, "Convenience store. Don't tell me you don't know what a convenience store is?"

"Yes, I know what it is, but I've never gone to one in the middle of the night like this."

Yukina spoke with a bounce in her voice, as if it contained expectation without any uneasiness mixed in. She had an expression like a girl keeping a prank secret from her parents. *Don't expect that much from a convenience store*, Kojou thought with a strained smile.

"Sorry about earlier. You must be exhausted."

"Eh?"

"Suppertime. Nagisa was really worked up."

"No, that was fun. The pot of stew was delicious, too."

Yukina smiled with what looked like a little blush. *Well, I'm glad*, Kojou thought as he smiled.

"We used to take turns cooking way back, but Nagisa's way better at it lately, so..."

"It's nice, being a brother and sister. I don't have any family, so I kind of admire it."

Yukina conveyed that with a casual tone.

"Don't have a family?"

Kojou looked at the side of Yukina's face in surprise. "No," replied Yukina, shaking her head without showing any real sentiment.

"Everyone at High God Forest is an orphan. The organization gathers children with potential together from all over the country and raises them to become Counter-Demon Attack Mages."

"That so...?"

Yukina's unexpectedly weighty personal history left Kojou at a loss for words.

"Then you were raised from the start to be an Attack Mage...?"

"Yes. Er, but it's not that I was lonely from not having family, or anything like that. All the staff at High God Forest are very kind; I didn't mind the Sword Shaman training, either."

Yukina amended herself in a hurry. It didn't feel to him that Yukina was lying; Kojou accepted her words at face value. He figured Yukina couldn't have learned martial arts at a high enough level to utterly dominate demons if she'd hated the training, anyway. But—

"What's…a Sword Shaman?"

Kojou tilted his head at the unfamiliar term.

"An Attack Mage who serves High God Forest. I think it's *supposed* to mean a shrine maiden trained in the art of the sword, though."

Yukina spoke with an unsure look. Apparently she didn't really understand it herself.

"Shrine maiden… Hey, Himeragi, does that mean you can do prayers and tell fortunes?"

"I can go through the motions. It's not really my specialty, though…"

"Hmm."

I see, Kojou thought, somehow accepting it. Now that she mentioned it, Yukina seemed prim and proper but had the air of someone who found stiff formalities difficult.

Either way, you could call her animalistic, or rather, the type to move based on instinct and intuition. Perhaps those were the very qualities that qualified her to be a Sword Shaman to begin with.

"Senpai… You were thinking something rather rude just now, weren't you?"

She unnerved Kojou with the timing of her question, as if she'd been looking right through his mind.

"Er, no, not at all."

"I am a rather skilled medium, you see. It is useless to lie to me."

"Eh…?! You really are like an animal…"

"So you were indeed thinking something like that…"

At some point during that conversation, the two of them arrived at the convenience store that was their destination.

Island South, the main residential Gigafloat where Kojou and Yukina's apartment complex was located, did not have many people walking about at night. Even so, things were fairly lively as they approached the train station.

Fast food and coffee shops. Even manga cafés and game centers—

"Ah…"

When they passed in front of the game center, Yukina suddenly came to a halt. That drew an over-the-shoulder look from Kojou. There was no way she didn't know what a game center was, for goodness' sakes, but…

"Ah, sorry. It's nothing."

"Something about that crane game there?"

Kojou asked as he realized Yukina was fixated on a cabinet at the front of the store. Yukina tilted her head a little.

"So that's a…crane game. It has a Nekoma-tan in it…"

"Nekoma-tan? That mascot plushie thingie?"

"Yes. Er… It was really popular at my old school."

Yukina made a small nod. It was a two-headed cat mascot waving a paw like a beckoning cat.

It featured a tail split in two, which probably accounted for the name. Yukina tried to speak like it wasn't anything special to her, but she looked at the mascot in the glass case with shining, glittering eyes.

"Well, we can nab it if it's just that."

A slightly strained smile came over Kojou as he took out a five-hundred-yen piece. Yukina looked up at Kojou with a surprised expression.

"What do you mean by *nab*? You can't mean…"

"No, no. I don't mean that in the sense of stealing; I mean, that's what the machine's for."

This said, Kojou inserted the coin into the game machine. As Kojou used button controls to make the crane's arm move, Yukina grasped the general idea, too. She gave the movements of the arm a much more serious look than when she'd fought those demons.

Since he'd been with Nagisa when she'd made plenty of high-handed requests, Kojou's skill with crane games was pretty decent. With precision, he placed the arm where it could easily grab, targeted the individual plushie, and lowered the crane.

Yukina held her breath as she watched the arm's unfaltering aim as it gripped the mascot, pulling it up and carrying to the drop box. Finally, the pseudo-beckoning cat mascot plushie dropped into the box. That moment…

"—You two there. You're Saikai Academy students, aren't you? What are you doing here at this hour?"

When Kojou and Yukina heard the calm voice coming from behind, they froze as if zapped by electricity.

Geh. Kojou sucked in his breath as he saw the silhouette reflected by the game machine's glass.

There stood Natsuki Minamiya. He didn't need to get a good look at her face; no one else on the Island of Everlasting Summer was crazy enough to wear something as stifling as a frilled dress. The parasol she held raised was out of place at night, but it seemed she was in the middle of making the rounds to give students proper guidance.

"You there, the boy. I think I've seen you before. Pull your hood down and turn toward me."

Natsuki spoke with a tone that somehow sounded amused. She seemed intent on cornering Kojou bit by bit, as if strangling his neck with silk lace.

When he glanced at Yukina, she was paralyzed with a pale look on her face. Having been raised to take being an honor student for granted, this situation was probably hitting her pretty hard.

This is bad, thought Kojou with a cold sweat.

It was already approaching midnight. Even if it was a game machine at the head of the store, *We were playing at a game center* wasn't any excuse. This was totally against school regulations. *And* he had a middle schooler with him.

"What's wrong? If you're going to be stubborn about turning around, I have ways to make you comply—"

It happened right after Natsuki spoke with a tone like she was toying with her prey.

Thump. A low vibration rocked the entire man-made island. A moment later, the sound of an explosion thundered.

"What the—?!"

Natsuki, also an Attack Mage, turned around in reaction to a strange presence.

Sounds of explosions continued to roar without end. No simple accident or natural phenomenon could account for this.

Someone was engaging in deliberate destruction. That was also conveyed by the fierce wave of magical energy that even normal people were able to sense. The moment Natsuki's attention was fully drawn away by that…

"Himeragi, run!"

Kojou instantly grabbed Yukina's hand and broke into a run.

"Eh, ah… Right!"

Understanding Kojou's intent, Yukina gripped his hand back.

"Ah, wait, you two—"

Natsuki yelled something at their backs, but both Yukina and Kojou possessed athletic ability incomparable to that of a normal person's. Kojou sensed a flash from Yukina, destroying the barrier Natsuki instantly stretched before them. Natsuki, taken completely off guard, no longer had any means with which to follow.

We made it, thought Kojou with relief. That moment…

"I'll remember this, Kojou Akatsuki!"

Natsuki's words, like those of a recurring villain, echoed throughout the night.

However, her voice vanished as the intermittent sounds of huge explosions continued once more.

Kojou's expression twisted as they ran. It wasn't that Natsuki's words bothered him. It was that he realized the true nature of the strange explosions occurring within the city.

This was a mass of sentient, overwhelmingly strong magical power running wild. An incarnation of destruction.

And a being all too close to Kojou Akatsuki's current existence—

A vampire's Beast Vassal.

5

"Senpai… Those explosions…"

Having continued to run all the way to the Gigafloat's cliffs, Yukina finally came to a stop. Her breathing was largely regular, but her cheeks had a slight redness to them—perhaps because she'd realized she was still holding Kojou's hand.

But she did not pull her hand back. From her posture, she seemed concerned Kojou would pull himself out of her grasp.

"Yeah. That was a Beast Vassal. Plus with that magic energy… The master's probably pretty up there."

Kojou spoke as his face continued to grimace. The next moment, a huge explosion erupted once more.

In the sky above the Gigafloat, a fireball several meters in diameter appeared; a sudden gust assaulted them a moment later. It was like a nighttime storm when white waves crashed against the artificial ground, making it creak and shake.

Bathed in exploding flames, they saw a jet-black bird-phantom rise up.

Kojou only saw it for an instant, but that was enough to know for certain: It was indeed a summoned beast born from dense magical energy. A vampire's Beast Vassal.

It wasn't a little one like the one Yukina had fought a few days before. Based on its having enough destructive power to shake the whole island, no doubt it was the familiar of someone from the Elder Days, with a name even wise men and nobles dared not speak.

It had been given form and was now on the rampage. A vampire was fighting someone.

Island East's warehouse district had become a battlefield. Though a largely unmanned industrial area, even from a distance Kojou could see damage equivalent to a large industrial fire taking place.

However, even with so much damage occurring, combat continued.

That fact could mean only one thing—whoever the vampire from the Elder Days was fighting also had combat capability equal to one from the Elder One itself.

So right now, someone somewhere in the city Kojou and Yukina lived was hunting down a powerful Elder vampire.

That was a pretty big deal.

"I'm sorry, Senpai. We part ways here. Please go on ahead back home."

Yukina, speaking one-sidedly, released his hand as she spoke. Kojou looked at her, dumbfounded.

"Himeragi?"

"I will go investigate what is happening. Once I confirm things are safe, I will return immediately."

"Hold on, Himeragi. If you're heading to take a look, I'll go w—"

Kojou called out to Yukina in a hurry. Yukina looked back at Kojou with an exasperated look.

"And what will you do if you go, Senpai? Please have a little consideration for the position you are in."

"P-position?"

"Yes. I mean your position as the Fourth Primogenitor, relative to the vampire who is fighting, Senpai."

"Um, er...?"

"What do you think will happen if you clumsily lay a hand on either side in an effort to stop them? If the Fourth Primogenitor attacks a vampire of another bloodline, it is a very large problem. The same would apply if you took his side."

Under Yukina's sharp glare, Kojou hemmed and hawed.

"The heck is all that... Well, what should I do, then...?!"

"You need not do anything at all. Please go home—you are in the way. I am here so that you do not do anything dangerous like that, Senpai."

"Hold on, that's no reason for you to force yourself to go, Himeragi. Watch me so I don't get involved, then!"

This time Kojou glared at Yukina as he spoke. However, Yukina shook her head without hesitation.

"If you were truly going to be cooperative, I would do just that, but... that is impossible, isn't it? After all, people you know might get drawn into combat, Senpai—"

As Yukina calmly pointed that out, Kojou went silent.

Even if the current battleground was outside of urban areas, there was no guarantee civilians wouldn't be caught up in it given the scale of the battle. And there were many people Kojou knew on the island. If he could at least guarantee their safety, Kojou would feel some measure of relief, but—

"I will go confirm things. It's connected to my assignment."

As he watched Yukina firmly cut off her words, Kojou unwittingly raised his voice.

"Why do you have to go that far, Himeragi?! Isn't upholding law and order in the Demon Sanctuary the job of the police and the Island Guard?!"

"Unless they have an Counter-Demon Attack Mage of no small strength, they cannot enter a battlefield with a Beast Vassal running wild. However, because I have this…"

As Yukina spoke, she drew her weapon from the guitar case on her back.

Making a tidy, metallic sound, the silver spear's blade deployed.

"This is equipment granted to me for fighting Primogenitors. A Beast Vassal of that level is no match for Snowdrift Wolf."

"Himeragi…"

"Therefore, please be by Nagisa-san's side, Senpai."

As an even more concerned expression came across Kojou, Yukina showed him a gentle smile.

That fleeting, smiling face gave Kojou pause.

"Eh?"

"The Holy Ground Treaty specifies the right to self-defense. If it is to protect your family or others who dwell under your protection, even if you use your power there's no problem at all, Senpai."

Thrusting through the opening made by Kojou's hesitation, Yukina broke into a hard sprint.

No doubt she'd chosen her timing from the beginning. As she vaulted down from the artificial island's cliff, there was a freight monorail passing beneath her feet. Yukina landed safely atop of the moving train. The automated monorail was heading toward Island East, where the combat was taking place.

"Himeragi…!"

Kojou, left alone atop the southern district's cliff, violently punched the fence standing before his eyes.

Combat in the warehouse district continued even now. The Beast Vassal floating up amid the blazing flames was pierced by an attack from someone, letting out a screaming howl.

After that, all that remained was a huge explosion—

6

A large-scale fire had erupted all over the warehouse district.

Streetlights extinguished, the district glowed crimson from the blazing flames. The automated fire-fighting gear was active, but the fire showed no sign of abating.

Fortunately, there was no sign of people within the district. It was a low-population sector to begin with; the people administrating the warehouse district seemed to have finished evacuating.

The explosions must have taken out the power supply. The monorail came to a halt the moment it arrived at Island East.

Yukina leaped down from the roof of the now-motionless train and headed to where the Beast Vassal was currently raging.

The Beast Vassal in combat was a ghostly, jet-black bird, resembling a giant raven.

Its wingspan easily exceeded ten meters. From time to time, its huge body, as if solidified darkness, glowed as if molten amber, bursting into a fireball that spawned ferocious explosions all around it. Its entire body was wrapped in a blast wind. Apparently this Beast Vassal was the incarnation of explosion itself.

The one controlling the Beast Vassal was a tall vampire in an expensive business suit standing on the roof of a building.

He looked like he was thirty years of age, give or take, but looking at his incredible magical energy, there was little doubt he'd lived several times that number. His overwhelming, intense presence was worthy of the moniker "Elder."

He could have been a manager in the employ of one of the corporations within Itogami City, a mercenary, or even a military officer dispatched by a Dominion. He was big game whatever the case.

However, in spite of the vampire unleashing such formidable attacks over and over, there was no sign combat was coming to a halt. To the contrary, signs of impatience and strain were clearly visible on the man's face.

He was an Elder, but he was being overwhelmed.

"That's…"

Yukina's bewildered voice came out as she noticed a flash tearing through the sky.

It was a giant, translucent arm, shining like the colors of the rainbow.

It wasn't flesh and blood. This was a mass of magical energy given physical form, just like a Beast Vassal. However, it had an aura that differed from any Beast Vassal that Yukina knew of.

That arm, some several meters long, made contact with the jet-black ghost bird in midair.

And the next moment, the ghost bird made an anguished howl.

The ghost bird's black wing had been ripped from its socket, sending fresh, magma-like incandescent blood scattering.

And, with the ghost bird's huge body having lost its balance, the rainbow-colored arm tore it apart as if feasting upon it.

Unable to maintain its physical form, the ghost bird fell to the ground as a simple mass of magical energy. However, the rainbow-colored arm did not halt its attacks. Like a scavenger, it violated the destroyed Beast Vassal's corpse.

"It's...*eating* the magic energy?!"

Yukina shuddered at the bizarre sight. Consuming a defeated Beast Vassal's magic energy—so far as Yukina knew, no one had ever heard of the existence of such a Beast Vassal.

And, when Yukina beheld the master controlling the Beast Vassal, she was further unnerved.

For the master of the rainbow-colored arm was a girl even smaller than Yukina. She was an indigo-haired girl wearing a cape coat over bare flesh. She had an artificially beautiful face. And those pale blue, emotionless eyes—

"She's...not a vampire?! It can't be... How can a homunculus control a Beast Vassal?!"

As Yukina stood in a daze, there was a heavy *thud* sound of something falling behind her.

Turning around in surprise, Yukina beheld the tall vampire, who had collapsed onto the ground and was gravely wounded.

The deep, slicing wound from his armpit stretched all the way to his heart.

A human being would have died instantly. The same went for the average vampire. To even be still breathing was testament to the hardiness of an Elder.

However, where normally he would have instantly begun to regenerate, his body showed no change. Surely it was not solely because he was weak from the loss of his Beast Vassal. He had taken damage from an attack that used extremely powerful magic.

The only type of human being capable of such an attack was a Counter-Demon Attack Mage—and even then, only those of the highest ability, known as Exorcists, but that simply wasn't possible.

An exorcist was, in other words, a holy man of the highest rank. Such men held the status of priests and bishops. There was no way one would willingly engage in a duel in an urban area. There was no way such a thing could be excused.

"—Hmm. A witness. Unexpected."

Hearing a low, male voice, Yukina gasped and lifted her face.

Standing with blazing flames at his back, he was a large-framed man more than a hundred and ninety centimeters tall. The blade of the bardiche held by his right hand, and the vestment he wore over his armored augmentation suit, were smeared red with fresh blood. Blood spatter from the vampire.

"Please end this fighting."

Yukina warned the man in the vestment with a glare.

As she did so, the man gazed at Yukina with contempt.

"Young, aren't you? An Attack Mage of this nation, yes… Not an ally of the demon, it would seem."

He spoke calmly, appraising her.

Feeling the bloodlust the man's body exuded, Yukina lowered her center of gravity.

"Atrocities toward incapacitated demons are forbidden by the Offensive Magic Special Measures Act."

"And do I have reason to obey laws passed by apostates that consort with demons?"

As the man easily dismissed her words, he raised his huge battle-axe high.

"Ngh, Snowdrift Wolf—!"

Spear in hand, Yukina sprinted. She ran under the battle-axe as it swung down toward the wounded vampire, just barely blocking it.

"My…!"

The man whose battle-axe had been thrown back murmured in apparent pleasure. Leaping back with agility unimaginable given his huge physique, the man faced off toward Yukina.

"Is that spear a Schneewalzer?! The Lion King Agency's DOE-inscribed secret weapon! To have a chance to see one here of all places!"

A delighted smile came over the man's lips. A red light pulsed from the eyepatch-like monocle he wore. It seemed to be projecting information directly into the man's field of vision.

"Very well; a Lion King Agency's Sword Shaman is a worthy opponent. Young woman, I, Rudolf Eustach, Lotharingian Armed Apostle, request a duel. Save this demon's life—if you can!"

"A Lotharingian Armed Apostle?! What is an exorcist of the European Church doing hunting demons—?!"

"I have no obligation to answer!"

The man's huge body kicked off the ground and fiercely accelerated. The battle-axe swung down, assaulting Yukina with the force of a guillotine. The force of the slice, assisted by his augmented armor, was sufficient to rip apart an armored car with ease. However, Yukina perfectly anticipated the strike, and slipped by it by a paper's width.

Then she counterattacked. The spinning Yukina stretched her spear toward Eustach's right arm just after it finished its attack.

Eustach, unable to evade the attack, blocked it with his armor-encased left arm instead.

The clash between enchanted weapon and armor sent pale sparks scattering.

"Hnng!"

As the man's left arm's armor plates were smashed apart, Yukina took the opportunity to put some space between them. With such a large, resilient man as her opponent, she was at a clear disadvantage in close combat. She judged she should bring him down with hit-and-run tactics.

"My holy armor's ward destroyed in a single blow?! I'd expect nothing less from a Schneewalzer… A truly fascinating enchantment. Splendid!"

Gazing at his destroyed left arm's armor, Eustach licked his lips in satisfaction. His monocle restlessly switched on and off.

Sensing a sinister aura from Eustach, Yukina's expression sharpened further.

I must defeat him here and now, she resolved. Her Sword Shaman intuition told her that if she let this Armed Apostle be, he would bring a great calamity down upon this land.

"—O purifying light, O divine wolf of the snowdrift, by your steel divine will, strike down the devils before me!"

"Hnn… This is…"

As Yukina chanted her solemn prayer, the ritual energy honed within her body amplified the Schneewalzer. Eustach's face twisted at the powerful ritual energy surge emitted from the spear.

The next moment, Yukina launched a ferocious attack against Eustach.

"Nuo…!"

The Armed Apostle blocked the beam of light that came from the silver spear with his battle-axe. A shocked look came over him at the impact conveyed to his arm. His augmented armor, able to easily fend off the attacks of a beast man, was pushed back several meters, unable to withstand the small girl's attack. Sparks flew from every joint from the intense strain.

Furthermore, Yukina's attacks did not end with that. She pressed on with a series of attacks at point-blank range like a storm, putting Eustach completely on the defensive. This fact shocked the Armed Apostle.

The truth was, in raw speed, the very human Yukina was very far from a beast man or vampire. However, with her spirit sight enabling her to see a moment into the future, Yukina ended up moving faster than anyone. Combined with various feints and a high level of weapons skill on top of that, Yukina possessed attack speed that was beyond what an armored augmentation suit's man-made abilities could evade. Only ceaseless training from a very young age made it possible. It was a superhuman skill only Sword Shamans could use.

"Mm, what power…and what speed! So this is a Sword Shaman of the Lion King Agency!"

Magnificent, extolled Eustach. Unable to withstand Snowdrift Wolf's attacks, the bardiche made a *crack*ing sound and broke apart.

That moment, Yukina's attacks came to a brief halt. She'd hesitated to attack the human Eustach directly for but a single moment. Eustach did not let the momentary opening slip away.

"Very well, I have beheld the Lion King Agency's secret ritual—slay her, Astarte!"

The Armed Apostole leaped back with the full might of his augmented armor. In his place, the young indigo-haired girl wearing a cape coat leaped before Yukina.

"Accept. Execute 'Rhododactylos.'"

The giant arm appeared, bursting out of the young girl's coat. It assaulted Yukina while emitting a rainbow-colored glow. Yukina counterattacked with Snowdrift Wolf. The giant magical energy and the ritual energy collided, causing an earsplitting ring to fill the air.

"Ugh…!"

"Aa…!"

Yukina won the exchange, but just barely. The silver spear slowly rent the Beast Vassal called "Rhododactylos." The girl called Astarte made frail, anguished pants, perhaps due to backlash from the damage sustained by the Beast Vassal. Then…

"Aaaaaaaaaaaaaaa—!"

The young girl screamed. A second arm emerged, seeming to rip its way out of the girl's slender back.

Yukina was sure it wasn't two Beast Vassals, but rather a single Beast Vassal with a pair of arms. However, the new arm attacked Yukina from above as if it were a completely separate creature.

"Oh n—"

Yukina's expression froze.

Snowdrift Wolf's spear tip was still impaling the Beast Vassal's *right arm*. If Yukina let up for even a single moment, the wounded *right arm* would crush the spear and Yukina both.

And, in this situation, Yukina could not evade the *left arm*'s attack—!

There was no way a fragile human body could withstand an attack that had bested even an Elder's Beast Vassal. If Yukina waited, she would most certainly perish.

Excellent Sword Shaman that she was, Yukina understood in a single moment how this would end.

She didn't even have time to resign herself to her death.

In that final moment, all that crossed the back of her mind was the sight of a familiar boy. A boy she had met only a few days before, always with a vague, listless look on his face.

He'd probably be sad if she died.

That's why I don't want to die, Yukina thought. Yukina was very surprised at herself for thinking it. And then…

"Himeragiiiiiii—!"

She heard the boy's voice from unexpectedly close range.

The voice of Kojou Akatsuki, the Fourth Primogenitor.

7

"Raaaaaaaagh!"

Kojou punched the Beast Vassal in the form of a giant arm with a simple, clenched fist.

It wasn't that he had any special or deep thought. He just figured that even against a materialized mass of magical energy like a Beast Vassal, punching it with a fist full of magical energy would probably do something.

The effect was greater than he had expected.

The *left arm* of the Beast Vassal with the rainbow-colored glow flew back as if a dump truck had crashed into it. And, as the young girl who was the Beast Vassal's master tumbled, dragged along by the impact, the *right arm* fighting Yukina vanished.

"Wha…"

As she stared at the nonsensical scene, Yukina's eyes widened in shock.

She seemed taken aback by Kojou's brute-force attack, which was far too crude and ridiculous to call *combat*. Kojou could understand how she felt. However, Kojou didn't know any magic; even if he was called the Fourth Primogenitor and stuff, he didn't know how to use a single special vampiric ability. He had no other means of attack.

"What do you think you're doing, Senpai?! In a place like this—?!"

"That's my line, Himeragi! You idiot!!"

"I, idiot?!"

"Didn't you say you were just checking things out? Why are you fighting!"

"Th, that's—"

"Uhh" was the only protest that came out of Yukina's mouth. It wasn't that Kojou understood the fine details, but he could imagine that a bunch of things were going on, at least.

Kojou couldn't fly through the sky; nor could he use teleportation magic and such. Sprinting full speed the whole sixteen kilometers across the bridge that connected the two Gigafloats had been as rough as he'd expected.

And, when Kojou had finally caught up, the Beast Vassal running wild at the start had already been defeated, and Yukina was in the middle of combat with the mysterious man in the vestment.

"So… Who the heck are these guys, anyway?"

"I do not know. That man seems to be a Lotharingian Armed Apostle, but…"

Yukina answered as she glared at the now-weaponless man in the vestment. Kojou was blunt with his confusion.

"Lotharingia? What the hell is he doing coming all the way from Europe to make a mess here?"

"Senpai, please be careful. They're still…"

The young girl in the cape coat rose faster than Yukina could finish her warning. The rainbow-colored Beast Vassal remained materialized behind her back. The damage from Kojou's punch apparently hadn't affected the Beast Vassal's core.

"That magical energy just now… You are no ordinary vampire, are you? Equal to the nobles, or beyond that… Perhaps the rumors of the Fourth Primogenitor are true, then?"

The Armed Apostle spoke while discarding his destroyed battle-axe.

The young indigo-haired girl stood before the Armed Apostle as if to shield him.

Kojou could not read any bloodlust from the girl's expressionless eyes. However, the words spun by her lips were calm.

"Restart, ready. Reexecute 'Rhododactylos'—"

Obeying the girl's words, the giant arm stretched upward, arching like a snake.

"Stop! I didn't come here to fight y—"

"Hold, Astarte. Now is *not yet* the time to fight a Primogenitor!"

Kojou and the Armed Apostle yelled simultaneously.

The young girl's eyes wavered, as if bewildered. However, the Beast Vassal, already commanded by its master, did not stop.

The rainbow-colored hooked claw dully glimmered as it descended, aiming at Kojou like a bird of prey.

"Stand back, Senpai!"

Spear in hand, Yukina leaped as if to thrust Kojou away.

However, as if anticipating Yukina's movements, the other arm came out from the girl's feet. As if snaking along the ground, the *right arm* came flying in a surprise attack, with even Yukina too slow to respond.

"Himeragi!"

Kojou instantly thrust Yukina away. Yukina had no way to prevent being brushed off by the impact to her defenseless back. Having lost its target, the *right arm* attacked Kojou from below as the *left arm* attacked him from above.

"*S-Senpai*?! What have you done—!"

Yukina broke her fall with a roll and regained her balance. However, she was too late to support Kojou.

"Ugh…!"

Kojou could only counterattack with his fist against the *right* arm. He was unable to evade the overhead attack, and blood spurted from his arm.

That's what Yukina thought, but that instant, Kojou yelled out with a voice so serious, it seemed to come from a completely different person.

"Wait… Doooooon't———!"

His voice seemed directed not at his enemies but at himself.

Kojou's eyes were dyed red; fangs protruded from his clenched mouth.

And what gushed out of Kojou's wounded arm was not blood.

What had appeared, seemingly ripping the skin, was a pale shine that dazzled the eyes. Its focus narrowed into an incandescent beam of light. It blew back the rainbow-colored Beast Vassal with an incredibly powerful shock wave.

"Nn, no good… Astarte!"

The Armed Apostle directed his shout at the young homunculus girl.

However, his bellow was erased by the explosive sound spawned by the shock wave.

What was emitted from Kojou's arm was a dense mass of magical energy in solid form. In other words, one of the beings called a Beast Vassal. However, it was not even in the same dimension as the Beast Vassals people knew about.

This was a lightning storm destroying everything in its path.

The giant, out-of-control lightning strike mowed down the buildings aboveground; the shock waves thus created became wildly blowing windstorms. Kojou was fully enveloped by the light as lightning arrows indiscriminately scattered all around him.

It was like a vast storm cloud had suddenly appeared at ground level.

All of Itogami Island shook as if it were being bombed. The surrounding sea raged like a tsunami.

Finally, the huge lightning and windstorm neatly vanished as if nothing had happened.

All that remained was the warehouse district and the fan-shaped swath of destruction through it.

Yukina was safe, if barely, protected by Snowdrift Wolf's ward. And, so was the "Old Guard" man on the verge of death, instantly covered by Yukina.

"So that's... Senpai's...the Fourth Primogenitor's Beast Vassal..."

Beholding the vestiges of the all-too-massive destruction, Yukina murmured in a quivering voice.

There was no sign of the Armed Apostle or the young homunculus girl.

The Gigafloat's surface had been thoroughly ripped away, leaving the underground-constructed section below exposed. It seemed they had fled there.

At what looked like "ground zero," Kojou, his strength exhausted, went limp and collapsed. The left sleeve of his parka had been destroyed, but his own body was unharmed. He'd just gone out like a light from exhaustion.

As Yukina sighed, she surveyed her surroundings once more.

The damage to the warehouse district was quite heavy, but it was considerable for other districts as well.

It would be hard to find a single ship moored in the harbor that had escaped damage; the monorail track had collapsed as well. As a result of the lightning strikes, there were power outages all over the island; she couldn't imagine how much industrial data loss had occurred as a result.

As Yukina returned her silver spear to its storage form, she walked over to the collapsed Kojou. Kojou was sleeping with a refreshed look on his face, as if he'd just finished venting all the stress he'd been holding in.

"...Goodness. What am I going to do with you?"

Gazing at Kojou's sleeping face, Yukina sighed a faint sigh.

Chapter Three
She's Crying

1

The next day, the mysterious explosion that occurred in Itogami City blanketed the news media.

The newspapers printed photographs of the demolished warehouse district on the front page; television and video sites had interviews with survivors on a continuous loop.

The sixty or so damaged buildings had all been warehouses belonging to a major food conglomerate. About twenty thousand households had lost power; of those, half had no scheduled date for restoration as of that morning. The monorail track connecting Island East to Island South had been destroyed; direct damage alone was estimated at seven billion yen. When indirect damage was included, the figure climbed to fifty billion yen. The lone saving grace was the complete absence of fatalities.

"Whoa, scary. And the cause remains unknown, they said."

With an apron over her school uniform, Nagisa was casually speaking while cleaning up after breakfast.

"Well, uh… It could be a warehouse fire started by lightning strikes, you know?"

Sipping on coffee to wake him up, Kojou replied with nervousness in his voice. His face seemed tired because he hadn't slept a single wink the night before.

In the process of escaping the scene of the incident with Yukina, making an anonymous tip to the police, and carrying the Elder vampire on the brink of death to the hospital, night had turned to dawn at some point.

"No one's gonna believe it was a lightning strike. Everyone's saying things, like it was a terrorist bombing or an accident from a cargo of rocket fuel, but *I* suspect it was a meteor strike. You know, like the Tunguska impact? Sudo said a big incident that happened in Russia a long time ago was a lot like this."

"Meteorite, huh... That's the good version, I suppose..."

Kojou gazed into the distance as he muttered to himself. Judging from what he saw on the news, the fact last night's widespread devastation was Kojou's work remained unexposed. The scale of the damage was so massive that it seemed no one could believe that the incident was brought about by a single vampire.

However, he couldn't be optimistic that would continue.

Surely there had been many witnesses who'd seen the Beast Vassal running wild right there just prior to the incident. It wouldn't be surprising for someone to deduce Kojou's existence from that. It was also possible Yukina would expose everything before anyone could; he hadn't felt like sleeping with that on his mind.

Fifty billion yen in total damage. *No way I can make up for that*, thought Kojou.

Incidentally, this Sudo character Nagisa had mentioned was an actor and radio personality local to Itogami City. Not that it mattered.

"Well, I have a Cheerleading Club meeting, so I'm going ahead."

Nagisa spoke as she ran out of the room with a patter. Kojou tossed a wave her way.

"'Kay."

"Close the door after, okay? And don't you be late, Kojou. Clean the mag cup and put it away when you're done drinking coffee. Make sure the lights are out before you go out the door... Ah, right, I put new handkerchiefs and tissues here in the hallway so—"

"Get going already!"

"'Kaaaay!"

After making sure Nagisa, boisterous to the very end, had left, Kojou limply exhaled.

September first. His first day of school since the end of summer break.

As Saikai Academy had two semesters, it didn't engage in any special commencement ceremony. After a long homeroom session, normal classes were scheduled to begin. Even if he felt like he hadn't gotten a break at all, his homework was nowhere near done, and last night's incident was guaranteed to add to it. He wanted to just skip class and go on a journey far, far away.

Just as Kojou began absentmindedly thinking about that, the chime in the entryway suddenly rang. Projected onto the intercom monitor was Yukina, in school uniform with the guitar case on her back.

"Himeragi…? What are you doing here at a time like this?" Kojou asked, suspecting it was an ill omen.

Yukina replied in her usual serene tone.

"I came for you. We'll be late if we don't finally get going, Senpai."

"For me…? What, you want to go to school together?"

"I don't mind if going together is too much, so I'll just watch you covertly if that is your preference."

"So I'm being watched either way, huh…? Fine, just hold on a sec."

Kojou cut the intercom and headed for the entrance with his usual schoolbag.

When he opened the door and went outside, Yukina was standing in the hallway, lowering her head with proper politeness.

"Good morning, Senpai."

"Ah yeah."

Even though, like Kojou, she'd probably barely slept at all, he could feel no sense of fatigue from Yukina's perfectly put-together look. No doubt her well-honed physique at work; that, or it was pure youth. However, even she could not conceal her weary expression.

"…You were rather extravagant last night, weren't you?"

Keeping silent until they boarded the elevator, Yukina spoke with apparent anger included in her tone.

Ugh, said Kojou, averting his eyes. Apparently, Yukina's real objective in having come to get him this morning was to chew him out on the way to school.

"They say the total damage is fifty billion yen."

"Ugh..."

"As you are an immortal vampire, Senpai, you might be able to pay that back in about five centuries or so. You'd still have to repay a hundred million every single year, though. Interest adds up, after all."

"...By any chance, you report on last night already to your higher-ups at the Lion King Agency?"

"I really must report to them about it, but I am somewhat hesitant."

"Hesitant?"

Kojou was surprised to hear that word coming from the overly serious girl's lips.

Yukina lowered her face, looking conflicted.

"Yes. I share responsibility for last night's incident, after all; I think it was absolutely not your fault alone, Senpai...and you did save me, after all... Um, thank you very much for that."

She conveyed the last phrase in a voice so tiny that it seemed like it'd vanish.

"I—I see. Well...when you think about it, it *was* legitimate defense and all. I had no choice but to take measures to protect myself, so, self-defense, right?"

Kojou unintentionally put great firmness into the words he spoke. Yukina made a disappointed shake of her head as she looked at him.

"However, there is no proof of that."

"Proof?"

"Yes. Of course, I would testify to that effect, but as to whether it would be believed... In the first place, the police and the Lion King Agency are on poor terms. My being on the scene might actually hurt more than it helps."

"Is that, ah, so...?"

Having reconfirmed the difficult situation he was in, Kojou deflated. He didn't know where the fault lines were exactly, but the departments within the government for demonic countermeasures apparently had various turf wars going on. When he thought about it, Yukina was still just a junior high schooler anyway; he could understand her testimony not carrying much weight. Of course, it wasn't likely they could get the "Old Guard" man on the verge of death to testify that Kojou engaged in legitimate defense.

The stifling atmosphere hung over them as they continued to walk, finally boarding the monorail headed toward the academy.

The devastated warehouse district was very visible from the train window. There was also the stark sight of the fracture midway along the bridge connecting the Gigafloats.

The greater-than-usual amount of chaos inside the monorail was no doubt due to the messed-up travel routes. This, too, was caused by last night's incident. As he was the responsible party, Kojou had no right to complain. As they squeezed aboard the tightly packed train, Yukina, too, made a rather sullen face.

"...The main thing is, you overdid it, Senpai. Certainly it was a dangerous situation, but that was clearly excessive defense. Surely you had no need to go that far."

"It's not like I did that because I wanted to, you know," Kojou muttered somberly as if sulking.

Perhaps taking that as him desperately making excuses, Yukina raised her eyebrows and glared at Kojou.

"So why did you command a Beast Vassal to engage in such excessive destruction?"

"I didn't order it to do anything. It's not like that live wire's my Beast Vassal anyway."

"Why are you telling me such an obvious lie?"

Yukina sighed, making an expression as if she was dealing with a wayward child.

"The Fourth Primogenitor, 'Kaleid Blood,' is said to possess twelve mighty Beast Vassals, each rivaling the monsters of myth and legend. Surely you are not telling me it is not so, given the damage that actually happened?"

"No, it's not like I'm trying to paper it over or something."

Kojou's voice was ragged from aggravation.

"They don't listen to any orders of mine. Now, if I could use the things like I want, that's a totally different story."

"...What do you mean by that?"

She must have sensed Kojou's words were not simply something made up at random. Realizing the seriousness of the situation, Yukina's expression turned quite sober. Kojou looked like this wasn't easy for him to talk about.

"They don't think of me as their master. Yeah, I did inherit twelve Beast Vassals from Avlora, but they don't accept that for themselves yet."

"Avlora…meaning, the previous Fourth Primogenitor you spoke of before, Senpai?"

Yukina looked up at Kojou to confirm. Kojou made a sloppy nod.

"So because of that, I can't control 'em. Usually I keep 'em under control somehow, but being attacked by other Beast Vassals is a bit much."

"And then they'll…go berserk like last night?"

"Well, maybe. Just because I come knocking doesn't mean they'll come out, I think. It's not like I've put it to the test, though."

"That is common sense. Please do not test it."

Yukina spoke with what seemed like sullen anger.

"…But, if what you're telling me right now is the truth, you are indeed a more dangerous being than I had thought, Senpai. If you do not somehow become able to properly control your familiars…"

As Yukina murmured, she sank deep into thought.

Kojou silently gazed at her for a while as she did so. Without thinking, he said what he really thought.

"You're quite an oddball, Himeragi."

"Eh? …Is that so?"

Yukina's eyes widened as if taken completely off guard.

"Although I do not want to hear that coming from you, Senpai, what is odd about me?"

"I mean…that's not what most people would think of if they heard me talking just now. They wouldn't think further than 'a vampire who can't control his Beast Vassals is dangerous; better stay away from him, or maybe destroy him sooner rather than later!' Stuff like that, I figure." Kojou spoke with a pained smile mixed in.

Yukina put a hand on her own chest as if reflecting on it.

"Is that so? Now that you mention it, I do feel like that, too, but… I mean, it's you, Senpai."

"...What do you mean?"

"Er, there's no deep meaning. It's just, I don't think you are all that bad a vampire. A little sloppy, occasionally lewd, but that's all."

Yukina's eyes narrowed as she spoke, as if replaying her memories since the moment they met. She wasn't speaking in a joking tone whatsoever. Apparently this was truly what she thought of him.

As any rebuttal would only kick up more trouble, Kojou twisted his lips without a word.

The monorail arrived in front of the academy; students wearing the same uniforms as Kojou and Yukina got off the train. Yukina took out her train pass case.

"But, if you inherited the power of the Fourth Primogenitor, Senpai, why can't you control the Beast Vassals, I wonder?"

"That's probably 'cause I'm a blood-drinking virgin."

Yukina tilted her head and looked at Kojou.

"Blood-drinking...virgin? What do you mean by *virgin*?"

Did she seriously just ask me that? Kojou thought, looking sharply at Yukina. However, Yukina simply blinked her eyes with a mystified look. Kojou remembered that she'd been raised at an all-girls school somewhere, and on top of that, she'd been training as a Sword Shaman from dawn to dusk.

"In other words, I have no experience. I've never drunk another person's blood before."

Kojou explained, picking the least offensive words he could find.

Actually, the fact that beside the Beast Vassals, Kojou couldn't use a single proper vampiric power was no doubt connected to that. Not that this had particularly bothered him until now.

"Ah, so *that's* what you meant by virgin...eh? You haven't done it?"

Yukina asked back in apparent surprise. Kojou's confession that he'd never experienced drinking blood was apparently hard for her to connect to her image of a vampiric Primogenitor.

"No 'experience,' Senpai...? Is that so...?"

"Come on, it can't be *that* strange. I mean, I was a normal human being till just lately."

"Well...that may be so...but..."

While perplexed, Yukina seemed vaguely pleased for some reason. For his part, Kojou's expression twisted in displeasure.

"Anyway, could you stop saying how I have 'no experience' and 'haven't done it' so loud in a place like this?"

"Eh, why? You said those things yourself, Senpai…"

"Er, well, that's because, um…"

As he made anguished thoughts about how he should explain this, Kojou drew his face close to Yukina's ear. A moment later…

"Heya, Kojou."

A sudden impact assaulted Kojou from the rear. A very familiar arm wrapped around Kojou's neck as an equally familiar voice spoke.

"Don't go sayin' suggestive words to a girl first thing in the morning like this, man."

"Y-Yaze?"

The voice speaking this cheerful, energetic tone first thing in the morning belonged to a male student with short-cropped hair and headphones down around his neck. He seemed to have been riding the same monorail.

Yaze went through the turnstile, still grappling with Kojou's shoulders.

"Heya… Wait, that's not Nagisa-chan. Who is that? We had a girl like this in our junior high?"

Noticing Yukina walking beside them, he looked at Kojou's face in what seemed a bit of surprise. Kojou gloomily thrust Yaze away.

"Transfer student. She's in Nagisa's class."

"Ohh, I see, I see. …So, Kojou, why are you going to school together with the little transfer here?"

"I just bumped into her on the way 'cause she lives close to us. A bit of talking's normal, geez," Kojou replied while keeping his cool. It's not like he was lying. He might've met her when leaving the entrance to his apartment, but that was still on the way to school, technically.

"I am Yukina Himeragi. And you are Yaze Motoki, right?"

Yukina spoke while lowering her head in perfect courtesy. Yaze suddenly made a very pleasant expression.

"Oh, what's this? So he's been talkin' about me?"

"No, there was information on you in Akatsuki-senpai's file."

"Ah? File?"

Looking at the question mark that came over Yaze's expression, Yukina apparently realized her mistake. Her blank expression twitched faintly as she shook her head.

"No, it's nothing at all. I'm kidding."

"R-right. Well, nice to meet ya."

Yaze made a friendly, smiling face while giving her a thumbs-up.

"Hey, so you're a musician girl? What kind of genres do you do?"

"Musician… Ah yes. Er, actually I'm not very knowledgeable about music."

"Eh? Ah, I mean, that's a guitar on your back, right? Maybe a bass?"

"Ah…yes. You're right."

Remembering she had a "guitar case" on her back, Yukina hurriedly tried to gloss over it.

And, when Yaze suspiciously raised an eyebrow, she awkwardly averted her eyes.

"Um, I'm sorry, Senpais. I have to go now."

"R-right. Later, Himeragi."

Kojou waved in recognition as Yukina ran off like that to the junior high school campus.

Yaze silently gazed, watching her for a while like that.

"Hey, Kojou. That girl, she's kinda mysterious, ain't she?"

"Nah, she just transferred, she's just a bit scrambled about stuff still."

"Is that so… Hmm. If this doesn't become trouble of some kind, then great," Yaze murmured in an oddly serious tone. Kojou shot his friend a doubtful look back.

"Trouble?"

"Yeah. Make sure you pull this off right, Kojou, for your sake *and* the sake of not messing up my peaceful, lively school life. I mean, you are kind of my precious childhood friend and stuff."

What's he talkin' about? thought Kojou, shifting his gaze to Yaze with a perplexed look.

Yaze was looking at the high school campus, at Kojou and Yaze's classroom on the second floor. Asagi, sitting right at the window, was waving her hand, having just noticed them arriving at school.

2

"Good morning, Kojou. You're really looking laid-back here first thing in the morning. Well, you always do."

Homeroom, right before classes began. As Kojou sat in his own seat, Asagi, sitting just ahead, spoke to him.

As usual, she was dressed in a gorgeous way with a hairstyle to match, but today, her usual liveliness served to conceal a shadow, as if an aura of ennui hung over her somehow.

Kojou waved back with the same listless expression.

"Gee, thanks. Hey, you look sleepy yourself."

"I am. Thanks to that, my makeup isn't sitting well… You saw about yesterday's explosion on the news, right?"

Asagi spoke while fussing over imperfections under her eyes with a hand mirror.

Gulp. Kojou was somewhat suspicious as he responded.

"Y-yeah. A little bit."

"Right after that, a big shot from the Gigafloat Management Corp was crying to me over the phone. Their mainframe for disaster countermeasures got blown away, and they had to put together a replacement system from scratch. That's what happens when you buy your hardware from the lowest bidder. It's not tuned at all, and its inbound filtering is like a sieve."

"I don't really follow, but…sounds like a big mess… Sorry."

As Kojou appropriately ignored Asagi's technobabble, he was tortured by a guilty conscience. To think that even people this close to him had been harmed by yesterday's incident.

Asagi shot Kojou a dubious look as he sunk into silence.

"Why are you apologizing?"

"Uh…no reason. So anyway, you're helping people across the whole island, then, Asagi?"

"It— It's not that huge a deal, though."

Asagi spoke quickly, seeming to blush a little. Then her usual leering grin emerged.

"But, maybe you should be thanking me all the same. There's a restaurant at Keystone Gate that has a cake buffet…"

"Yeah, sometime, sure. I'll think about it once I get my summer break homework settled."

Kojou tried to paper it all over. Keystone Gate was the section where the four Gigafloats connected—the giant building literally at the center of Itogami Island. It was the island's most fashionable spot, brimming with high-end brands and specialty stores. And this restaurant was right there. An expensive one, no doubt.

"Homework, huh."

As Asagi rested her chin on her hands, she muttered in an indifferent tone, seemingly on purpose. For some reason, she was glancing sideways at Kojou intermittently.

"B-by the way Kojou, I thought I'd ask… Whatever happened after that?"

"After that?"

"You know, yesterday, the girl you were at the station with. Nagisa-chan's classmate, you said?

"I mean, not that it matters to me either way."

"Oh yeah."

Something like that happened, too, didn't it? Kojou recalled. Thanks to the intensity of the disturbance that followed, he felt like it was already something in the distant past.

"Oh, we just went home like normal."

"Is that…so?"

"Yeah, I was just helping her carry back the stuff she bought."

"Th-that so? Hmm… I see."

Asagi's expression seemed to brighten as she lifted her face.

Right around then, in a corner of the classroom, there was a small commotion punctuated by *ooh*s. Several boys had gathered in the corner around a single raised cell phone.

"What's that all about?"

Kojou watched his worked-up classmates looking as if he'd spotted something unpleasant in a train station washroom.

Asagi called out to Rin Tsukishima, a friend of hers who just happened to be passing by.

"Hey, Rin. What's up? What are the guys getting all worked up about?"

"Ah, that? Seems some girl transferred into junior high."

Rin Tsukishima was the class representative. She was a student whose height and style made her seem very adult.

She had meager social graces and was a girl of few words, but there were surprisingly many boys who went for that. Among first-year high school boys, she was number one in the Girls I Wanna Be Walked All Over By rankings by a rather glowing margin; she had apparently been rather shocked to learn of that result.

"A junior high school transfer student…?"

Kojou's face grimaced a bit as he made a low murmur. "Good grief," Rin murmured, watching the boys in exasperation.

"Apparently the rumor is that she's extremely cute, so they've ordered the juniors in their clubs to send them pictures."

As Asagi's brow furled, she drew her face close to Kojou.

"Hey, this transfer student, is that the one in Nagisa-chan's class?"

"Yeah, probably."

Kojou nodded with a pained expression. It was a pretty safe bet it was Yukina.

Rin watched the exchange between Kojou and Asagi with mild amusement.

"Not going to go and look, Akatsuki?"

"Nah, not interested."

As Kojou tossed his reply, Rin said, "I see," nodding with apparent satisfaction.

"I suppose. You have Asagi, after all, Akatsuki."

"Huh?"

Kojou looked up in surprise. He met the very close Asagi's eyes, and both hurriedly separated simultaneously.

Asagi, even with her cheeks reddening, maintained her cool attitude as she looked up at Rin.

"There you go again, Rin… Kojou and I aren't like that. We're just friends from back in junior high. Right?"

"R-right. Asagi hangs out with me and Yaze a lot. It's just natural."

Kojou, too, conveyed it as the plain truth. For some reason, Rin made a disappointed-looking face as she listened.

"So, in the end, no progress this summer, either? Even though Yaze seems to be making out fine with an older girlfriend?"

"That's 'cause Yaze and his girlfriend are both weirdos." Kojou nonchalantly asserted it like it was inconvenient to be compared to either.

Certainly, in spite of appearances, it was a fact that Yaze had a girlfriend. As soon as he'd graduated to high school in April, he'd fallen in love at first sight with a third-year senior. After a number of passionate approaches straight out of a romantic comedy, they'd finally become a couple just before summer vacation.

"I suppose so," Rin agreed, looking at Kojou with a meaningful expression.

"Certainly I think she is a bit eccentric, too, but, Akatsuki-kun, I don't think I want to hear *you* calling anyone odd. I have the feeling you have some very interesting secrets yourself."

"No idea what you're talkin' about, Tsukishima."

"Heh-heh." As Rin watched Kojou feign ignorance, seemingly sulking, she narrowed her eyes and laughed.

Her grandfather was a famous scholar of demonic ecology. Perhaps due to that, Rin was very learned about the characteristics of various demons; sometimes she acted as if she realized Kojou was not a normal human being.

However, Rin did not regard Kojou with enmity; she seemed disinclined to raise any special fuss in any case. It seemed like she was observing Kojou simply because she found him interesting. Here in Itogami City, where there were more demons, etc., than foreign residents, it wasn't a big deal.

Saikai Academy had a number of demonic students, after all; they weren't looked at in any special way, enough that a beautiful girl transferring into junior high attracted far more attention.

That said, even Rin would surely be surprised to know that Kojou was actually the Fourth Primogenitor.

"Oh yeah, Kojou. I brought that World History report I mentioned yesterday… You wanna look?" Asagi, whose mood had improved slightly at some point, spoke as she fished a pile of copying paper out of her bag.

Kojou nodded in a flash. "Yeah. Of course."

"So! Cake buffet at Keystone Gate!"

"Ugh… All right already…"

Heartbroken, Kojou nodded. It was a matter of priorities; he was more worried about how he was going to do the homework in front of his face than the condition of his wallet.

"Good, good," Asagi replied, nodding with a smiling face as she handed the copying paper to Kojou.

"Ah? I wonder what's with Natsuki-chan?"

That moment, Rin quietly muttered. It was too early for the homeroom session, but the class's homeroom teacher, wearing a stifling, jet-black dress, entered the classroom with an expression of displeasure.

"Kojou Akatsuki, are you here?"

The charismatic homeroom teacher, small enough she looked like a little girl, called for Kojou at the classroom entrance with the aura of a ferocious deity. Kojou had a bad feeling about it as he sluggishly waved back.

"...'Sup?"

"Come to the student guidance room at noon. I need a word with you."

Natsuki made a frigid declaration. Incidentally, her outfit on this day was a miniskirted, goth loli–style dress and socks with black-and-white borders. It was completely stifling as per usual, but it looked nice and cool compared to most of what she usually wore.

The frostiness and bloodlust of Natsuki's implied threat sent a small shudder through Kojou.

"Eh? Er, you said I had until the first class of the last day of the week to turn in that English homework..."

"Also, bring that junior high transfer student with you."

"Himeragi...? Why?"

Kojou's voice unwittingly slipped.

The murmurs among the students broadened as the name of the much-rumored transfer student emerged from his lips.

"Would you understand if I said, last night's incident?"

"Er, ah... No idea what you're talkin' ab—"

"Don't play dumb with me. I'm going to speak to you very thoroughly about what the two of you were doing after running out of the game center late at night."

Natsuki left that monologue behind her before departing without waiting for Kojou's reply. After that, Kojou was sweating bullets while bloodlust-filled glares from the male students poured upon him. And then…

"Akatsuki… What was she speaking of just now? Could you explain, in detail?"

The tall Rin stood beside the seated Kojou, leering down at him as she asked. She was so quiet normally, but at times like this, she was impressively intimidating.

"T-Tsukishima… Er, Asagi?"

Kojou spontaneously called for an assist. However, Asagi, who should have been sitting right there, had vanished at some point.

"If you want Asagi, she's over there."

Rin pointed to the back of the class with a straight face.

For some reason, Asagi was standing right by the garbage bin, innocently ripping to shreds the pile of paper in her hands over and over.

Geh! As the sheets turned into shreds, Kojou sucked in his breath as he realized what the pile of paper was.

"W-wait. That wouldn't be the World History report I asked you for, would it…"

As Kojou hurried to his feet, Asagi glared at him, eyes half-closed and filled with silent rage. Without saying a word…

"Hmph!"

…she made a hard snort, tossing the thoroughly destroyed paper into the garbage bin.

3

As soon as lunch break began, Kojou darted out of the classroom and rendezvoused with Yukina in the corridor in front of the staff room.

By the end of morning classes Kojou was tired enough to keel over, but Yukina looked considerably weakened as well, enough that she'd actually forgotten to bring that guitar case with her. Having seen his own classmates' excitement, Kojou could largely picture what had happened, but being the center of the school's attention seemed to have been quite an ordeal for her.

Since Yukina didn't have a cell phone, Kojou had to go through Nagisa to call her over. Thanks to that, Nagisa had insistently grilled them about this and that, adding one more reason for them to be exhausted.

Somehow, Kojou and Yukina finally arrived at the student guidance room together.

When Kojou and Yukina knocked and entered, Natsuki was already sitting on the sofa, waiting for them.

"So you came, Akatsuki."

Natsuki spoke as she reclined with her legs crossed like she was some sort of princess. *Huh.* And, as she noticed that Yukina was standing behind Kojou, the corners of her lips curled upward.

"So you're the transfer student in Misaki's class."

"Yes... Himeragi, junior high, third year."

Speechless for a moment as she beheld Natsuki's beautiful, doll-like looks, she replied in an overly serious tone. Natsuki, her behavior filled with an air of charisma, seemed satisfied as she looked back at Yukina.

"Welcome to Saikai Academy. It's a pleasure to have you, particularly if you do not stir up any unnecessary trouble."

"Y-yes."

Yukina's faltering reply was likely due to remembering the top class trouble that had stirred up just the day before. The warehouse district destroyed; fifty billion yen in damage. It wasn't the level of problem you got called in by your homeroom teacher for. And so...

"Now then, both of you. You know about the fireworks that occurred on Island East yesterday, yes?"

"Well, uh, yeah, sure."

Kojou nodded with an uneasy feeling as Natsuki's question got right to the point. The cold sweat moistening his back made his uniform shirt cling uncomfortably.

"Actually, an Elder vampire was secured near the scene. He was gravely wounded and on the verge of death, but someone apparently made an anonymous tip to the fire department. This information hasn't been released to the public yet. Does any of this ring a bell with either of you?"

Shudder. Kojou heavily shook his head. Beside him, Yukina was like a statue, paralyzed.

"That Elder was a trading company executive on the surface but police seem to have long suspected he's part of the leadership of a smuggling ring. It would seem yesterday he was in the warehouse district in a place where he'd done many deals in the past. The underlings apparently say they don't know anything about the other party for this deal."

"...Oookay."

Kojou watched Natsuki with a guarded expression. He was pretty interested in this information, but he didn't know what Natsuki was telling Yukina and him all this for.

"Witnesses saw a Beast Vassal on a rampage in the area a short time before the explosion. In other words, the nearly dead man who was found had been fighting someone, an enemy who could push an 'Old Guard' vampire to a comatose state. I believe it is extremely likely that this person was involved in the explosion... I wonder who?"

"Wh-who knows?"

As Kojou twisted his neck, seemingly on purpose, he remembered "Eustach," the Lotharingian Armed Apostle, and the homunculus he had with him. Who they were, why they were fighting, and what it was they desired remained mysteries to Kojou and Yukina.

Seemingly finding both of their reactions interesting to watch, Natsuki continued in a blunt tone, "Indeed... Actually, yesterday was not the first time a vampire was found on this island on the brink of death."

"Eh...?"

"In the last two months, the police have ascertained that at least six similar incidents have occurred. That makes this the seventh, though, of course, this is the first time an Elder was involved."

As Natsuki said all that, she roughly tossed a thick pile of files onto the table.

He didn't want to know how she obtained all that, but they seemed to be copies of police investigation files. There was a jagged photograph attached, an enlarged image from city surveillance camera footage.

"Wai...! Natsuki, what is this?"

Kojou's expression hardened as he looked at the men depicted in the photo. The charismatic homeroom teacher glared at Kojou, looking displeased at being addressed by her first name.

"This is the list of demons assaulted to date. The ones displayed here are victims of the sixth incident. They were found two days ago, but... Do you know them, Kojou Akatsuki?"

"No, I don't *know* them…but…"

Kojou's lips twisted unpleasantly. When he stole a glance at Yukina beside him, Yukina's face was pale as she clenched her fists without a word.

The men depicted in the photo were the beast-man-and-vampire team. The men Yukina had sent flying for flirting with her the day he and she had first met. At some point after they'd fled Kojou and Yukina's presence, someone had assaulted them and inflicted nearly fatal wounds.

If this was somehow related to the combat in the warehouse district the night before, chances were very high that Eustach was the one who'd assaulted the two of them. Either way, Kojou and Yukina had become more deeply involved in this incident without ever realizing it.

"So what…happened to all of these people?"

"Hospitalized. They're in no danger of dying, but none have regained consciousness as of yet. Not that I know what could do that to a dog with a powerful life force and a nonaging bat."

Natsuki elegantly rested her chin on her hands as she glared at Kojou with sharp eyes.

"This is why I called both of you here."

"Eh?"

"I don't know the purpose is, but whoever's been indiscriminately hunting demons remains at large. In other words, Kojou Akatsuki, it is possible that you, too, may be assaulted."

"A-ah… I see. Suppose so."

Having little self-awareness of his being a vampire, he hadn't realized it until Natsuki said it, but she had a point.

Eustach already knew Kojou was the Fourth Primogenitor. If his objective really was to hunt demons indiscriminately, Kojou might well be his next target.

In fact, when Eustach had encountered Kojou, he'd said as much.

That it was *not yet* time to fight a Primogenitor—

"Corporation-raised demons and their families have apparently already been warned to beware of demon hunting. I'm sure you don't know anyone that high up, so I'm warning you instead. You should thank me."

"Uh-huh. Well, thanks."

"So for that reason, no more playing around at night like you did yesterday. At least until this matter is resolved."

"R..."

Natsuki's tone had been so nonchalant that Kojou had almost unwittingly replied, *Right*, and was on the verge of nodding. However, just before he did, he noticed Yukina's reproachful glare and caught himself.

"Er, ah, what do you mean, playing around at night?"

"...Hmph, very well. Anyway, you have been warned."

Natsuki, speaking like she was bored with it all, dismissed them with a wave of her hand.

Kojou and Yukina did as she indicated, rising up and leaving the student guidance room together.

"Ah, right. Wait a moment, transfer student."

That moment, Natsuki suddenly called out to Yukina.

Huh? Yukina turned around and looked at Natuski, seemingly on her guard.

Natsuki pulled something out of the breast of her black dress and lightly tossed it over to Yukina.

It was a tiny mascot doll, small enough to fit in the palm of Yukina's hand. She caught it by reflex, unwittingly speaking the doll's name.

"...Nekoma-tan..."

Gasp! Looking up at how Yukina covered her mouth, Natuski made a broad, leering smile.

"You forgot this. It *is* yours, isn't it?"

Yukina said nothing in response to Natsuki's question. A puzzled expression came over Kojou as he watched Natsuki and Yukina glare at each other, tension hanging in the air for some unfathomable reason.

Finally, Yukina made a polite nod and left the room.

Watching Yukina as she left until the very end, Natsuki seemed quite pleased with herself for some reason.

4

"So Ms. Minamiya knew."

Yukina spoke as she walked along a corner of a passageway, as if to hide from prying eyes. The oddly happy way she gazed at the doll she'd received from Natsuki made her truly look like a regular female junior high school student.

"Guess so… We really slipped up, leaving the doll behind like that."

Kojou replied with a serious expression. He'd meant to make a clean getaway the night before, but Natsuki seemed to have indeed known it was him from the start. *Now she has something else on me*, he thought, deflating somewhat. Yukina made a somewhat exasperated sigh as she looked at Kojou.

"No. Not that. About the opponent we fought last night."

"Eh? That old man, Eustach or something?"

"Yes. And that homunculus girl, too… Apparently the police already knew about their engaging in demon hunting."

Kojou nodded as he remembered the photograph Natsuki possessed. If the assaulted demons had been caught on camera, it wouldn't be a surprise if the same surveillance camera had filmed Eustach and the girl. So the police no doubt knew about them.

"However, it seems they do not as yet know their identities."

"Identities?"

"That the perpetrator is a Lotharingian Armed Apostle."

"I see… She said the guys who'd been attacked are still unconscious…"

"Yes. It would seem that we are the only ones to have directly fought them unscathed."

Yukina calmly pointed it out. At the time, Eustach had readily exposed his name and title because he was confident in the certainty he would defeat Yukina then and there. When one considered the combat capability of the girl called Astarte, it couldn't be dismissed as overconfidence. However, Kojou intruded, and consequently, Yukina made it back safe and sound. To them it was no doubt a grave miscalculation.

"Why didn't you say that to Natsuki earlier? Appearances aside, she is a C-card holder. She has her Counter-Demon Attack Mage license. She seems to know the police pretty well, too."

"Senpai…are you serious?"

"Huh?"

Yukina glared at him eyes half-closed, throwing Kojou off. She seemed angry for some reason.

"I have a C-card, too. Why does someone from the Lion King Agency need to go crying to the police?"

"Er, it's not really a 'why' thing, but…"

Come to think of it, Natsuki said the Lion King Agency and the cops don't get along, Kojou recalled. Perhaps that accounted for the odd tension in the air between Yukina and Natsuki.

"Geez," Yukina exhaled.

"A simple serial killer case is a job for the police, but since this was someone from the Lotharingian Orthodox Church, an Armed Apostle–class man no less, it is very much an international sorcerous crime. That's in our jurisdiction."

"O-oh. So it's not just a turf thing."

"Of course it isn't. Also, Senpai, have you forgotten?"

"Eh? Forgotten what?"

"About how to get what you did recognized as legitimate defense."

"Ah… And about there being no proof. Huh. And you said your testimony won't be enough, Himeragi… Ah!"

That's when Kojou finally grasped what Yukina had in mind.

"Himeragi, you can't mean…"

"Yes. This opponent has been indiscriminately hunting demons and even defeated an 'Old Guard' vampire. Anyone would recognize the danger he poses, so if you can prove he attacked you, I think something can be done about your own crime, Senpai. You are technically a Primogenitor, after all."

"The gist being, if we can catch the Armed Apostle geezer and his girl, it's all good…?"

Oh boy. Kojou made a sigh. So capturing Eustach would cancel out his own crime. The opposite was also true: Until they were captured, he couldn't go to the police for help.

If Kojou explained about last night to the police, the chances were high he'd be detained on the spot, no longer able to move freely. It would also expose to Nagisa the fact he was a vampire.

"Either way, the police are not equipped to deal with that Lotharingian Armed Apostle. I believe it would only add more casualties."

Yukina, who held the trump card called "Schneewalzer," conveyed that plainly, with no elation whatsoever. Her tone conveyed that it was simply her calm analysis of the facts as a Counter-Demon Attack Mage.

Fed up with it all, Kojou scrutinized her eyes.

"Bottom line is, if we don't find the old man and the girl before the cops, nothin' we can do, huh?"

"I do not believe this is impossible. We are the only ones who know the perpetrator is a Lotharingian Armed Apostle. And given their distinctive appearance, the places he can hide in are limited."

"Well, you're right about that... Imagine walkin' around the city dressed like that."

And that's another thing, Kojou grasped.

He was a middle-aged man almost two meters tall going around with a half-naked girl. That was almost a crime by itself. You could get arrested at any moment like that.

"Actually, thinking along those lines, I sent for data this morning."

"Data?"

"A list of Western European Church facilities on this island."

As Yukina spoke, she fished a notepad out of her pocket. It was a fancy notepad with Nekoma-tan drawn on it. However, it had a dreary list of church names and street addresses written on it.

"There is a single Lotharingian Orthodox church. There are also seven facilities belonging to other sects. No doubt he is hiding in one of them with his associate."

"...I wonder," Kojou muttered offhand.

Yukina blinked in apparent surprise. No doubt she never imagined he'd contradict her.

"Is there something mistaken?"

"No, it's not that, but just wondering if we should be going about it so simply."

"Hmm?"

Yukina's lips tapered in what looked like a small pout. Kojou's face grimaced.

"I mean, even if they don't know they're Lotharingian, I think they at least know what those two look like. That includes the old man wearing that vestment."

"I see... You might be right..."

"If that's the case, wouldn't the police have investigated the Western European Church already?"

"Ah..."

Yukina inhaled slightly. She shook her head, seemingly mildly confused.

"B-but if that's so, where are they now?"

"Yeah... Hmm, maybe a foreign branch company?"

As he tried to think of where Eustach could walk in broad daylight without anyone being suspicious, he said the first thing he could think of.

"What?"

"I mean, just 'cause he's an Armed Apostle doesn't mean he can't be somewhere other than a church. In the first place, we don't know that the old man's an actual Armed Apostle. He might just have claimed to be one."

"I—I see..."

A perplexed expression came over Yukina as she politely conceded the point.

No matter how great her combat capability, she was still an inexperienced, apprentice Attack Mage. Having such a frank personality to begin with, she might well have been particularly vulnerable to maliciously spread misinformation.

"Having said that, I don't think he can really hide with looks like that. I think he's gotta have some kind of trick. The easiest place for a Lotharingian to avoid suspicion is in the middle of other Lotharingians, so somewhere like a Lotharingian embassy... Well, there probably isn't one in the city, though."

"So a branch company headquartered in Lotharingia...or such?"

"Right, right. That's what I mean."

Kojou nodded without a conscience. He did feel like it made sense, but the idea lacked even one shred of evidence supporting it. If anybody asked, he wasn't confident enough to say he was absolutely sure.

But Yukina had a serious expression as she thought about something.

"Senpai...I'm impressed."

"Eh?"

"I'm quite surprised. To think that even you are capable of logical thought like this, Senpai."

She looked up at Kojou with sparkles in her eyes. Without thinking, Kojou averted his face from her radiant gaze.

"Is—is that so… Kind of doesn't feel like much of a compliment, but…"

"However, if it is a branch company inside Itogami City headquartered elsewhere, how should we investigate, I wonder?" Yukina spoke as she immediately snapped back to a serious expression.

"Yeah, that has me stumped, too… The Gigafloat Management Corp must have data on all the corps, but they won't hand that out to just anyone, after all…"

"Wait," Kojou muttered as he remembered something. "The Gigafloat Management Corp, huh?"

From the back of Kojou's mind emerged the face of a very familiar classmate.

5

It was just before the end of lunch break. Kojou, his breath ragged as he returned to the classroom, rushed over to Asagi's seat.

Ever since the incident that morning, Asagi had clearly been in a foul mood for some reason, but noticing that Kojou seemed serious for once, she reluctantly raised her face. Apparently they were at least on speaking terms. And then…

"—Lotharingian-based corporations? Why do you want to know about that?"

When Asagi finished listening to Kojou laying out the bare essentials, she asked back rather dubiously.

"Er, that's… It's not a really big deal, but…"

Kojou hemmed and hawed rather than saying, *I'm looking for a guy indiscriminately hunting demons.* Asagi glared with annoyance at Kojou's halfhearted posture.

"This isn't…something that Himeragi girl put you up to, is it?"

"Wha? No, that'd be ridiculous. No, no."

"…"

"It's really not that! Right, I'm doing personal research on Lotharingia for summer break homework."

"Ah? Personal research?"

Is there such a thing? Asagi wondered, tilting her head, but it was a fact that Kojou, serial skipper, had a huge pile of extra homework dumped on him. As if giving up on pressing the point further, Asagi fished out her smartphone and started it up with a sigh.

"I guess I have to. Yes. Yes, I'll look it up."

"Oh, thanks a ton, Asagi."

"You're gonna have to show your gratitude. Lotharingian corporations, huh? ...There are none. Not on the island." Tapping the keyboard like a first-class pianist, Asagi easily extracted the confidential information. Her answer threw Kojou off.

"None? Not even one?"

"There's a bunch of companies that do business with Lotharingian corporations under subcontracting agreements, but all the workers are Japanese. I mean, there's no reason for European corporations to have branches on Itogami Island in the first place. They have Demon Sanctuaries over there, too, and with the yen's value being high lately, wouldn't most have pulled out?"

"...Pulled out?"

A light went off in the back of Kojou's mind. Eustach was lying low; he didn't need a corporation that was actually in business. The opposite was no doubt all the better.

"I see... Asagi, can you look into ones that pulled out, ones that have shut-down offices still here?"

"Hmm, I feel like if it's within five years in the past, there should still be records, but..."

Asagi operated her keyboard once more. This time there was a short wait. It apparently took time to squeeze the data out. Finally the screen switched, with detailed data now filling it.

"Here we are. There's just one, though: the Sfelde Pharmaceutical Lab. The head office is in Lotharingia. It was mainly researching new, experimental drugs used for homunculi. Two years ago the lab was closed; looks as if the building's been seized by creditors."

"...That's it, Asagi! Where is it?"

Kojou leaned over to peek at the screen of the smartphone. Asagi blushed a little at Kojou's innocently getting so close, they were practically touching.

"Err, Island North, second level, section B. It's a corporate lab district."

"Got it. Thanks."

As Kojou spoke, he turned his back on Asagi all of a sudden like he was brushing her off.

"H-hold on, Kojou. Where do you think you're going?"

"Something just came up. I'm headin' out!"

"Huh?! What are you talking about? What about afternoon classes?!"

"Make a good excuse for me. Please!"

Kojou made a pose like a pleading bow, leaving behind only those words as he really did leave the classroom this time. Realizing that Yukina was waiting for Kojou in the hallway, Asagi kicked her chair back as she rose up.

"H-hey you…! What the hell is this?! I'm really going to kill you! You jerk—!"

As Asagi yelled in the direction of the corridor, her fearful classmates hurriedly averted their eyes. *So that is how it is*, Yaze's face seemed to say, having watched the whole thing from start to finish.

And, without anyone noticing, Rin Tsukishima, the class representative, gave a gentle sigh.

6

Island North—Itogami Island's northern R&D district, with corporate labs lined up one after another. The abandoned laboratory site remained standing here, in a corner of the futuristic district that felt the most artificial of the entire man-made island.

It was a four-story building largely shaped like a box.

It had no windows, perhaps to protect trade secrets. For that reason, it didn't really feel like the place had been shut down. It was an ideal environment for a criminal hideout.

"So that is the pharmaceutical company laboratory?"

Peeking out from behind the shadow of a roadside tree, Yukina asked with a guarded expression, "Probably," said Kojou with an uncertain nod.

"The parent company pulled out, and the lab was apparently close. But since the word is that the place was seized, I think the facilities in it are still intact. The one for homunculus adjustment included."

"A homunculus adjustment facility… That's just what they'd need, isn't it?" Yukina murmured with a serious expression.

Homunculus was a title given to an artificial life-form constructed via biotechnology.

Though completely artificially designed down to the genetic level, there were fundamental differences between them and chimera.

The technological difficulty was higher, but the level of freedom in design was larger as well.

The first methods for producing homunculi were supposedly established by the sixteenth century. Research had long continued at the hands of a wide variety of people, either to produce a cheap labor force or to develop a partner for mankind.

However, in the end, widespread use of homunculi never happened.

There were two rather large reasons people cited for that.

The first was the ethical problem.

There was deep-seated opposition centered on religious institutions against creating life, viewing such behavior as humans intruding upon the realm of the divine. Furthermore, a fierce debate raged as to whether homunculi should be granted human rights; the debate remained unsettled to this day.

And the other reason was a simple matter of construction cost.

The methods for producing homunculi simply cost too much to use them for labor or sending them onto the battlefield as soldiers. Cloning technology, etc., using genuine human beings, was decisively cheaper.

For that reason, homunculi production was now rarely undertaken, and the number of scientists researching it had greatly dwindled.

However, even now, there was one exception: a field that incorporated homunculus research. That was using homunculus technology in the development of pharmaceuticals. Homunculi, whose genetic construction could be artificially altered, were optimal for clinical trials and researching immune responses and so on; criticism had been blunted to a degree because it was for the just cause of the advancement of medicine. For that reason, most large pharmaceutical firms had their own facilities for the construction and research of homunculi.

The Sfelde Pharmaceutical Laboratory had apparently once been one such medical research facility.

"—We'll never be able to tell what's inside from here, will we..."

As Yukina spoke, she lowered the guitar case from her back. She gently withdrew the silver spear, deploying the blades of the spear tip.

"I'll go look. Please wait right here, Senpai."

"Eh? Hold on, Himeragi. You don't plan on going in there alone?"

"Yes. I intend to do just that."

Of course I do, Yukina's gaze seemed to say as she looked up at Kojou.

"Why?!"

Oh dear. As Kojou's eyes widened in surprise, Yukina made a loud sigh and shook her head.

"And what will you do if you come with me, Senpai? You'd only be in the way, so please behave."

"Er, in the way...? What if you bump into the old man and the girl inside? You gonna fight them alone, Himeragi?"

"Of course. And what would you intend to do if you came with me, Senpai?"

"Stop talkin' like I'm thinking of doing something dirty. Geez."

Kojou spoke with a tone of displeasure. However, unlike Yukina, who had a considerable amount of training as a Counter-Demon Attack Mage, Kojou was only a rank amateur who'd obtained vampire powers. Even if he was called the Fourth Primogenitor, he wasn't even able to control a single Beast Vassal as he pleased. Given that, he couldn't help being called "in the way."

"And what could you do as a vampire in the first place, Senpai? You cannot use a Beast Vassal; you cannot fly through the sky; you cannot even turn into mist or the like."

"H-hey, only a few vampires have special powers like that. It's not like I can't do anything."

"Certainly your raw strength is considerable, but you cannot use it in actual combat with moves like an amateur. Also, you lack caution and presence of mind."

"U...gh..."

"If you truly understand, then please behave. Do not do anything rash."

Yukina spoke with a tone like she was brushing him off.

What she'd said was pretty harsh, but she was in no way being deliberately malicious. To her, she was just pointing out the obvious so that Kojou would not place himself in danger.

"But I'll be worried about you, Himeragi!"

Kojou spoke in a rough, nervous tone.

Those words made Yukina's eyes go wide. Her cheeks reddened a little.

"Wh-what are you saying…?! I'm the one worried about you, Senpai! If your Beast Vassal runs wild like last night in the middle of the city like this, how much damage do you think will occur then?"

"You do have a point there, but it's not right for everything to fall on just your shoulders, Himeragi! I don't like that one bit. In the first place, it's not like I've got nothin' to do with this whole thing."

Kojou watched Yukina with a serious look. That vigor awed Yukina into silence.

"I… I understand. I do think you have a point there, Senpai."

Ahem. With a small clearing of her throat, Yukina made a serious expression. "Well, yeah," said Kojou as he nodded.

"So long as it is possible you will be hunted as a vampire, you certainly have something to do with this, Senpai."

"Wait, you think *that's* the point I have?"

"In the first place, my original mission is to watch over you; I really should not take my eyes off you, Senpai. Let's act together as much as we can. However, if we encounter the Armed Apostle—"

"Yeah. I'll run to safer ground right away. I don't wanna get in your way, Himeragi."

"Good. Please do."

After sighing those words, Yukina went silent as she looked up at Kojou. After a bit of hesitation, she spoke in a voice so faint as to barely be audible.

"Um, Senpai…"

"Mm?"

"Thank you very much."

"Eh? What for?"

Kojou asked back with a dubious face. However, Yukina gently smiled and shook her head.

"No. It is nothing at all. Let us be off."

Whoosh. Swinging her spear, seemingly severing all doubt with it, she walked toward the building.

7

It went without saying, but the shut-down lab building was locked. Of course that went for the glass doors of the front entrance, but the service entrance was also sealed with a padlock and chains.

The cheap padlock was red with rust, indicating it hadn't been used in a long time.

"Isn't this the place the old man and the girl are hiding...?"

Kojou spoke in a discouraged tone.

From what they could see, this was the only way into the building. It wasn't the kind of building you could access from the roof or from underground, either. Even the homunculus girl couldn't have made it in through the vents, let alone Eustach, with his huge frame.

That would mean that Kojou and Yukina's hypothesis that they'd been using the lab as their hideout had been mistaken. *Whew.* However, Yukina made a satisfied smile.

"No, Senpai. We were right."

The silver spear suddenly thrust through the service entrance's door.

Chingg! That instant, with a high-pitched metallic ring, Kojou felt like glass was shattering before his eyes. The chain and padlock that should have been locking the service entrance vanished; the door slowly opened.

"Himeragi? What just...?"

"A novice-level illusion spell. Senpai...falling for magic this simple makes you a failure of a Primogenitor."

Yukina made an exasperated-seeming sigh. Kojou was silent. His heart murmured as if excusing him, *It's not like I want a passing grade for that!*

The building interior was dark. However, Yukina seemed untroubled as she walked within.

Somehow she seemed to have better night vision than the vampiric Kojou. Perhaps this, too, was the special Sword Shaman power Yukina had referred to as spiritual sight.

Certainly, with that much power at Yukina's disposal, Kojou could understand why she felt he was in the way.

However, that very thing made Kojou vaguely nervous. It was the truth that Kojou was an untalented vampire, but he thought that even so, Yukina was just too perfect.

He didn't think Yukina's abundance of combat power and intellect was something a girl fourteen to fifteen years of age could acquire *by any sane method.*

"…"

While Kojou walked, thinking absentmindedly about that, Yukina suddenly came to a halt. Kojou inadvertently bumped into Yukina, drawing a silent glare from her.

"What is it, Himeragi?"

"Senpai… This is…"

Yukina pointed to the scene spread before their eyes.

It was a room with a high ceiling, like the chapel of a church.

Instead of stained glass, the walls were lined with cylindrical vats.

Each was about a meter in diameter. They were probably just under two meters tall. A total of twenty were arrayed from left to right at regular intervals.

The vats were filled with a slimy, amber-colored solution.

Light emitted from illuminated panels made the liquid shine faintly, but the sight was far from what one could call *beautiful.*

This was a simple lab room. Abandoned vats for homunculus adjustment. But…

"This is…a homunculus…? This…?"

Kojou exclaimed as he looked up at the vats. His voice shook slightly in anger.

Suspended within the amber-colored solution were bizarre life-forms about the size of a puppy. Some, one might guess, were like demonic beasts; others, like beautiful faeries. Either way, these were life-forms that did not exist in nature.

"Senpai…?"

A surprised expression came over Yukina as she watched Kojou display fierce anger. Yukina wanted to ask him the reason for that anger, but she turned her back on him instead. She poised her silver spear and lowered her posture.

She'd noticed someone's presence emerge from the shadows of a vat.

She was a petite girl with indigo hair. She had splendid, pale blue eyes, but they gazed expressionlessly at the spear Yukina pointed toward her. She was the homunculus girl called Astarte.

"That's…"

Noticing Astarte's presence, Kojou turned as well. *Gasp!* However, Yukina spread her left palm before Kojou's eyes.

"Don't look, Senpai!"

"Eh? Uh, but…"

"Do *not* look. Don't turn this way, please!"

"Himeragi? What are you ta—"

"Uhh!" Kojou exclaimed in a low voice as he looked at Astarte's appearance past Yukina's palm.

The first thing his gaze fell upon was skin so white, it was almost transparent.

Transparent drops fell at Astarte's feet. The homunculus girl seemed to have just emerged from a vat, her adjustment complete.

The only thing she had over her body was a thin cloth, like a surgical gown. That cloth was equally soaked, clinging right to her bare flesh. She was as good as naked.

"Senpai…"

As Kojou continued to stare dumbfounded at Astarte, Yukina glared at him, speaking in a low voice. Kojou's expression stiffened as he shook his head.

"No, you're wrong…! I'm not, Himeragi!"

"Wrong about what? Goodness… You truly are indecent."

Letting out a single, ragged sigh, Yukina seemed angry as she looked the other way.

However, Kojou did not shift his gaze away from the sight of Astarte's flesh, easily visible through the cloth. For under her white, transparent-like flesh, a rainbow-colored shadow flickered.

Abruptly, Astarte calmly opened her mouth.

"…*Warning*. Please leave this place immediately."

"Eh?"

The girl's somewhat unexpected words shook Kojou back to his senses. In the meantime, Yukina altered how she poised her spear, shifting to a posture from which she could preemptively attack without warning.

However, Astarte continued to speak, still appearing completely defenseless.

"This island will soon sink. Before this occurs, please flee as far as you can..."

"The island... Sink?! The heck does that mean...?!"

Shudder. Kojou exclaimed as he felt a chill run up his spine. Perhaps the low-inflection, robotic voice made Astarte's words more trustworthy. A homunculus like her had no reason to lie to Kojou or Yukina.

" 'This island is a transient land floating where the dragon lines cross the southern sea. Without its nucleus it shall simply collapse...' "

"Eh?"

Yukina let out a surprised voice at the homunculus's recited words. Kojou couldn't follow, but the dialogue with Astarte apparently included information that seemed to shock Yukina.

Then, behind Astarte, a huge shadow slowly emerged.

He was a huge man wearing a solemn vestment over his armored augmentation suit. The Lotharingian Armed Apostle Rudolf Eustach.

As he coldly gazed down at the homunculus girl, she turned around, seeming fearful.

"—Indeed. We desire the most valuable, immutable treasure that is the nucleus. And it is thanks to you, Sword Shaman of the Lion King Agency, that we have the power to achieve our long-wished aspiration."

He turned the blade of his bardiche toward the spear-poising Yukina as he spoke.

The Armed Apostle's riddling words brought a look of confusion over Yukina.

However, it was not she who replied to Eustach, but Kojou.

"Gained the power...you said...? You mean, you stuffed it into that girl's body?"

"Senpai?"

The smothered anger in Kojou's voice clearly unnerved Yukina.

Kojou stepped in front of Yukina, glaring at Eustach with anger-filled eyes. The Lotharingian Armed Apostle stared indifferently at Kojou.

"So you noticed. As expected of the Fourth Primogenitor, I should say. However, even you are no longer any threat to us. We are invincible."

"Don't toy with me—!"

Kojou's thunderous roar shook the air in the tranquil lab.

"Old man, why, you, you planted a Beast Vassal into this girl, didn't you?"

"Eh…?!"

Listening to Kojou's angry voice, Yukina looked at Astarte's slender body in apparent surprise. Then she looked at the bizarre life-forms in the cultivation vats to the left and right of Astarte.

They resembled demonic beasts and faeries, distorted life-forms that should not exist in this world. But could an artificial life-form become host to a Beast Vassal—?

"It is just as you say."

Eustach conveyed pride with his words.

"The only blood that flows through her veins is that of vampires who make vassals of these beasts. Through implantation of Beast Vassals before they hatch, I have succeeded in creating a homunculus that is host to a Beast Vassal—although Astarte here is my lone success."

"Shut up!!" Kojou interrupted the bishop's words. "Don't tell me you don't know why no demons other than vampires can use Beast Vassals!! You knew that and still did this—?!"

"Of course I do. When a Beast Vassal materializes, it consumes its host's life force at an incredible rate. You wish to say that only vampires with an infinite 'negative' life force may tame them?"

"Then this girl—"

"No doubt, so long as Rhodaktylos resides in her, her remaining life span shall not be long. She might hold on for another two weeks or so. And that was lengthened greatly via the consuming of the demons we defeated… However, it is sufficient to fulfill our objective."

Eustach spoke in a tone that lacked a single shred of anguish or guilt.

Kojou was so angry, he was at a loss for words.

Yukina opened her mouth in his place. She gripped her spear as if shaken by the image.

"Consumed the…demons…? You don't mean, were attacking demons on this island to…"

"Yes. First, their magical energy served as live bait for the Beast Vassal. And the second reason, to complete the technique infused into Astarte... Sword Shaman of the Lion King Agency, the battle with you and the spear you hold provided splendid, precious data for this purpose."

Yukina's shoulders shook as he addressed her by her title.

"For this...did you raise that girl for the sake of this alone—?! It's like you're using her as a tool!"

Eustach watched Yukina's display of anger with what seemed like amusement.

"Why are you indignant, Sword Shaman? Did the Lion King Agency not raise you to be a tool as well?"

"...That's...!"

"Purchased as an unwanted child, instilled solely with skills to oppose demons, and sent into combat like a disposable tool—that is the way of the Lion King Agency, is it not? Sword Shaman, to obtain counter-demon techniques of such proficiency, surely you had to sacrifice something?"

As Eustach calmly pointed it out, Yukina's entire body froze. She wordlessly bit her lip as her cheeks lost their color, becoming pale.

"Shut up, old man..."

Kojou murmured as if to shield Yukina. However, Eustach's expression was unmoved.

"I use as a tool that which I created to be a tool; you take those born with the blessing of God and degrade them into tools. I wonder whose sin is the graver?"

"I told you to shut up, you rotten priest—!"

As Kojou roared, his entire body was shrouded in pale lightning. Dazzling lightning emanated from Kojou's right fist. Kojou should have appeared no more than an average high schooler, but thanks to the dense magical energy he was giving off, his Beast Vassal had partially materialized, using his own flesh as a medium.

"Senpai...?!"

Yukina made a weak exclamation, as if completely overwhelmed by the density of the magical energy he was giving off.

His battle-axe poised, Eustach's face scowled a little in surprise.

"My. So a Beast Vassal's magical energy responds to the anger of its host… So this is the Fourth Primogenitor's power. Very well—Astarte! Grant them mercy!"

"—Accept."

Obeying the command of her master and creator, the homunculus girl blocked Kojou's path.

From her small body, a giant, haze-like Beast Vassal emerged.

It was a translucent giant, glittering with the colors of the rainbow. It was no longer just arms, but a nearly complete body that emerged. It was a giant between four and five meters in height. It was faceless golem with a thick armor of flesh all over its body.

The humanoid Beast Vassal took the girl that was its host within it as it howled.

"Don't just do whatever the hell he says—!"

Kojou moved to pound the golem with his lightning-infused fist.

Even if it was but a little leaking out, this lightning attack was the power of a Beast Vassal of the Fourth Primogenitor. Surely its might surpassed that of an ordinary vampire's Beast Vassal. However—

"Senpai, don't!"

The moment Yukina beheld the scene, she spontaneously cried out.

The next moment, it was Kojou, wrapped in light, who was sent flying.

"Gu…aa!!"

As Kojou let out a loud scream, his body flew back like a piece of tattered cloth.

The moment Kojou appeared to have punched Astarte's Beast Vassal, a fierce explosion erupted, blowing him back nearly ten meters.

The fallen Kojou's entire body was shrouded in a white vapor that carried the stench of burn flesh.

It was as if he'd been struck by lightning—as if the magical energy in Kojou's body had backlashed against him.

"Senpai!!"

Yukina poised her spear and charged toward Astarte, seemingly to shield Kojou.

In concert with Yukina's ritual energy, the silver-colored spear tip was enveloped in a pale white flash.

It was the holy, purifying light that could destroy even a Primogenitor's

Beast Vassal. No abilities that demons possessed could withstand a single blow. It should not have been withstood. However...

"Snowdrift Wolf's...been stopped?!" Yukina exclaimed in response to the strange resistance she felt through the spear.

Snowdrift Wolf's blade halted just a tiny bit short of touching the Beast Vassal that enveloped Astarte. The spear, able to penetrate any demonic ward, had been stopped cold.

In their previous battle Yukina had felt a similar resistance, but now she completely understood the reason why.

The surface of Astarte's Beast Vassal, "Rhododactylos," was surrounded in the same white light as Snowdrift Wolf. Indeed, by the exact same holy, purifying radiance.

"Resonance...?! This power is...!"

"You are correct, Sword Shaman. 'Divine Oscillation Effect'—the power to neutralize magical energy and tear apart any ward, successfully implemented solely by the Lion King Agency, its trump card for anti-demon combat. Using your combat data as a reference, I was finally able to complete my own."

Eustach made a satisfied smile.

Severely shaken, Yukina barely managed to continue to fend off Astarte's counterattacks.

Eustach had said that he'd engaged in repeated combat with demons to perfect the incomplete technique.

It was the "Divine Oscillation Effect," the power to completely neutralize any attack by magical energy, the secret ritual said to be the ultimate counter-demon combat technique, which he had sought.

And then they encountered Yukina.

A Sword Shaman who had come to the island bearing a Schneewalzer—the Lion King Agency's secret weapons, the world's only successful implementation of the "Divine Oscillation Effect."

"No... It's my fault that..."

Yukina, having lost her will to fight, was being overwhelmed by Astarte.

Even if incomplete, Astarte's DOE used very similar technology; by combining data obtained from Snowdrift Wolf, it had finally become complete—enough to make the magical energy of Kojou Akatsuki, the

Fourth Primogenitor, bounce off. Yukina's actions had consequently helped them complete it.

Eustach had obtained the power he desired. Kojou was wounded and on the ground. All because Yukina had come to Itogami Island—

As a hollow expression came over Yukina, Eustach hoisted his battle-axe before her.

"...!"

Yukina, her mental concentration disturbed, noticed the Armed Apostle's attack too late. By the time she reacted, the battle-axe's massive blade was already right before her eyes.

Perceiving that it was not possible for her to either evade or block the attack, Yukina instantly resigned herself. An impact rocked Yukina; her entire body was drenched in lukewarm blood.

However, it had not hurt as she had expected.

Instead, Yukina felt warmth envelop her all over, along with a gentle heaviness.

"Koff...!"

Kojou made a small cough into Yukina's ear. There was a great deal of fresh blood pouring from his lips.

Already heavily wounded in battle with Astarte, Kojou had thrust Yukina back to shield her, sustaining Eustach's attack in her place.

"S...Senpai...?!"

Yukina's voice shook. She supported Kojou as he collapsed.

Kojou's body was unusually light. From his arm, seemingly desperately embracing Yukina, his shredded torso slipped downward.

A single blow of the massive battle-axe had smashed Kojou's ribs and spine, turning Kojou's torso into small pieces of meat. The shattered bones fell to the floor as bloody fragments.

With a dry ripping sound, his damaged blood vessels and muscles tore apart.

The spurting, fresh blood formed a blood pool at Yukina's feet.

The final skin connecting Kojou's head to his torso, unable to bear the weight of the body, tore apart with a sound like thin paper ripping. All that remained in Yukina's hands was Kojou's severed head, his eyes open and vacant.

Kojou's body rolled onto the floor, his spine, his lungs, his heart, everything smashed and torn into unrecognizable pieces.

Vampires were unaging immortals. However, a single blow from the Armed Apostle had destroyed his heart, the source of that power; his blood, the foundation of his magical energy, now merely poured out in vain…

"Senpai… Why… Oh no…no… Aaaaaaaah…!"

The spear fell from Yukina's hands. She desperately embraced Kojou, reduced to his head alone, with both arms. However, Kojou of course made no reply.

Eustach gazed at the scene with a neutral expression, lowering his battle-axe.

No doubt he had judged that Yukina no longer had the strength to continue combat. Having now perfected the DOE, Eustach no longer had any reason to fight Yukina.

"Let us go, Astarte… We shall take back our most valued treasure."

"*—Accept*," Astarte murmured with a neutral expression, enveloped by the humanoid Beast Vassal.

The Beast Vassal's giant arms let loose a pale light, blowing apart the laboratory's outer wall with an explosion. Yukina turned her back to shield Kojou's severed head from the dust and debris dancing in the fierce blast wind, bent over him like the Virgin Mary.

For a single, final moment, the faceless golem that served the Armed Apostle remained crouched, watching Yukina.

Appearing sad somehow, her look seemed to desperately convey, *Run, quickly*.

Chapter Four
The Right Arm of the Saint

1

That day, after school. Asagi Aiba was arriving at her part-time job, still in her school uniform.

Twelve levels under the Keystone Gate. The Security Section of the Gigafloat Management Public Corporation.

As what one might call the nucleus of Itogami Island, security was extremely strict in this area, but Asagi easily passed through each gate with one swipe of the System Administrator ID Card prepared just for her.

Though normally, such a card was not issued to anyone short of the mayor, the blunt truth was that if Asagi was serious, she could easily disable security of this magnitude. Knowing this full well, the public corporation's director had given her the card as a special case. Such special privilege was recognition of Asagi's superior genius as a programmer.

"Hiya, m'lady. You seem displeased. Your fine beauty will go to waste."

As Asagi sat down and logged in at her terminal, her assistant AI spoke to her in an overly familiar manner.

The artificial intelligence Asagi had dubbed *Mogwai* was the avatar of five supercomputers holding all of Itogami Island's city functions within their grasp. Though its operational capacity was no doubt on par with the world's most powerful computers, it was said to be difficult to handle because of its...quirks. But for some mysterious reason, Asagi rather liked it.

"Oh, shut up. Cut the boring flattery and the helpful spirit act, 'kay?"

"Heh-heh. Concerns about love, I presume? It seems that genius programmers' affairs of the heart are different from those of mere mortals."

"Oh, stuff it or I'll upload a virus."

Asagi began her work while shooting the breeze with the AI.

The job she'd accepted for today was cleaning up after the explosion incident in the warehouse district the night before. Hundreds of detailed subjects, such as managing the maintenance of destroyed pieces of the electrical grid and water and sewer systems, rearranging the service schedules of transport facilities, calculating restoration estimates, and so on, all required the writing of new, custom programs.

It was a job that would take a group of dozens of excellent programmers a full half year, but Asagi and Mogwai teamed up would need about three days.

With Asagi's skill, she could have chosen any number of higher-profile jobs, but Asagi rather liked having a part-time job where she could use one of the world's top supercomputers as her personal chew toy.

Her lone regret was that taking this job meant she had no free time to help Kojou with his homework. She thought, feeling a bit wistful, it was a bit of a shame to have ripped up and tossed away that World History report…

But that was Kojou's fault any way you sliced it. Plus the idiot had skipped school so early in the term and never even made it back.

She didn't even need to confirm it. That transfer student Himeragi had been with him, after all.

What surprised Asagi had been how much it burned her inside.

A disagreeable thing was a disagreeable thing, but she didn't think that Kojou, of all people, had the resourcefulness to skip a class to go out on a date with a younger girl. There had to be some circumstances involved.

What put Asagi in a bad mood was that Kojou hadn't told her those circumstances, instead trying to cover things up with a clumsy lie. She vaguely realized Kojou was just trying to be considerate of her feelings, but she *really* didn't like *that*.

There was one other thing she didn't like: the girl, Yukina Himeragi.

Asagi had no evidence to back her intuition, but Kojou probably had a weakness for her type.

She behaved with a resoluteness that didn't feel feminine in the slightest and spoke very frankly. No doubt the athletic aura she gave off appealed to Kojou, who'd played basketball day and night when he was in middle high.

On top of that, Yukina looked beautiful to Asagi even in spite of their being the same gender. Though Kojou didn't appear to pay attention to the opposite sex at all, even he might fall for an opponent of that level.

"Not that I think I'm giving up anything in style points..."

Lost in her work, she didn't even seem to realize she'd spoken out loud. The AI's sharp ears picked up on it.

"Well, in this world there are rascals who go for all *kinds* of things."

"Don't answer when I'm talking to myself."

"I'm just having a conversation with my partner."

"None of your business. And when did I turn into your partner, anyway?"

"Isn't the reason it's not going smoothly because you're not honest with yourself?"

"Y-you don't have to tell me something obvious like that. But...!"

Asagi's hands unwittingly stopped tapping the keyboard as she raised her eyebrows in annoyance.

It was the moment right after when a dull vibration and impact shook the room Asagi was in.

Asagi let out a brief yelp. Itogami Island, floating on top of the Pacific Ocean, didn't have any earthquakes. It was the first impact Asagi had felt since she'd immigrated to the island.

"Mogwai, what was that just now?"

"...Well, this is unexpected. Intruders."

The AI spoke with something like admiration. Asagi furrowed her eyebrows in surprise.

"Intruders?"

"Yes. They are in combat with this building's security forces. The vibration from just now was from a support pillar being cleanly broken during combat."

"Broken... You're kidding, right?" Asagi murmured in a low voice as her face changed color.

This was no ordinary building. This was the Gigafloat's underground infrastructure section. Its main support pillars, designed to hold up tens of thousands of tons, were not so easily destroyed, even with explosives.

"It's not just the support pillar. There's quite a bit of damage to the upper floors as well. I believe it is still safe here for now, but it might not be possible to escape. The elevator shaft was also destroyed."

"You mean I'm shut in here?"

"The emergency stairs are still intact, but I do not recommend using them right now. Not unless you want to meet the intruders in person. The security forces have already been routed."

"Routed?" Asagi asked back, dumbfounded. Even in peacetime, the Keystone Gate was garrisoned with nearly a hundred and fifty security personnel. And they had been beaten?

"Who are these intruders? A terrorist group? Or are we under attack by a Dominion army?"

"Err, no. Neither..."

The AI replied to Asagi, who'd expected some kind of demonic military incursion, with an oddly human-sounding tone.

A fierce explosion shook the room once more.

"...There are only two intruders. One a mere human; the other, a homunculus."

2

Keystone Gate was the name of the giant composite structure located at the center of Itogami Island.

At twelve stories, its aboveground section was the tallest building on the island. You could look up from pretty much anywhere on the island and see its majestic reverse-pyramid shape.

Within the facility were government administration offices, including city hall, and numerous hotels and commercial facilities built one after another, functioning as the island's nucleus in both name and fact.

On the other hand, the giant construct also fulfilled one other, crucially important role, performed by the forty levels under the surface of the water as well as the Gigafloat Management Facility.

This structure, just under two kilometers in diameter, bound together the four Gigafloats that together composed Itogami Island.

Keystone Gate was designed to absorb the effects of ocean currents, wind, waves, and so forth, such as bending and vibrations between the Gigafloats. Without this, the four districts of Itogami Island would suddenly collide, or perhaps break apart, drifting atop the Pacific Ocean. It was a critical facility, truly worthy of the name *keystone*.

Furthermore, it was heavily defended.

Itogami City was under the jurisdiction of the Island Guard, four hundred and forty men strong, divided into three battalions. One of those battalions was assigned to guarding Keystone Gate. This included a platoon of sixty Counter-Demon Agents, numbers equal to those of all CDAs under the jurisdiction of a typical midsized prefectural police headquarters.

Such a large number of personnel had been assigned to protecting Keystone Gate in anticipation of assaults by large-scale terrorist organizations.

In simulations, they could hold out for several days, even against a company of beast men troops from the Dominion.

That was why, that day, people were in utter shock.

That a mere two intruders had shattered the security forces and penetrated the gate—

They had already broken through the tenth underwater level's airtight bulkhead, heading for the gate's central section, having not made a single demand.

"—*Complete*. The airtight bulkhead's seal has been destroyed."

The homunculus girl, shrouded in Beast Vassal armor, made an austere report.

Right now the girl appeared to be wearing a twelve-foot-tall golem, glittering in rainbow colors, as armor. A single brush of its fingertips instantly destroyed the barrier protecting the seventh level's airlock.

This was the work of the DOE sealed within Astarte's body.

Completely merged with the man-made Beast Vassal "Rhododactylos," she was able to neutralize various mystical forces and slice through barriers.

It was this ability in particular that Eustach the Armed Apostle had long sought. For it was this, *the power to destroy barriers*, that was indispensable for the achievement of his fondest wish.

"Go, Astarte. That which we seek lies beyond."

"Accept."

Quietly murmuring, Astarte climbed over the destroyed bulkhead.

Ahead was the central section, under the jurisdiction of the Gigafloat Management Corporation, extending down to the twenty-fifth floor underwater.

If damage was inflicted on this block, it was possible that severe damage would be caused to the inhabitants of Itogami Island.

For hospitalized patients, a power outage could be fatal; food could no longer be preserved in the fierce heat of Itogami Island. Here on the Pacific Ocean, three hundred kilometers from the mainland, it was not possible to evacuate some five hundred and sixty thousand inhabitants in a short time frame.

That was the very reason why it had been a target of terrorism time and time again and why security had been beefed up to cope with it.

It had been the Island Guard's finest that awaited Eustach and Astarte's arrival into the central section. There were two CDA squads and one heavy, mechanized platoon.

"Hmm… An adequate response for an emergency situation. They are well trained."

As they spotted Eusatch and Astarte on the path below, they engaged with one great volley.

These were Blessed Bullets for use against demons. Even Eustach's armor-enhanced clothing would not emerge unscathed from a straight-up hit. Eustach slipped behind a wall to avoid direct hits but appraised with a very calm voice, "Still, it is all for naught. Exterminate them, Astarte."

"—Accept. Execute 'Rhododactylos.'"

The humanoid Beast Vassal, glimmering in rainbow colors, assailed the mechanized troops as they continued to fire.

The giant moved with unimaginable agility. The Beast Vassal's overwhelming power mowed them down.

The barriers that protected the mechanized forces shattered like thin glass; now defenseless, they were dispatched with the greatest of ease.

Having determined that normal Blessed Bullets were having no effect, the CDA fired ballista at Astarte. These were small-scale siege weapons that launched javelins, but when their heads were charged with ritual power, they became powerful weapons against demonkind—enough that their use had been treaty-restricted, being able to inflict lethal wounds to beast men and vampires in a single blow. The javelins, glimmering with a dark gray light, assaulted the humanoid Beast Vassal with a speed rivaling that of a bullet.

And then the armor deflected them as easily as raindrops.

The unbelievable display made the CDAs stop dumbfounded in their tracks.

Only Eustach made a quiet smile.

A Beast Vassal, being a mass of magical power, could not be damaged save by even greater magical power.

However, Rhododactylos was now neutralizing the magic power of all attacks, and reflecting them back.

Now no one could stop the Vassal Beast—or its lord, Astarte. Not even the Beast Vassal of a Primogenitor.

The CDA continued to resist, but with their most powerful weapons rendered powerless, their chances of victory were nil.

With overwhelming physical might, Astarte's Beast Vassal annihilated them.

This was no longer combat. It was a one-sided slaughter.

"Hmm, a wise decision."

No doubt they'd noticed that Eustach was the one giving orders to Astarte the homunculus. The several surviving CDAs attacked Eustach directly.

"However, I cannot be defeated by such dull skills. Compared to that Sword Shaman girl, 'tis mere child's play."

A grand smile came over Eustach's face as he struck back.

His physical strength amplified by his augmented robe, swinging his metal bardiche, swept the security force's Counter-Demon Agents away. He had been an exorcist sufficient to be granted the title of Armed Apostle by Lotharingia. His might far surpassed that of the average for National Counter-Demon Agent.

"—Perhaps things have been put in order?"

Eustach spoke coldly as he looked around at the completely silent security forces.

The vestiges of scattered bullets and of the Beast Vassal's destruction had changed the floor from a battlefield into a ghastly ruin. All members of the elite force, over sixty strong, had fallen, heavily wounded. No one moved aside from the two intruders.

No—

In a place a short way from the battleground, one girl stood.

She was unarmed. All she had was a cell phone and a little notepad computer. From her posture, she had no combat training; he felt no magic power from her. She was neither combat personnel nor demon, a mere human being.

She had the aura of someone in the passageway by chance who'd come to see what was going on and had happened upon the battle.

As Eustach gazed at her trembling form, his face scowled in suspicion, for the uniform she wore greatly resembled that of the Lion King Agency's Sword Shaman.

Though the chance they were comrades was not high, perhaps it was best to neutralize her just in—

Amid his thoughts, Eustach shook his head.

It was not necessary. Even if the Sword Shaman herself came after him, she could do nothing against Eustach and Astarte. Not anymore.

Besides, to take the girl's life here was meaningless.

She would die soon enough as it was. Not only her but every person who lived on this island.

Yes. This forsaken land built by criminals, Itogami Island, would soon sink into the sea.

3

Kojou Akatsuki awoke amid the thin darkness of twilight.

He faintly heard a sound. He didn't recognize the landscape, but it seemed to be a park near the coast.

His outstretched arm felt cold, perhaps because he was lying atop the concrete on his side. That made it a less comfortable place to sleep. His cheek conveyed pleasant warmth.

"Senpai… Would you mind getting up already?"

Kojou suddenly heard a voice above his head. It was Yukina's voice, seeming to pout somehow.

"Sorry… Five more minutes."

Feeling like he was watching a dream, Kojou's lips meekly made the request. It'd be a waste to pull away from this tranquil warmth that seemed to envelop his head. But…

As Kojou heard a "Good grief" and a light sigh above his head, something pinched his cheek.

"Do not get carried away. This isn't the time or place to be doing this."

With an "*Ow,*" Kojou opened his eyes without thinking, realizing the unexpected existence of a girl at point-blank range looking down at him.

"H-Himeragi?"

"Are you finally awake, Senpai? Making someone worry about you that much… You're really quite something."

Yukina spoke in an uncommonly sarcastic tone.

Seeing her expression, Kojou remembered what had happened. He and Himeragi had encountered Eustach at the pharmaceutical company lab; then he'd sustained an attack from a battle-axe meant for Yukina.

A blow powerful enough to slice through his heart and smash his torso to bits.

It wasn't a wound even a vampire could survive.

"I see… I died, didn't I?"

"Yes."

Yukina bit her lip as if remembering what she'd seen at the time. And as her face seemed close to tears once more…

"A little while after you died, your wounds healed on their own… Even the blood spatter came back, as if time was rewinding itself…"

"So that's why I've been sleeping here for a while, huh?" Kojou asked while pressing on his right shoulder. The shoulder, which ought to have been severed by the bardiche, was attached to his torso, which should have been torn to pieces, not even a flesh wound remaining on either of them.

Of course, his uniform shirt was still wrecked, but it was still wearable—as long as he didn't mind looking a bit like an anarchist.

As Kojou's fingers wandered, seemingly confirming the state of his wounds, Yukina glared bitterly.

"If you're going to come back to life, please say that *before* you die. How much do you think I worried about you…!"

As Yukina spoke, she held Kojou's head and began beating it with her fist. As Kojou was about to object to the absurdity of that, he realized his head had been resting on her lap. Yukina had been here the whole time until Kojou revived.

As Kojou looked up at Yukina's tear-filled eyes, he made an exasperated sigh.

"Sorry I made you worry, but I didn't know. So this is what that Avlora was talking about."

"Avlora? The prior Fourth Primogenitor said something about…?"

As Kojou slowly rose up, Yukina watched blankly with wavering eyes.

"Yeah… She said, to the Primogenitors, immortality isn't a power, it's just a curse."

"Curse?"

"Primogenitors don't die. Even if you impale their hearts or crush their heads, they still live on. To live alone for centuries or even millennia, even if you *want* to die… Yeah, you can't call that anything but a curse."

Yukina watched silently while Kojou grumbled as if making a sigh.

Even though vampires were said to be ageless and undying, that did not mean they were completely invulnerable. In particular, their brains, which controlled their magic power, and their hearts, which governed the circulation of their blood, were lethal vulnerabilities.

Even for the Elders, receiving severe damage to either meant certain death.

However, as the Fourth Primogenitor, Kojou's body was different.

Even his completely destroyed heart had regenerated; most of the blood he had lost had flowed right back into him.

But there would be no coming back if he managed to get himself turned to ash like vampires in legend.

"Even so, why did you shield me like that?! Curse or not, you had no proof you could come back for sure! What if you didn't come back to life?!" Yukina asked Kojou with a tone of genuine anger.

"Well, that's true, but I'm still glad."

"What are you glad for?!"

"Er, that you're all right."

A curious expression came over Yukina as the words came casually out of Kojou's mouth.

She had an expression like that of a broken doll, too anguished to either laugh or cry.

"...And...that makes you glad?"

Yukina's lips weaved the words without emotion. Kojou tilted his neck a bit, seeming perplexed.

"Eh?"

"You would have been better off not shielding me. Have you forgotten already? I came here to kill you, Senpai."

Yukina murmured expressionlessly, seemingly without emotion.

Kojou's eyebrows grimaced as if to say, *The heck are you talking about?*

The aura Yukina gave off that moment was just like that of the girl called Astarte. Just like the sad homunculus girl, bound by the orders of her creator.

"What that Armed Apostle said is the truth. I'm a disposable tool. I realized it long before, but I just didn't want to admit it. My biological parents sold me for money; I was raised as a mere tool for fighting demons... That's why, even if I die, no one will be sad, but you're different, aren't you, Senpai...?"

"Himeragi..."

Hanging her head in shame, Yukina turned away from Kojou, seemingly holding back tears.

Kojou finally understood why Yukina had hesitated in the middle of the battle with Eustach.

Only fourteen years of age, a Lion King Agency Sword Shaman bearing enough combat ability to overwhelm a Lotharingian Armed Apostle. Wielder of a demon-slaying spear, a combat expert raised solely to fight demonkind.

That was why, faced with Astarte, likewise constructed as a tool for combat, Yukina had seen that they were alike. That was why Eustach's words had hurt Yukina so much—they'd hit too close to home. That was the cause of her hesitation.

Kojou thought that maybe *he* had been the reason Yukina was so hard on herself. In the several days since he'd met her, she'd continued to watch him the whole time, seeing him struggle to live as an ordinary human being in spite of having obtained the power of the Fourth Primogenitor.

Yukina had abandoned a normal, everyday life to obtain her combat prowess.

And here was Kojou, who had been granted power mightier than anyone's, who'd chosen that banal, everyday life.

Perhaps to Yukina, Kojou's actions looked like a rejection of how she'd lived her life until now.

That's why she'd said it.

That it should have been her who died, not Kojou…

"…"

As Yukina remained motionless, still covering her face, Kojou gazed at her with a puzzled expression.

And he realized he was faintly indignant.

It wasn't that he didn't understand how Yukina felt, but her reasoning was messed up any way you looked at it.

It wasn't a good thing for her to be hurt instead of Kojou. *What the heck is she saying?* he thought to himself. However, right now it was probably difficult for Kojou to convince Yukina with mere words. After all, in a manner of speaking, his very existence was causing her pain.

The sight of Yukina's curled back felt all too ephemeral, as if she'd disappear the moment he took her eyes off her. She was like a little lost girl in tears.

That was irritating Kojou more and more.

"Now, hold on here, Himera…gi!"

"Eh…?"

As Yukina kept her back to him, Kojou tried to gently reach out and touch her shoulder. However, sensation apparently hadn't returned in full to Kojou's barely regenerated flesh and blood. As he tried to stand up, he lost his balance, falling right on top of Yukina.

Yukina's body went rigid at Kojou's completely unanticipated action. Pressing down on her as if embracing her tightly, the incident put Kojou in rigor as well.

Even so, Kojou couldn't abandon Yukina now, so he remained locked like this without moving.

"Um… What are you doing, Senpai?"

After a while, Yukina asked him with a low voice that seemed angry. Kojou replied with an intentionally pained-sounding voice.

"Er, it's aftereffects from when I almost died earlier, so…"

"You're lying, aren't you?"

"Er… Yeah."

Without a word, Yukina, still held down, continued to glare at the silent Kojou. For a while Kojou wondered how he could excuse himself, but he changed his mind midway.

In this situation, he thought it best to lift Yukina's spirits, even if it made her a little angry in the process.

And so, with Yukina's body still rigid, Kojou gently brought his face to her neck. He took in a deep whiff of the scent of her hair. The odd sensation from the nape of her neck made Yukina let out a yelp.

"You smell good, Himeragi."

Kojou informed her of his thoughts with frightening bluntness. Yukina's shoulders trembled a little.

"Wh-what are you saying, all of a sudden?!"

"Your hair's so silky, too. It feels good."

"Please stop that! Wh-where are you touching?!"

"You're softer than I expected, Himeragi. And really light…"

"S-Senpai! Th-that tickles, geez!"

"…You really do smell great."

"So you really are a pervert…!"

With tears welling up at the edges of her eyes, Yukina made a yell devoid of strength.

Kojou still had his lips right at Yukina's ear.

"Yeah, that's right. *Pervert* is fine. So don't go saying you should've died instead of a pervert like me."

"Th…that has nothing to do with it, does… Ah, aah!"

As Yukina attempted her rebuttal, Kojou put his tongue against Yukina's neck and blew his breath onto her. Yukina's body twisted as if desperately trying to escape from within Kojou's arms, but her struggles were weakening.

"Besides, I don't at all get this thing of you being raised to be a tool, Himeragi."

"Eh?"

"I mean, you're so cute, Himeragi."

"Quit saying things like that right n… A!… St!"

As Kojou gave the nape of Yukina's neck a long-winded lick, strength drained out of Yukina's entire body. Somewhere along the way, her white skin had developed a pinkish tinge.

"Yeah, maybe it wasn't your parents who raised you, Himeragi, but I can tell just by looking that the folks at High God Forest took really good care of you. I mean, you said yourself you had fun training to be a Sword Shaman, didn't you?"

"I get it… I get it already, Senpai… Please forgive me! I can't take any more of…!"

"R-right."

As Yukina asked in a frail voice, Kojou's arms around her loosened a little.

After all, if he'd let her go completely, he'd have fallen right on top of the exhausted girl.

"…"

Breathing rather roughly, Yukina touched up her uniform without a word.

Then, her eyes still moist from tears, she glared sharply at Kojou.

"This time I know for certain. You truly are an indecent person, Senpai."

"Er, no, I don't really think so. Besides, what you were doing there, Himeragi—"

"Hai? I did…what?"

"…Er, never…mind. Sorry, I got carried away."

"Well, reflect on it! Goodness…"

Yukina made a violent sigh as she spoke.

Seeing that Yukina was somewhat noisy and rather resolute, and therefore back to her usual self, a smile spontaneously came over Kojou.

Seeing this, Yukina glared at Kojou with her eyes half-closed.

"And what are *you* grinning at?"

"Er, I was thinking you really are cute, Himeragi."

"………"

Yukina silently poised Snowdrift Wolf. Kojou inhaled as his expression changed.

"W-wait… Put that spear away!"

"Seriously, cut it out already! This *really* isn't the time and place for us to be doing this. Have you forgotten *why* you almost died?"

Yukina spoke with a hard voice, her blade still aimed at the nape of Kojou's neck. She seemed quite confused as to whether she should be angry at him or at herself, or simply blush. Judging that it would not be wise to provoke her further, Kojou tightened up his expression.

"Okay, got it. Suppose you're right… Er, by the way, where is this? Where'd the old man and the girl go?"

"This is a public park behind the Sfelde Pharmaceutical Lab."

Yukina slowly lowered her spear.

As she'd indicated, Kojou could make out the outline of a familiar building behind him.

"As that artificial Beast Vassal's attack set off the building's alarm systems, I carried you here while you slept, Senpai. I do not know where the Lotharingian Armed Apostle and the girl have gone."

"I see… Kinda worried about that. They said something weird, after all."

Kojou's face grimaced as he muttered.

They'd said, take the treasure, sink the island. Certainly that's what they'd said.

From the words alone, it sounded like nothing but a foolish fantasy, but it was beyond dispute that Eustach had a clear objective and had prepared accordingly. There was every possibility they'd already made their move.

The sun was already sinking under the waterline; darkness was enveloping the area.

Having been killed by Eustach, it'd taken Kojou some four or five hours to recover. He hoped it would not prove a fatal delay.

"Right… The news…"

"Huh?"

Kojou dug out his cell phone and looked it over as Yukina made a somewhat dubious face. Maybe she didn't know that you *could* check the news with your cell phone, but he had no time to explain now. If Eustach had already started a disturbance, there was a high probability there were already reports about the incident.

With that thought, Kojou looked over the screen, inhaling a bit.

What he saw was an endless list of e-mail notifications…

The senders were mostly Yaze and Rin.

Their e-mails were to tell him that Keystone Gate had been assaulted by someone and that Asagi, at her part-time job inside the Gate, was still trapped inside.

4

On the floor the intruders had passed through, they saw a tragic scene.

More than sixty security personnel were laying all over the area, gravely wounded, the scent of their lost blood filling the air. About ten of them could somehow move on their own power. However, they no longer had any combat ability remaining; their hands were full from performing field medicine for their comrades.

The only unwounded person left was Asagi, gazing at the tragedy in a daze, half-absentmindedly.

That was when Asagi's cell phone rang. The facilities within the Gate had suffered severe damage from combat with the intruders, but somehow the cell phone relay station had emerged unscathed.

With a sluggish, robotic motion, Asagi checked the screen of the cell phone.

When she saw the name that was displayed, her eyes suddenly came back to life.

"—Kojou?!"

"Asagi…! I'm so glad! Are you all right?"

She heard Kojou's voice via the cell phone. For no real reason, that somehow brought tears of relief pouring out of Asagi. Her voice rose shrilly, as if she'd plotted to vent her anger the entire time.

"Geez, what the hell…? I'm not all right at all! The Public Corporation got attacked, there's a lot of people hurt. I'm trapped in the rubble of a building… What's wrong with those people?!"

"You saw the people who attacked? A hard-ass old man in priest robes, right? A humanoid Beast Vassal, too."

"You know them?!" Asagi asked back, dumbfounded. At the same time, fierce concern advanced upon her.

Why would Kojou know what those who'd attacked Keystone Gate looked like unless he'd somehow come across them before Asagi had? If that was the case—

"Yeah. I almost died thanks to those two."

"Almost died…?! Kojou, you…," Asagi simply exclaimed at Kojou's blunt confession. Normally he'd just make some banal joke to make light of it, not that she'd have believed a word of it, having seen the atrocity the intruders had committed with her own eyes. There was no doubt Kojou really had stared death in the eye.

But Kojou spoke with the same laid-back tone he always did.

"Anyway, looks like you're okay right now. More important, where'd those two go?"

"Down. They seem to be headed toward the lowest level of the Gate."

Asagi spoke as she got back on her normal track. She wasn't the only one who'd been through something horrible. Kojou understood. She felt like that thought alone had rescued her.

Asagi opened the notebook computer that she'd been hugging like a protective charm the entire time.

She accessed the maintenance division's server and checked the situation inside the Gate.

Opening every bulkhead along the way, the intruders had already reached the thirteenth level. What lay ahead was a structurally reinforced area, but their arrival at the bottommost level was now a simple matter of time. It might have taken them two hours at the most.

"The lowest level… Huh. Do you know what's there, Asagi?"

"Like I should know. The only thing that should be on the lowest level is the Anchor," Asagi answered while tapping her keyboard.

"Anchor?"

"Anchor Block. You know that Itogami Island is formed of East/West/North/South Gigafloats, right? It's kind of like a platform for holding the linked main cables in place."

"…And there's something real important about that?"

Kojou asked like something in his gut just wouldn't settle down. With a "Huh?" Asagi scowled.

"As if. It's just a stupidly tough mass of steel. It soaks up all the Gigafloat shocks and vibrations from waves and wind to keep Itogami Island from breaking apart."

Itogami Island's four Gigafloats separating was a last resort to avoid the sinking of the entire island. Furthermore, the connecting sections had gaps and flexibility suitable to protect against dangerous vibrations from windstorms and uncomfortably high waves. That meant the four Gigafloats were always supporting one another, just like how a table's four legs kept it stable.

Put another way, the entire burden of keeping Itogami Island together fell on the place where the Gigafloats were connected.

"...So what's that precious treasure the old man talked about...?"

"Precious treasure? Whaddya mean?"

"I dunno, but apparently the old man came to this island to get it back..."

"Even if he said that, no one would put anything valuable like that in the Anchor Block. You wouldn't be able to look at it or take it back, after all...?"

Asagi sank into thought as she realized Kojou's words were bugging her in an odd way.

The *precious treasure* part bothered her. It was difficult to believe a priest learned in the strict tenets of Western religion would go raiding the Demon Sanctuary of another country out of lust for material possessions.

No, in the first place, what did *treasure* mean to a man of the cloth...?

"Asagi?"

Concerned that Asagi had gone quiet, Kojou called out to her.

Asagi took a deep breath as if to shake off her doubts.

"Hold on. I'm checking something—wait, the hell?! This is military secret–level firewall, isn't it?!"

Asagi was beside herself at the deep red alert displayed on her computer screen. There was a happy glint resting somewhere in her eyes. Her competitive spirit had been piqued.

"So you can't find out what it is?"

"Like hell I can't. Who do you think you're talking to—Mogwai!"

Asagi summoned the AI, which had settled on silence, with one press of a hot key. The supercomputer's avatar casually appeared atop her screen.

"You're a real slavedriver, m'lady. Really, I was built so that I couldn't lay my paws on something like this, but…my partner requests it, so I guess I must."

"Ah, you get it, don't you? So break that firewall, now!"

The AI grumbled in a listless tone as Asagi punched in her administrator override code.

Before the AI executed the order, its aura shifted for just a moment.

"I'll break it, but…you'll regret this."

What does he mean? thought Asagi. A moment later, her eyebrows shot up.

"Eh? This is… No way, you're kidding me…"

All Asagi could do was murmur as she looked at the image from the Anchor Block in shock.

5

"So that's…what it is…"

Kojou slowly lowered his cell phone, his call to Asagi finished.

They'd finally solved the puzzle. Everything was connected together.

Eustach's objective in coming to Itogami Island. Why he sought the power to break barriers.

Kojou understood all of it.

Certainly it was as the man had said. If he succeeded in his objective, an unbelievable disaster would befall this island. The island really might sink.

What Eustach was after was in Itogami Island's lowest section, the Anchor Block—and within it, the keystone at the center of the main pillar from which Keystone Gate derived its name.

"Senpai…let's go. We have to stop them."

Yukina got up, staring intently at Kojou as she spoke. Kojou looked back as if perplexed by her words.

"Stop? Us, stop that old man…?"

"Yes. According to Aiba, it'll still take a little time before they arrive at the lowermost level. We can probably still reach them in time with Aiba's cooperation."

Yukina looked dead serious. With Asagi able to access the management corporation's main server, they'd know every route in the entire Gate. On the other hand, Eustach and Astarte seemed to be taking a stupidly blunt, straightforward approach, breaking every bulkhead along the way. With Asagi farming out the shortest routes to them, they should be able to circle ahead with time to spare.

"But the two of us go, and do what...?"

He spoke with honest doubt. Seemingly in surprise, Yukina stopped moving.

"I'll go save Asagi. On the way I'll get Nagisa and my mom, who has a lifestyle like a stray cat, off the island. But that's the most I can do."

"Senpai...what are you saying? Itogami City's Island Guard can't stop that homunculus's Beast Vassal!"

"Haven't you lost sight of what you're here for, Himeragi? I tried to catch the old guy because it was legitimate self-defense, but that's not necessary now."

Kojou spoke with a devil-may-care tone.

Though the culprits in the demon hunting case, they'd revealed themselves through causing such a huge uproar. There was no longer any reason for Kojou and Yukina to apprehend them.

For that matter, since the damage to the Island Guard had demonstrated how dangerous Eustach and Astarte were, Kojou's actions in wrecking the warehouse district would be accepted as unavoidable much more easily.

"I can't stop the Armed Apostle old man... I know that all too well from what Asagi told me. And I don't understand it, but what the old man's doing, in one sense it's *just*...!"

"Even if that's the case, to put everyone living on this island in danger is..."

"Wrong... Yeah, it might well be...but who's right can't be decided by me. I can't make that choice. I...mustn't make that choice!"

Kojou groaned his words as if someone were wringing them out of him. Yukina listened in silence.

It'd be like declaring himself emperor.

An emperor's decision set people in motion. An emperor's decision changed history.

But was there any evidence to prove that decision had been just?

To set the world in motion meant the consequences for the world were on your shoulders alone.

A normal human being couldn't prepare himself for that. He'd break under the weight of the decision.

The battle with Eustach was no longer a duel between him and Kojou Akatsuki.

That Lotharingian Armed Apostle had declared war against all of Itogami City.

This wasn't a battle a mere high school student was permitted to involve himself in.

Kojou Akatsuki could no longer fight him. To challenge Eustach in battle, Kojou would have to himself accept that he was not a mere high school student but a being equal to an entire national army by himself—a Primogenitor, he who should rule a Dominion.

Yukina preserved her silence, seemingly seeing through all that troubled Kojou.

"..."

Finally, without a word, she lightly spun the silver spear she held.

The spear turned one and a half times—turning the spear tip toward her.

And so, Yukina rested the blade on the part of her neck.

Without a sound, she gently pulled the spear.

A thin red line ran across Yukina's skin. Drops of blood finally began to emerge.

"Himeragi...wh-what are you doing?"

Kojou was seized by shock as he watched Yukina's bizarre conduct. She seemed to have lost her mind, as if that austere expression she'd worn up until now was just a lie. Yukina's breathing was ragged as she looked back at him.

"Senpai. Please...drink my blood."

Her voice conveyed quiet determination.

Kojou stiffened completely. He couldn't understand why Yukina would say such a thing.

"Senpai, you said that…your Beast Vassals didn't recognize you as their lord because you have not yet drunk human blood, yes?"

"Y-yeah. I did say that, but…"

"So please drink my blood, here and now."

"Hold on. It's just a hypothesis; there's no guarantee that just by my drinking blood they'll serve here and now…"

"If the possibility exists, that is enough."

"Why do I have to do a thing like that?… Even if the Beast Vassals won't serve me—"

"That is a problem, since I cannot stop Armed Apostle Eustach by my power alone."

Yukina spoke, interrupting Kojou's words midway.

"Huh?"

"To defeat a Beast Vassal with magic-canceling ability on par with Snowdrift Wolf's, a stronger mass of magical energy is necessary—a Primogenitor-class Beast Vassal. Senpai, you're the only one who can stop them."

Yukina's intensity, leaving no room for dissent, made Kojou recoil in spite of himself.

"Er, but…I don't intend to fight the old man and the girl. That's for people who aren't us to think about, isn't—"

"You're lying."

"Yeah?"

Kojou began an immediate rebuttal to Yukina's one-sided scolding, but his argument died on his lips.

That was because Yukina's eyes were gently watching him as blood continued to flow from her neck.

"I don't have any doubt you really do want to stop them, for you have that power, Senpai… Deep down inside, even you want to use the power of the Fourth Primogenitor any way you like, don't you, Senpai?"

"No way. Since when have I wanted to do something as bothersome as that…?!"

"Senpai, if you want to protect the people of the island, please do as you like. If you can't bear the responsibility by yourself, I'll bear it with you."

"Huh…?"

For some reason, Yukina smiled gently as Kojou stared at her.

"Of course I will. Have you forgotten? It's my duty to watch you, after all—"

As she made her declaration with an unruffled expression, Kojou watched her for a while, dumbfounded.

Thrusting her spear into the ground, Yukina loosened the chest ribbon of her uniform.

Then she undid the buttons, exposing her breasts.

In so doing, she exposed her white flesh, her slender collarbone, and, of course, her slender neck.

And Yukina slowly stepped forward, as if posing for Kojou to admire.

As she looked down at Kojou, his vision was compelled toward the tidy underwear she wore and the modest bulge of her breasts. He let out a light yelp.

"H-Himeragi…?"

"Senpai, you said earlier that I'm cute, didn't you…"

"Y-yeah…I think I might have, but that and this are—"

"So please take responsibility and act accordingly."

"Wha…? Whaaa?!"

"Or…am I just not…good enough?"

Yukina softly pressed her own breasts as she murmured in a timid voice.

Kojou realized that her slender shoulders were trembling bit by bit.

Bashfulness…or rather, fright, he thought. Yukina was really afraid, too. Afraid of offering her own blood to a vampire and afraid of exposing her flesh before Kojou like this—

She was a Sword Shaman of the Lion King Agency. A Counter-Demon Attack Mage dispatched solely for the purpose of watching Kojou—a vampire who, originally, would have been merely a target for her to destroy.

And now it was as if she was offering up her own body to Kojou.

Surely this was more for Kojou's sake than for protecting the people of Itogami Island, so that Kojou would not someday regret his decision—his decision not to wield the power of the Fourth Primogenitor.

"S-Senpai?" Yukina called out in a voice of surprise as Kojou suddenly embraced her.

Kojou could feel faintly warm, pleasant scents coming from her slender, quivering body. The clean scent of her hair, and other sweet scents of her body. And the smell of blood—

His canines, no, his *fangs* ached. Lust was the trigger for vampiric behavior. Vampires only drank blood from targets they recognized as desirable. Surely Yukina had seduced him with all her might in full knowledge of that. But…

She doesn't get it, Kojou thought.

"Ah, ow… Sen…pai…"

Yukina didn't understand just how desirable she was. She didn't understand at all just how hard it had been for Kojou to restrain his vampiric impulses around her.

Yukina closed her eyes intensely, enduring the pain. Yukina's lips let out frail sighs.

Finally, embraced by Kojou's arms, all strength drained out of Yukina's body. It was as if both of their shadows melted together under the peaceful crimson moonlight.

6

This place, constructed too deep underwater for light to reach it, was easy to think of as an eternal prison.

Keystone Gate's bottommost level was in the middle of the ocean, some two hundred and twenty meters below sea level.

The exterior wall, built in the shape of a cone to resist high water pressure, gave off an aura a bit like the biblical Tower of Babel.

The level's role was much like how the head of a violin held the spools for the violin strings. By keeping the connecting wires from the four Gigafloats in tune, the entire island's vibrations could be controlled and rendered harmless.

The wire cables arrived via the Gate's walls and were wrapped around the lowest level's supporting pillars. The cables were composed of about sixty-five thousand steel strands. The ridiculously huge winch was controlled by a motor with an output equal to a power plant's.

It gave off the oppressive feeling of an engineering room with an overwhelming mass of steel and imbued with an explosive level of power. And the building was enveloped by fierce water pressure. All of these things seemed to change the atmosphere drifting over the level into something…denser.

The bulkhead sealing off the lowest level gave off a creak somewhat like a shrieking sound as it was wrenched open.

The rainbow-colored, glimmering, humanoid Beast Vassal had ripped open the seventeen centimeters thick armored wall like it was a tin can.

The Beast Vassal's lord was visible, shut away in the center of its torso.

She was a girl with long, velvet hair and pale blue eyes. The homunculus, Astarte.

The form of a man with a muscular body, wrapped in the robes of a priest, appeared behind her—

Having arrived at the Gate's lowermost level, the Lotharingian Armed Apostle, Rudolf Eustach, was deeply moved as he slowly looked all around.

"*Complete.* Objective has been confirmed."

Astarte made her report while still enveloped by her own Beast Vassal.

The infection in her voice, meager to begin with, had now completely lost all emotion.

A Beast Vassal was a beast summoned from another realm. To give it physical form, its lord had to shave off a piece of his own life span. Though there were different varieties of Beast Vassals, it was said that a normal human would lose his entire life from summoning one for but an instant. To a Beast Vassal, its lord's life was simple food.

Even a homunculus lord was no exception.

Astarte had been granted a life span far in excess of a normal human's to attune her to symbiotic life with a Beast Vassal; however, little remained even of that. She had used too much of the Beast Vassal's power to invade Keystone Gate.

"..."

However, Eustach walked toward the center of the lowermost level without even a passing glance at Astarte.

There rested the end point of the four wire cables stretching from each of the four Gigafloats.

All were secured with an anchor with a machined head. It was a metal platform built in the shape of a small reversed pyramid.

Like a post, a single pillar was thrust down into the center of the anchor to secure it.

The diameter was not even one meter wide.

However, to link Itogami Island together, it continued to support the weight of several million tons, even now.

A translucent stone pillar resembling obsidian. A *keystone.*

"Oh… Ohh…"

Eustach's mouth let out a voice containing both grief and delight.

His entire body shaking, he fell to his knees on the spot. Tears poured ceaselessly from his eyes as he gazed up at the stone pillar. Then his sadness and happiness finally turned into loud, ragged laughter.

"The immutable body stolen from the Lotharingian Church… Long have we awaited the day when it shall be returned to us! Astarte! Nothing remains in our path any longer. Tear apart that accursed linchpin and bring justice upon this degenerate island!"

As Eustach commanded his homunculus servant, his voice rose in loud laughter.

However, Astarte did not move. In an emotionless voice, she reported, still enveloped by the materialized Beast Vassal's armor.

"*Reject.* Error in preliminary conditions. Further, request reselection of command."

"What?"

Clutching his giant battle-axe, Eustach rose to his feet. He realized why Astarte had refused his command. There was someone standing atop the stone pillar secured by the anchor.

A boy wearing a shredded uniform and a girl wielding a silver spear.

"Sorry, gonna have to make you cancel that order, old man."

The Fourth Primogenitor—Kojou Akatsuki—smiled with a languid expression.

"The relic of a saint who serves the Western European Church's 'God'…"

Kojou seemed to be looking at the stone pillar known as the Keystone with compassion.

Someone's "arm" was floating within the translucent pillar.

It was a slender arm, dried up like a mummy's.

Its wrist bore a cruel scar that seemed like a vestige of crucifixion. This was the corpse of a martyr who had suffered and lost his life for his beliefs.

It was a manifestation of the holiness of God within this world and an object of worship to many.

It was a corpse said to be so holy that it would never rot and said to have brought about numerous miracles.

One part of that saint's corpse was sealed within the stone pillar.

"They call this a 'holy relic,' huh. So this is what you're after."

Kojou spoke as if in a sigh.

The existence of this holy relic was the secret Asagi had discovered through breaching a powerful firewall. Itogami Island, a giant, artificial city, was being supported by a "miracle" brought about by this holy relic.

"The city you now call Itogami Island was designed over forty years ago."

Eustach recited the tale in a low, solemn voice.

His tone carried dignity worthy of a Lotharingian bishop whose teachings guided a multitude of believers.

"It was a design to build a new city, an artificial floating island atop the ley lines—dragon lines in the Orient—that ran *on top of the ocean*. At the time, this was an epochal concept. As spiritual energy flowing along dragon lines is linked to the liveliness of the residents, everyone thought this would lead the city to prosperity. However, the construction went poorly, for the naked power of the dragon lines that flowed over the ocean far exceeded people's expectations."

Kojou nodded silently at his words.

So that was the reason Itogami Island had been constructed above water far to the south of the mainland: the existence of dragon lines—giant spiritual channels that flowed across the surface of the earth.

Places built on top of dragon lines were full of spiritual energy. That alone made possible spiritual techniques and magical experiments more powerful than the norm. These were ideal conditions for the research on demons conducted in the Demon Sanctuary. So the Gigafloat project was indispensable for constructing a city on top of dragon lines.

"The city's designer, Senra Itogami, knew this very well. He elected to separate the Gigafloats into four—representing the four Celestial Animals of feng shui governing east, west, north, and south, using them to attempt to control the linked dragon lines in a more harmonious manner. However, even so, a single, insurmountable problem remained."

"The strength of the keystone, huh…"

Eustach replied to Kojou's murmur with a solemn nod.

"Precisely as you say. The designer, Senra Itogami, required a keystone in the center of the island to represent the Yellow Dragon—he who governs the four Celestial Animals. However, the technology of that time could not construct materials strong enough to withstand that. Consequently, he stained his hands with an abominable heresy."

"Sacrificial components…"

It was Yukina who made the frail utterance.

The designer of Itogami Island had resolved a question of engineering through reliance on necromancy.

Human sacrifice.

He realized he could he could employ the heresy of sacrificing living humans to increase the strength of his structures. However, dragon lines were flows of natural energy; their untamed power placed an enormous burden on the Gigafloats' connecting section.

The keystone needed to withstand that burden; half-baked necromancy wasn't going to cut it. He needed power on par with a miracle from God himself. Hence…

"What he selected as the sacrifice to support his city was the relic of our patron saint, usurped from our Church. This deed—the trampling of our faith for the creation of an island where foul demons may run rampant—cannot be forgiven."

Eustach declared this in a calm, reverberating voice as he poised his battle-axe.

His actions indicated the end of the tale. Eustach's objective was to recover the holy relic. He had no reason to force combat with Kojou and Yukina. That's why he answered Kojou's question.

At the same time, it was to demonstrate his justice—to prove he was in the right.

He could no longer be dissuaded. There was no way to overcome his determination.

"Consequently, we shall recover the holy relic by force. You would do well to withdraw, Fourth Primogenitor. This is a holy war between us and this city. We shall brook no interference, even from you—"

"I understand how you feel, old man. What that Senra Itogami guy did was definitely the lowest of the low."

Even so, Kojou stood before the bishop, protecting the keystone.

"But does that justify killing five hundred and sixty thousand people living on this island, not knowing a thing, for the sake of your revenge? The same goes for the people you hurt to get here. Don't go dragging in people who've got nothing to do with it!"

Perhaps what Eustach was doing *was* just. Or perhaps he truly was mistaken, but that didn't matter anymore.

If it was the decision of Rudolf Eustach to destroy the city…

It was the decision of Kojou Akatsuki, of his own free will, to stop him.

"If one compares this scale of sacrifice to what would be required to redeem this city, it is not even a speck," Eustach announced coldly.

It was Yukina who blocked his path. Her silver spear facing the armed apostle, seemingly to restrain his movements, she yelled out in a voice as clear as a bell, "The use of sacrificial components is now forbidden by international treaty. The usurping of a holy relic for that purpose all the more so…!"

"And what of it, Sword Shaman? Are you saying I should sue in the courts of this nation?"

"With the technology that now exists, it is surely possible to construct a keystone strong enough to link the island together. The keystone can be exchanged and the holy relic returned to—"

"Would you say the same thing if it were your own blood relatives suffering from being trampled upon by others?"

Unconcealed anger seethed out of Eustach's voice.

Momentary hesitation ran down Yukina's back. Raised as a Sword Shaman, Yukina did not know the faces of her relatives.

Eustach was provoking Yukina in the full knowledge of that.

"Old man… Why, you…"

Kojou, indignant, moved to close the distance with Eustach.

However, Yukina stretched out her left arm to stop him. She made a strong smile, as if to say, *I'm okay*. The eyes she looked at Kojou with contained a mysterious gentleness.

Hmph, Eustach crudely snorted.

"It seems any further words shall be fruitless. We shall recover the holy relic. If you stand in our way, we shall simply remove you by force—Astarte!"

"*Accept. Execute 'Rhododactylos,'*" Astarte, who had maintained her silence, responded with a twinge of sadness in her voice.

The glimmering of the rainbow-colored Beast Vassal increased proportionately to the increase in the force of the magic energy spread about by it.

"So it's this in the end, is it…?"

Aah, said Kojou, smiling with a heavy sigh.

His fangs peeked out from between his ferociously twisted lips. His eyes were dyed a dazzling crimson.

"…But have you forgotten, old man? I still owe you one for you slicing my chest apart. Let's get that settled before all this stuff about revenge on a guy who bought it ages ago."

"Damn you… That ability has…"

Eustach's expression twisted.

Lightning enveloped Kojou's entire body. This was not anger allowed to run amok. This was a Beast Vassal that had awakened with its lord's blood, responding to his will.

"So, let's get this party started, old man—from here on, this is *my* fight."

Kojou roared as he presented his lightning-shrouded right arm.

At Kojou's side, Yukina wielded her silver spear with a teasing smile, as if cuddling up beside him.

"No, Senpai. This is *our* fight—!"

7

It was Yukina who struck first.

Wielding her silver spear, the Sword Maiden headed toward Astarte at what seemed like the speed of light. The homunculus girl used the Beast Vassal, whose giant humanoid form enveloped her, to counterattack.

The great blows of its fist caused the entire structure to shake.

Astarte's Beast Vassal was not a humanoid-shaped life form. It was a dense mass of magical energy materialized in that shape.

Its fists were equal to the rounds from the most powerful of Black Magic Cannons; its kicks, superior to the explosions brought about with arcane rituals.

And its arms were able to rip apart thick bulkheads made of specially reinforced alloys.

This was the overwhelming power that pulverized the Island Guard's CDAs in a single blow…

But Yukina deftly deflected the attack.

Snowdrift Wolf—or rather, the DOE infused into the Schneewalzer, fended off the materialized Beast Vassal's tyranny and aimed to rip its flesh apart instead.

However, the Beast Vassal's flesh, enveloped with an identical divine oscillation, withstood Snowdrift Wolf's slicing blow.

Snowdrift Wolf's attack, powerful enough to inflict fatal damage to a demon, made only a shallow wound upon the Beast Vassal's body, which it regenerated instantly.

Yukina was superior in combat skill, but she did not possess the offensive power to destroy her opponent.

On the other side, though Astarte possessed overwhelming destructive power, Yukina's skill with the spear and unarmed martial arts made her all but untouchable. Their duel was at a complete stalemate.

However, that was what Kojou and Yukina had been aiming for.

"Ooooooh—!"

Pale blue lightning scattering about, Kojou rushed Eustach with his fist.

While Yukina drew Astarte off, Kojou would defeat the homunculus's master, Eustach. That was the plan Kojou and Yukina had thought up.

Kojou couldn't fight Astarte's Beast Vassal with its magic energy reflection. Having said that, even Yukina's weapon couldn't defeat it, either.

However, if Eustach, who was dishing out the orders, fell, Astarte would surely halt. After all, Astarte herself had no desire to bring harm to the residents of Itogami Island. The short conversation Kojou and Yukina had shared with her made them certain of that.

Therefore, for her sake as well, Kojou had to defeat Eustach here and now. However…

"Hnn!"

With unimaginable nimbleness, Eustach's huge body evaded Kojou's blow, counterattacking with his battle-axe. The air pressure from the axe alone ripped the cuffs from Kojou's school uniform. He could taste the axe's sharpness on his tongue.

Fast and heavy. If it hit Kojou cleanly, no doubt it'd split his body in two just like it had during the day. So there was no way he could let that attack hit him.

Eustach made a hearty laugh as if Kojou's impatience was all too clear to him.

"Certainly that is impressive magical energy, but such clumsy attacks cannot touch me. Your thoughtless movements are like those of an amateur, Fourth Primogenitor!"

"They're not *like*—I really am an amateur!"

As Kojou rebutted, he increased his speed. Certainly, in terms of martial arts Kojou was an amateur; in terms of a vampire, incompetent. However, though he had a few blanks, the footwork he'd honed in basketball was still good to go. Evade the pick, defend your own goal. Move quickly and balanced. And feint. Kojou was well versed in how to fight bigger and tougher opponents than he was.

"Hn… This is—!"

He tossed the ball of magical lightning he'd created at Eustach like a sharp pass. The frivolous attack gave off an air of Kojou borderline playing around. However, it made the Armed Apostle's expression stiffen.

"I take back what I said. I accept that you are not an enemy to underestimate… Consequently, I shall face thee with appropriate resolve!"

"What…?!"

The incredible dark energy bursting from Eustach's entire body drained the blood from Kojou's face.

Radiance leaked out from every gap of the Armed Apostle's vestment. The armor-reinforced clothing under the vestment emitted a golden light. Sharp pain ran through Kojou's eyes as they looked upon that radiance; Kojou's light-bathed skin burned.

"O holy garb, 'Alcazava,' crafted by the technology of Lotharingia—may thy light remove all obstacles before me!"

Eustach increased the speed of his attacks. His plated armor augmented his physical strength. Kojou, his vision robbed by the golden light, evaded his attacks mostly on intuition. Fresh blood scattered from his cut cheek.

"That's playing dirty, old man—so you still had a trump card like that hidden away!"

Kojou unwittingly raised his voice in rebuke. However, Eustach did not halt his attacks. He leaped around time after time but the slices had both power and speed behind them. However unsightly, it was all Kojou could do to run and escape.

"Senpai…?!" Yukina yelled out as she looked at Kojou, now purely on defense. However, she, too, was at her limits just to contain Astarte. Besides that, with Eustach strengthened by the armor's power, even Yukina probably had little chance of victory.

Kojou winked at Yukina, as if to say, *Don't worry*, as he slowly rose upright.

Eustach stayed his attack, probably out of prudence at the strange aura Kojou gave off.

"If that's how it's gonna be, I'll use this with no restraint, either. Don't die on me, old man!"

"Hnng…?!"

Eustach leaped back, instinctively sensing danger.

His eyes beheld Kojou thrusting his right arm out, fresh blood spurting from it.

"Kojou Akatsuki, successor to the bloodline of the 'Kaleid Blood,' releases thee from thy bonds—!"

That fresh blood transformed into glimmering lightning. The light, heat, and shock wave of the lightning was incomparable to that which had come before. This was the same Beast Vassal of the Fourth Primogenitor that had devastated the warehouse district.

But unlike before, the light did not burst indiscriminately in all directions; instead, its shape condensed, changing into that of a giant beast.

This was the Beast Vassal's proper form. The true form of a Beast Vassal of the Fourth Primogenitor, completely within Kojou's grasp.

"C'mon, Beast Vassal Number Five, 'Regulus Aurum'—!"

What had appeared was the Lightning Lion—a mass of magical energy in the form of raging lightning, as huge as a main battle tank. Its entire body emanated a radiance that dazzled the eyes; its roar shook the air like thunder itself.

Kojou had inherited twelve Beast Vassals from the previous Fourth Primogenitor.

But, in the end, drinking Yukina's blood had only made this Beast Vassal of lightning recognize Kojou as its lord.

However, he had expected as much.

For, over the space of several days since meeting Yukina, the Beast Vassal of lightning had become livelier for some reason, to a very unusual degree.

And at the warehouse district, it had run amok for the sake of protecting Yukina.

Now he understood the reason full well. This Beast Vassal had been fond of Yukina since the moment they'd met. For it was attracted to the scent of her blood—

"So this is your Vassal Beast—! It is reckless to use such power in an enclosed space such as this!"

One of the Lightning Lion's front paws swung downward, aimed at Eustach.

The attack only scratched him. From that alone, Eustach's huge physique was thrown several meters back.

A lightning-generating shock wave scattered sparks all over his plated armor; the lightning's high temperature melted the blade of his battle-axe.

The attack's aftereffects were felt by Keystone Gate as well.

The great electrical currents released ran along the Gate's exterior wall in all directions. The emergency lights and security cameras placed across the area were blown away without a trace. The winch that secured the wired cables let out a groan as well. Neither would emerge unscathed from prolonged combat.

"Astarte—!"

The Armed Apostle finally called his servant. Nothing existed that could counter the tyranny of Kojou's Beast Vassal, waving around explosive magical energy rivaling a natural disaster, save her Beast Vassal's "Rhododactylos." Surely he had determined it was so.

Shrugging off Yukina's attacks, the Beast Vassal-shrouded Astarte stood before Kojou's own Beast Vassal.

Partially disregarding Kojou's will, "Regulus Aurum" went on the attack. The giant Beast Vassal's front paw turned into lightning and slammed down upon the Beast Vassal in humanoid form.

That instant, the rainbow-colored light that enveloped Astarte's Beast Vassal increased in radiance.

The spiritual resonance wave barrier withstood the attack of Kojou's Beast Vassal and reflected it back—!

"Whoooah?!"

"Eyaaaaah!!"

The uncontrolled magical lightning discharged, raking the ceiling, punching through and breaking apart the thick ceiling of the Gate's lowermost level with ease. Kojou and Yukina yelled out as they ran around to escape from the incessant downpour of debris.

"Shit...! No good?! So even my Beast Vassal can't break her barrier...!"

Kojou groaned as fierce uneasiness assaulted him.

Even having taken a blow from "Regulus Aurum," Astarte's Beast Vassal was undamaged. Even if the attack was repeated over and over, it would probably end with the same result.

And the structure probably couldn't endure further combat. If the exterior walls of Keystone Gate were breached, seawater, propelled by the water pressure at two hundred and twenty meters below sea level, would no doubt rush in all at once, crushing Kojou and the others. Yukina would definitely die instantly; even Kojou's fate was uncertain.

"Senpai..."

Yukina gently approached as if to support Kojou against the debris trying to bury him. Even her expression bore heavy signs of fatigue—naturally, having been fighting such a powerful opponent in the flesh.

"Sorry, Himeragi. We might not be able to beat them...!"

Kojou's voice shook with anger, as if directed at his own inadequacy.

One step. Just one step farther, and they could save the island. And yet they could not reach it.

However, Yukina, looking up at the frustrated Kojou, smiled vividly.

"No, Senpai. In this fight, victory is ours."

As Kojou said, "Eh?" Yukina stepped in front of him, leaving no time for a rebuttal.

"—I, Maiden of the Lion, Sword Shaman of the High God, beseech thee."

She danced with the silver-colored spear, like a swordsman praying to the gods for victory. Or perhaps like a maiden to whom victory was foretold.

"O purifying light, O divine wolf of the snowdrift, by your steel divine will, strike down the devils before me!"

Alongside her solemn chant, the snowflake spear began to emit a shine.

That dim white light was a spiritual resonance wave that could rip apart any barrier. However, its form was different from Astarte's. It was slender, sharp, like a shining, glittering fang—

"...No!!"

Having realized Yukina's objective, Eustach heaved back his axe to throw it at Yukina while she was defenseless. However, a sphere of lightning released by Kojou attacked Eustach as he did so. Protected by plated armor as he was, it was not a fatal blow. However, it interrupted his motion for an instant.

That instant, Yukina dashed. Like a supple, pale white she-wolf, she danced in the sky without a sound.

Astarte's response lagged behind Yukina's speed.

Both were imprinted with the same DOE. However, while Astarte's was a huge Beast Vassal with a barrier enveloping its whole body, Yukina's spear's power was concentrated on a single point: slender, sharp, for the sole purpose of penetrating the opponent's barrier.

"Snowdrift Wolf!"

The next moment, the silver-colored spear pierced Astarte's defensive barrier, deeply impaling the faceless head of the human-shaped Beast Vassal. That moment, Kojou, too, finally understood the meaning of Yukina's words.

Even though the barrier had been pierced, Yukina's spear had done little damage to the giant Beast Vassal. However, the spear continued to deeply impale the Beast Vassal's head, even now, inside the materialized Beast Vassal's body, where the defensive barrier would have no effect.

The long metal shaft was as if a lightning rod, beckoning for the lightning—

"*'Regulus Aurum'!*"

Faster than Kojou's command, the Lightning Lion moved at the speed of light.

Yukina had already released her spear, leaping in midair.

And then Kojou's Beast Vassal bit down on the shaft of the spear she had left behind.

The magical energy of the Beast Vassal transformed into lightning form poured into "Rhododactylos's" body.

The way to defeat a mass of magical energy was to smash it with stronger magical energy—

This time, the overwhelming magical power of the Primogenitor's Beast Vassal instantly burned away and annihilated Astarte's.

"Astarte—?!"

Having lost her Beast Vassal armor, the homunculus girl slowly collapsed onto the floor.

Eustach moaned, dumbfounded, as he gazed upon the scene.

The annihilation of Astarte's Beast Vassal, with the ability to destroy any barrier, meant the collapse of Eustach's ambition to release the holy relic from the keystone.

Before Eustach's wavering eyes, Yukina landed without a sound.

The distracted Eustach was slow to react.

Yukina pressed her palms against the torso portion of the armor-reinforced garb that shrouded him.

"Distort—!"

It was the Sword Maiden palm strike that penetrated armor to convey damage directly to the human body within.

As Eustach made a pained *guhh*, his tall body bent over. And—

"—It's over, old man!"

Kojou added his own strike, punching the Armed Apostle in the face.

It was a forceful blow with only might behind it, not magic or spells or any other power of a Primogenitor. Consequently, it was an attack no arcane art could defend against.

Eustach's sturdy body flew back. It bounced several times over, finally collapsing onto the floor.

He slowly outstretched his hand toward the keystone; then, his strength seemingly exhausted, he fell silent.

8

An eerie silence came over the Keystone Gate's lowermost level.

Eustach did not move. Even if he regained consciousness, most likely he had no intention of continuing to fight. His defeat had been assured the moment Astarte had fallen.

Eustach's holy war was over.

Even so, Yukina remained in a fighting stance, as if to guard against a counterattack from him.

"..."

Without a word, Kojou looked over the area. The Gate's bottommost level had taken severe damage. Even so, the keystone was intact; the wire cables were virtually undamaged. They'd protected the island, if barely.

Having confirmed this, Kojou met Yukina's eyes.

He unwittingly let out a small smile.

Yukina did the same. Yet in an instant, like a flower blooming shyly in winter, her beautiful smile inevitably vanished from her lips.

They had won a victory. However, that didn't mean they'd achieved anything in the process.

A great many people had been hurt. And even now, the holy relic slept within the keystone. None of the distortions that enveloped Itogami Island had been resolved.

Even so, having seen her smiling face just now, Kojou was just a little satisfied. Just for that, he thought, this battle was not in vain.

And, it wasn't as if he hadn't saved anyone—

"..."

Kojou made a shallow sigh as he looked over the fallen Astarte.

She was heavily exhausted, but she was still alive.

She didn't seem to be suffering any significant effect from the lightning released by Kojou's Beast Vassal, either.

When surrounded by metal, a substance that easily conducts electricity,

the person on the inside is unaffected by lightning strikes. The phenomenon was known as "Faraday's cage"; likely the Beast Vassal surrounding Astarte had produced the same effect.

The girl was a homunculus, granted a life span far in excess of that of a human being.

However, so long as the Beast Vassal dwelled within her, her life span wouldn't last beyond a few days.

But, if something could be done about the Beast Vassal, she'd be able to live a longer life.

The fallen Astarte was clothed in something like a thin surgical gown.

However, with her now seeming like a wounded fairy, he couldn't form any lewd feelings while looking her over; it was painful just looking at her all-too-frail form.

Well, can't be helped, Kojou thought. He turned toward Yukina.

"Himeragi."

"Yes?"

"Sorry. Just for a sec…okay?"

Yukina gave a mystified look back as Kojou walked closer, speaking those words as he strongly embraced her.

Yukina's lips let out a *Wha?* in a small voice.

She seemed in quite a bit of confusion at Kojou's unanticipated behavior, but her body only stiffened a little bit; she didn't really try to resist. She awkwardly leaned toward Kojou, entrusting the weight of her body to him.

"S-Senpai…"

Yukina seemed bewildered as her body quivered. She was so soft. So warm. She smelled faintly of sweat and blood. Kojou's entire body took it all in, seemingly coveting everything about her.

He understood the reason why Yukina was bewildered.

It wasn't an issue of what would happen to her right away from having a vampire drink her blood. It was said humans felt pleasure and ecstasy from being drunk from, but that was as simple as that.

The problem was if blood plasma from the vampire's own body flowed from his fangs as they still pierced, and into the other person's body. Those who received blood from vampires became "Blood Servants."

That didn't mean it was guaranteed to happen. That probably changed according to the phases of the moon, the condition of the human being's body, and one's ability to resist dark forces. However, if vampiric behavior was done over and over, eventually the other person would become one of the undead.

That meant living together as partners for the rest of one's eternal life.

"Senpai...you can't... We're not...ready for..."

Yukina tried to rebuke Kojou, her voice frail.

But contrary to Yukina's words, there was no resistance in how she acted. As Kojou thought that a rather mysterious thing, he squeezed Yukina strongly. Yukina gently moved her hands to Kojou's back as well.

"—Thanks, Yukina. I can do this now."

His vampiric impulses having been sufficiently heightened, Kojou promptly let go of Yukina.

"Eh...? D-do what?"

Yukina looked back at Kojou with an absentminded expression. The slight flush on her face was rather cute.

"Er, um... Senpai?"

However, as Yukina did so, Kojou quickly turned his back on her, leaning over the fallen Astarte.

Kojou gently picked up the slender homunculus girl, piercing the girl's exposed neck with his fangs. He then drank up the girl's body fluids.

After a long, long silence, he slowly drew his lips back from Astarte.

There was no change in the fallen Astarte's form. However, he had surely finished all of what he had to do.

Still holding the half-naked Astarte, Kojou sighed with relief.

Next to him, Yukina remained impressively unemotional as she picked up the silver spear.

"Senpai...what are you doing?"

The cold tone in Yukina's voice was identical to that from when they had first met.

Somehow, Kojou felt a glacial chill up his spine as he turned his face to her.

"I, ah, I thought I'd put her Beast Vassal under my dominion. It's like a magical energy allowance, or a Beast Vassal rental, see... In other words, if this girl's Beast Vassal isn't draining its direct host's life directly, but consumes my life force instead, this girl's life span will be a lot longer than it is now, right?"

"So you're saying that, in other words, you drank her blood to save her life."

The tone of Yukina's voice was filled with unconcealed, cold anger. Kojou, not understanding the reason she'd become angry, made a timid nod.

"Th-that's what it is. To seize control rights over her Beast Vassal, I had no choice. Right, no choice."

With his words, he firmly pressed the justice of his own cause. Surely there had been nothing mistaken about what he'd done. To the contrary, it should have been praiseworthy behavior.

However, Yukina's expression did not change. Indeed, emotion had completely vanished from her.

"I see. If that is so, why did you direct such lewd behavior at me?"

"Er, ah. I didn't do that out of any lewd feelings, but… In other words, to drink blood, I have to work myself up a bit—"

Kojou's unsteady words faltered. Sexual arousal was the trigger for vampiric impulses. Having said that, he couldn't just feel up Astarte's frail, wounded body like that, so he had no choice but to elicit Yukina's cooperation.

"I mean, certainly you're not an all that sexy type, Himeragi, but there wasn't anyone else, so I had to work with what I had… I just needed to get your help, a bit."

"…Work with what you have…is it? There was no one else, so you had no choice…"

Yukina was looking down as her shoulders began to tremble. As she did so, Kojou realized his verbal slip. The way he'd put that just now was mean-spirited, but he didn't know how else to explain it.

Finally, Yukina's icy expression shattered, her eyebrows shooting up as she glared.

Her face was in a rage, even as she seemed she might to cry at any moment.

"Senpai, you can sink to the bottom of the sea for all I care! Idiot—!"

As she yelled, Yukina swung the broken Snowdrift Wolf downward.

It was Itogami Island's deepest section. On the lowest level, some two hundred and twenty meters below sea level, the cries of the Fourth Primogenitor reverberated all around—

9

Island South, residential district. There was a lone girl at the edge of a window of a nine-story apartment complex.

She was a girl in the low teens who gave the impression of being a bit underdeveloped—

Nagisa Akatsuki.

All she had on was a thin shirt in place of pajamas.

The silver moonlight passed through the material, highlighting the contours of her slender body.

Her hair, worn down, was unusually long. It reached almost all the way to her hips.

Perhaps that was why she gave a different impression than her usual appearance, with her hair worn up. Her usual aura of cheerfulness was hidden away; her cherubic face had an adultlike calm across it.

Her long hair swayed without a sound from the sea breeze that blew in through the open window.

She was looking at the inverted-pyramid-shaped building at the center of Itogami Island—Keystone Gate.

Being the highest building on the entire island, she could see it quite well from the edge of the window.

Nagisa Akatsuki silently gazed at the building.

Tonight, the night of Itogami Island was dark.

With its lights extinguished, one could think of the majestic Keystone Gate as melting into the night sky.

For just a single instant, there was a pale glow, as if it had been struck by lightning.

Watching this, the girl's lips formed a mysterious expression.

She made a smile as if she knew what that glow represented.

"Regulus Aurum… So you have finally awakened…"

Nagisa's tongue calmly spun the words.

It was a calm voice, as if it were not her speaking, but another person.

But her expression seemed somehow amused.

"So even that boy finally got a little motivated. Heh-heh… Wouldn't be any fun if he weren't…"

A fiercely mischievous light dwelled within her refined eyes—a light that resembled flickering flames.

However, when the breeze blew next, both the adultlike calm and the ferociousness vanished from her body. Seemingly forgetting why she'd been there to begin with, the girl closed the window and let out a small yawn. Rubbing her sleepy eyes, she returned to her own bedroom and bed.

Her face was the same as always: that of an innocent, young girl.

"Mm, Kojou-kun…"

Mumbling her big brother's name, seemingly out of habit, she closed her eyes.

Looking like she was watching a pleasant dream, Nagisa Akatsuki fell asleep.

OUTRO

Yukina Himeragi was sitting alone as the rays of the setting sun filtered into her room.

It was room 705, the far-too-big-for-one-person apartment next to the Akatsuki family residence.

There were signs of life: curtains, cushions, magnetic cups with black tea in them. She'd bought them together with Kojou. In just a few days, she'd gotten completely used to seeing them, yet no doubt she would soon be leaving them behind.

Thinking that, she felt very lonely for some reason.

"..."

Outside the window was the expanse of the twilight sky.

Looking down at Itogami City from here, nothing seemed to have particularly changed. It was a peaceful scene, as if the battle that had occurred in this island's lowermost section had been all a lie.

Three days had passed since Armed Apostle Eustach's raid on Keystone Gate came to an end. Now that the chaos had calmed down somewhat, the residents of Itogami City seemed to think it was time to go on with their normal lives.

In the end, Yukina and Kojou had escaped after the battle before the Island Guard made it to the lowest level. So all the security force personnel saw when they reached the lowest level were traces of incredible destruction and Eustach and Astarte's unconscious bodies. Apparently Eustach had not spoken of Kojou or Yukina after his arrest, either.

His recovery of the saint's corpse having thus ended in failure, Eustach's conduct grew into a global-scale incident.

The Gigafloats were held up by a miracle from a holy relic. That Itogami City had been designed this way brought a flood of condemnation from not only the Western European Church but a wide variety of kingdoms and organizations. Simultaneously, there was a widespread demand to pardon Eustach for his crime. It was not possible for the government of Japan to ignore the controversy.

As a result, what had been Itogami Island's keystone for over two decades would be replaced by one constructed by conventional means. The government publicly committed to return the currently used holy relic to Lotharingia.

Eustach was declared persona non grata and expelled, and Astarte, a homunculus, having merely been obeying her master's commands, would be treated as under probation. The formalities had yet to take place, but it was a fair and just conclusion that managed to mollify world opinion.

The next morning, Kojou Akatsuki went to school as usual as if nothing had happened at all.

After his having skipped class on the first day after summer break, his charismatic homeroom teacher wrung him dry. She added to his unfinished pile of summer break homework, which made him look a bit like the dead.

However, that was probably a normal, everyday thing to him.

It was boring, day-to-day life like this that he had used the power of the Fourth Primogenitor, the world's mightiest vampire, to protect—

"...He really is quite a piece of work..."

As Yukina murmured, she unwittingly let out a small giggle as well.

Her laughing voice, containing so much fun it shocked even her, immediately changed to a deep sigh.

Yukina, too, would soon return to her normal daily existence.

Her training as an apprentice Sword Maiden at High God Forest. Though severe, there was nothing perplexing or confounding about it. It was tranquil and never-changing, day after day. That was Yukina's old daily existence.

Yukina had failed too many times to continue watching over Kojou.

The Fourth Primogenitor's Beast Vassal went berserk, reducing the warehouse district to ashes.

The Fourth Primogenitor she was watching over had been in great danger and nearly slain.

When the Fourth Primogenitor rejected combat, she spurred him on and brought him to the battlefield with her.

And on top of that, so that he could become able to use his Beast Vassal, she had granted him her own blood—

Any one of those actions made her unworthy of being a watcher.

Even more, as a result of combat unrelated to her mission, Snowdrift Wolf, the Lion King Agency's secret weapon, had been wrecked.

Yukina was not skillful enough to gloss all this over with a suitable report. She reported what had occurred to the Lion King Agency, leaving out the minor details.

Yukina would no doubt be recalled by the Lion King Agency for failure as a watcher. Probably soon.

If it ended in no more but discipline that would be fine, but it would not be strange for her Attack Mage qualification to be revoked and for her name to be stricken from the Lion King Agency's rolls. That, too, would be Yukina's sole responsibility. It was the result of her own conduct, so it could not be helped. Besides, Yukina did not regret what she had done.

If she had any regrets, she regretted only that she would never meet Kojou Akatsuki again.

He was a flake, so she worried about him. After all, if she wasn't by his side, there was no telling what he might do—

"—!"

The intercom's chime caught her by surprise.

The monitor displayed a man in a home delivery company uniform, no doubt working for the Lion King Agency.

Yukina unlocked the door for him and went into the entryway. However, by then the deliveryman had already vanished. In his place, a large package had been left in front of the apartment's entrance.

It was a long aluminum case. It was a trunk called a tour case, used for transporting guitars and other musical instruments. Yukina was perplexed as she brought the case into the room.

She undid the clasp and opened the case.

Then Yukina sucked in her breath.

Inside the case was a silver-colored spear, all repairs complete, every bit as good as new.

"A lot happened, but the result was as you expected...I would suppose?"

Nighttime, Saikai Academy, high school section. A lone male student was in a classroom that should have been empty.

As he leaned against a wall, there was a crow right beside him.

The young man spoke casually to the bird, which was considered an ill omen, as it rested on the windowsill.

"Having thus obtained a blood partner, Kojou Akatsuki gained a single Beast Vassal. So he's one step closer to becoming a full Fourth Primogenitor, but what I don't get is why you'd go out of your way to wake up a monster that can raze a city without blinking..."

The crow silently listened to the young man's words. Its body, covered in jet-black feathers, was strangely flat and smooth. From its angles and lack of thickness, it looked like it had been simply crafted from paper. This was not a real bird. It was a shikigami born from ritual energy.

"The timing's too convenient in the first place. Surely you knew of the Lotharingian Armed Apostle hunting demons, and his objective of seizing back the holy relic, from the beginning?"

The young asked the crow with a critiquing tone.

"And sending an apprentice Sword Shaman with a strong sense of justice to watch over Kojou at a time like that, it's really transparent. So, Kojou drinking that girl's blood was part of your scheme from the beginning. Geez, you sure put that serious girl through the wringer here."

"...However, thanks to this, the Fourth Primogenitor's awakening has been hastened."

The crow suddenly opened its mouth and spoke with an elderly voice.

"He already exists, whether we reach out to him or not. Therefore, it is best to control him and have one more card to play."

"So, Yukina Himeragi is the bell around the neck of the sleeping beast."

Making a heavy sigh, as if pitying her, the young man shifted his gaze beyond the window.

"Certainly given Kojou's personality, no doubt he'd never do anything cruel to the valiant girl, but…I'm sure she has no idea the Lion King Agency sent her to be the Fourth Primogenitor's lover. Poor thing."

"There has never been a Primogenitor born to rule a Dominion in this nation's entire history. National survival is at stake; may she play her role very nicely."

Something like a chuckle came out of the crow's throat.

The tone had been a jesting one, but there was no concealing the gloom that came with it.

Even to them, this plan was a double-edged sword that could invite a great calamity. She must have felt like she was tossing a lit lighter into a warehouse full of gunpowder and taking her chances.

However, it seemed that for the moment, things were proceeding as they had hoped.

Yukina Himeragi had most certainly closed the distance between her and Kojou Akatsuki.

"And not all that may befall her deserves pity. To be the partner of an emperor means to be an empress."

"Well, that might be so, but…it does give me a somewhat conflicted feeling."

As he spoke, the young man looked at a table in the center of the classroom. That was where his childhood friend sat.

If she ever found out that he was *the actual watcher of Kojou Akatsuki*, no doubt she'd fly into a rage. He really wasn't looking forward to that.

"Now then, the Fourth Primogenitor appears at turning points in history. Does his appearance portend good or evil? …Kojou Akatsuki. At times the Western European Church refers to the Lightbringer, another name for the fallen angel Lucifer… Hmm, very interesting…"

So a servant of God, or the Devil who would destroy the Earth—

Leaving those words behind, the crow was undone.

It became a simple sheet of paper, dancing atop the wind.

Watching it go until it faded into the dark nighttime sky, the young man stroked his hair as if fed up with it all.

"Sheesh… You've got a rough road ahead of you, buddy."

His utterance was somehow playful, but the sound was wasted on an empty classroom.

Kojou Akatsuki was lying on his face, sitting in a terrace seat in the corner of the student cafeteria.

It was Monday, after class, having surmounted a weekend immersed in homework. Here in the terrace-style café of the student cafeteria, male students who'd spotted unsold bread at fire sale prices and athletic club members before practice made the place unusually lively.

Looking at them from the side, Kojou made a deep sigh.

"So hot… I'm melting. Burning. Turning to ash… And what's with *more* supplemental exams? That little shrimp homeroom teacher's doing it to have fun tormenting me, I just know it!"

He complained to no one in particular as he gazed at the textbooks spread over the table.

Apparently the results of the last make-up test during summer vacation were far from the necessary number of points to make up for the piles and piles of days of missed attendance. On top of that, they'd looked into the issue of his skipping class on the first day after summer break, with even more make-up exams being assigned as a result. *Not much of a reward for saving Itogami Island from almost sinking*, thought Kojou.

The only saving grace was that since that incident, Asagi had been oddly kind toward him.

Even that very day, she'd gone out of her way, staying after class to help him study for the extra make-up tests.

Having been caught up in the Keystone Gate incident, she knew that it'd been Kojou and Yukina who'd stopped Eustach and saved Itogami Island. Perhaps as a result, from Asagi's point of view, Kojou had risked his own life to save hers.

That was actually just Kojou's arbitrary decision, not something Asagi should think of as a debt to be repaid, but Kojou was grateful for the study help all the same.

Asagi was currently away, off to buy something to drink from the counter.

"…"

"Now get these done before I come back," she'd said of the pile of problems from which Kojou was subconsciously averting his eyes.

Asagi had incredibly good grades, but perhaps thanks to her being a genius, she wasn't all that good at teaching others, to the degree he could understand the younger Yukina's explanations a lot better.

But, he couldn't rely on Yukina, either.

She'd said she'd no doubt be removed from watch duty over Kojou. She'd probably return to High God Forest and resume her training as a Sword Shaman.

Kojou had no reason to stop her. A girl like her being sent to watch over him had been a strange situation to begin with.

However, the idea of an Attack Mage being assigned to watch duty in her stead rubbed him the wrong way somehow. He didn't like it.

And Kojou liked even less the idea of Yukina being assigned to another mission he'd know nothing about.

When he pictured her fighting alone and being hurt, he had unpleasant feeling, like something heavy was sinking inside his chest.

Unable to explain why he felt so irritated, Kojou made an anguished groan.

"Studying for exams, Akatsuki-senpai? This formula is wrong."

Suddenly, he heard a familiar voice close to him. It was a somewhat blunt, and so, serious-sounding voice.

When Kojou raised his head in surprise, there stood Yukina, the setting sun at her back.

Of course, she was wearing a school uniform with a black guitar case on her back. A doll looking something like a beckoning cat mascot had been tied to a corner of the case, dangling.

"H-Himeragi?"

"Hello, Senpai. What's wrong? You look so surprised."

"Er...so then, inside that guitar case is...?"

"Yes, Snowdrift Wolf. Yesterday, it came back from repairs."

"Er...um, why?"

"I suppose because it's necessary for watch duty over you, Senpai. After all, this is equipment for fighting the Fourth Primogenitor."

Yukina conveyed that in her usual serene tone. However, she was smiling, her eyes looking a bit happy.

Perplexed, Kojou slapped his cheek.

"Wait, this means you're gonna keep watching over me, Himeragi?"

"Apparently so. Actually, I'm not really certain why they granted permission for that either but…are you disappointed, Senpai?"

As Yukina spoke, she made a small giggle with a teasing expression.

Kojou made a strained smile and shook his head.

"Nah. I'm glad… I mean, you look excited, too, Himeragi."

"Eh? I do? Er, yes, well, really it's all the same to…"

"I mean, um, hey. After all, I did *that* in the park with you, Himeragi."

"*That*…meaning?"

As Yukina tilted her head with a dubious look, redness seemed to suddenly explode over her cheeks. No doubt she'd finally remembered what she'd done to get Kojou to drink her blood.

"Ah, er… That's… If at all possible, I'd like you to forget about that…"

"No way that's gonna happen. Nothing going on with your body?" Kojou asked with a serious expression for once.

He'd been told that just having a vampire drink your blood had no great effect. But there were rare exceptions. Making someone a "Blood Servant" who wasn't prepared for eternal life with him would've been a huge problem.

"Don't worry," Yukina said with a nod. "I did check with a testing kit, but it's all right. I already knew that according to the phase of the moon, it was a comparatively safe day."

"I, ah, see… Well, I'm glad you're safe, Himeragi."

Kojou breathed a sigh of relief.

"Yes," Yukina said with a smile. "Sorry for making you worry like that."

"Nah… I'm the one who should say I'm sorry."

"S-Senpai, I don't think you have anything to apologize for. At the time, I was the one who said I wanted you to do it…"

As if embarrassed, Yukina lowered her face, speaking in a low voice. Kojou ran a hand over his head, feeling very awkward himself.

"Well, I suppose that's true, but it must've been a painful experience for you, too, Himeragi."

"It's all right. All that happened was a tiny bit of blood loss, and the mark from where you sucked is nearly gone already."

Yukina touched her hand to her neck. There was only a small, unobtrusive adhesive on it. "Well, I'm glad," Kojou said as he nodded, when…

"—?!"

His entire body froze instantly.

A shadow slowly rose, like a zombie, from the plant behind Yukina. It was a female student wearing the same junior high uniform as Yukina. She wore her long hair tied up, giving her a lively aura.

"Hmm… Kojou-kun sucked something of Yukina's?" she asked in a low voice that seemed to seethe with anger.

Kojou went pale as he looked up at the speaker's face.

"N-Nagisa?! What are you doing here…?"

"I met Asagi-chan at the counter earlier and heard you're studying for exams, so I thought I'd come and encourage you, but then you two were having a conversation I couldn't ignore. So I wanted to come ask for a few more *details*."

Nagisa Akatsuki turned an aggressive, smiling face toward her older brother. It was her habit to put on a broad smile that twitched at the edges of her lips when she was at the peak of her anger.

"W-wait, Nagisa. I think you are probably misunderstanding something. Right, Himeragi?"

Kojou desperately tried to hold his little sister at bay. Yukina, standing beside him, nodded her head up and down as well.

However, Kojou and Yukina's united front only seemed to deepen Nagisa's anger.

"Hmm, a misunderstanding? Where's the misunderstanding? Kojou was Yukina's first time, it hurt, and on top of that you're worried about her physical condition, so what am I misunderstanding exactly…?"

"I'm saying, everything you're imagining is a complete misunderstanding, but…"

Midway, a conflicted expression came over Kojou.

He couldn't tell Nagisa what had really happened. She didn't know that Kojou was a vampire. If at all possible, he didn't want her to know that for a while longer.

"Wait, you said you met Asagi. Where'd she go?" Kojou asked back as calmly as he could to somehow change the subject.

However, Nagisa replied in a chilly tone…

"Asagi has been right here listening to you and Yukina talking the whole time."

"Huh?"

Kojou finally realized that there was another female student standing next to Nagisa.

Because she'd splendidly kept her aura in check, he had not realized she was present.

She wore her uniform stylishly and had an eye-catching face. However, those beautiful features now burned with a frigid, angry fire that made her look like a goddess of vengeance.

"W-wait, Asagi. I thought I'd explain this to you sometime, but there are some very deep circumstances involved in—wait, why are you angry anyway?"

Kojou instantly tried to apologize with all his might. However…

"You're the worst!"

Speaking with no expression on her face, she dumped the contents of the paper cup in her hand over Kojou's head without mercy. It had a sour smell to it. Cranberry soda and grape juice, apparently.

"S-Senpai?!"

Yukina took her handkerchief out in a hurry as she saw the red liquid dripping down Kojou as if it were a large amount of blood. Asagi drew near Yukina as well in a show of hostility.

"You, too. This is a good opportunity for me to ask, so what exactly is your relationship to Kojou?"

"I'm Akatsuki-senpai's watcher."

Yukina replied calmly. Her demeanor looked gentle on the surface, but Yukina was really a martial artist as well. Invisible sparks scattered about as the two glared at each other.

"Watch? So like a stalker?"

"You are mistaken. I simply thought I'd watch so that Senpai does not commit any wrongdoing—"

"Then what are you doing seducing this idiot?!"

"W, well… You have a…point there…"

Perhaps feeling pangs of guilt, Yukina seemed to concede the issue.

"It's not like that! Deny it, Himeragi!"

Kojou unwittingly shouted as he wiped the juice from his eyes.

"Everyone, this is an incubus! A sex fiend who laid a hand on his little sister's classmate—!"

"Stop it, Asagi! Listen to me a little!!"

Shocked, Kojou got up with all his might, hoping to silence Asagi's outcry with his loud voice, to no avail.

"Kojou, you big lecher! Deviant! Pervert! This is filthy even for you!"

"P-please stop this, both of you. Certainly Akatsuki-senpai has some lewdness about him, but..."

"Nagisa, you pipe down, too. Himeragi, you're not helping at all here!"

Attracted by the clamor of the girls' voices, the eyes of the students nearby converged onto Kojou.

The male students bore expressions of envy and jealousy, but disgust came over the female students' faces like they were looking at a filthy criminal. As Kojou felt their gazes prick his back, he unwittingly looked out the window.

Someone kill me, now.

So long as his flesh bore the curse of immortality, that was a prayer that would go unanswered.

However, he did not yet realize...

...That the daily travails of the world's mightiest vampire, the Fourth Primogenitor, Kojou Akatsuki, had only just begun...

Afterword

Maybe it was because I watched spirit TV specials before the era of CG, but even though I was a smart-aleck brat who didn't believe in ghosts and specters one whit, I became very fond of monsters that had acquired strange powers and the sense they were much stronger than people.

This is just my arbitrary imagination at work, but I think monsters are divided into two broad categories, with one being the lone villain or hero who walks a lonely path beyond our image of the human norm. The other is fear of a phenomenon beyond human comprehension, such as natural disaster or "death," given physical form. And I feel that some things mix the two together. Yes, for example, a hybrid monster such as the vampire.

While similar to humans, they are beings that have obtained powers beyond human control. What do they desire? How do they live? These themes have been repeated time and time again since the age of myth, yet how such beings live still tugs strongly at our hearts.

And so, I deliver unto you *Strike the Blood*, Vol. 1.

It's been a while since I had a new series. The main character is the world's mightiest vampire. Having said that, he does give off a feeling of *uwaa, he's not that bright*, but on the inside, it's a pretty straightforward school action fantasy. Incidentally, in baseball, the straight pitches come with a few curveballs mixed in…but anyway, if you're having fun, that's great.

And this work is also another kind of tale, that of the out-of-control monster and the people who accept him, and who are in turn saved by him. This is a myth that has been handed down in many flavors, but I really like stories like that. Sometimes it's a nameless boy or girl who stands up the monster beyond human comprehension, and it is they who come to be called *heroes* afterward.

Often, their weapons are youth, reckless courage, and love. That's why, even if the main characters look like a pair of idiots causing trouble to everyone around them, it can't really be helped. A lot of flirting is a good thing.

Now then, getting this novel published was thanks to the aid of a great many people.

In particular, Hideyuki Furuhashi-sensei first proposed the "Fourth Primogenitor" naming and offered many suggestions and pieces of advice for the content of the work. Thank you as always.

I want to thank Manyako-sama very much for providing such wonderful illustrations for this work. Please take such good care of me in the future as well. Also, to all those I caused trouble to, and everyone who helped me, let me take this opportunity to say my thanks.

And to all the readers who took the plunge and bought the first novel of a new series, I thank you from the bottom of my heart. Really, thanks.

This is the last part, but on March 11, 2011, a large earthquake occurred known as the Great East Japan Earthquake.

I am writing this afterword several days after it occurred.

Thus, as I write this, there are still many people involved in emergency disaster relief, dealing with the aftermath at the epicenter. I'm worried that there are still many people missing. I pray in the hope that as many people as possible may yet be saved. I also wish that everyone will be able to return to their peaceful daily lives as quickly as possible.

This work is a story about monsters and heroes. However, I think that natural disasters and scientific technology running amok are very much monsters of the modern age, and those who stand against them are the true heroes.

In the movie *Spider-Man 2*, one of the characters says, "I believe there's a hero in all of us."

This work is a story about monsters and heroes. Because of circumstances like these, if you, in reading this, have felt tranquility and courage for even a single moment, I have no greater delight.

HAVE YOU BEEN TURNED ON TO LIGHT NOVELS YET?

IN STORES NOW!

SWORD ART ONLINE, VOL. 1–5
SWORD ART ONLINE, PROGRESSIVE 1–2

The chart-topping light novel series that spawned the explosively popular anime and manga adaptations!

MANGA ADAPTATION AVAILABLE NOW!

SWORD ART ONLINE © Reki Kawahara ILLUSTRATION: abec
KADOKAWA CORPORATION ASCII MEDIA WORKS

ACCEL WORLD, VOL. 1–4

Prepare to accelerate with an action-packed cyber-thriller from the bestselling author of *Sword Art Online*.

MANGA ADAPTATION AVAILABLE NOW!

ACCEL WORLD © Reki Kawahara ILLUSTRATION: HIMA
KADOKAWA CORPORATION ASCII MEDIA WORKS

SPICE AND WOLF, VOL. 1–15

A disgruntled goddess joins a traveling merchant in this light novel series that inspired the *New York Times* bestselling manga.

MANGA ADAPTATION AVAILABLE NOW!

SPICE AND WOLF © Isuna Hasekura ILLUSTRATION: Jyuu Ayakura
KADOKAWA CORPORATION ASCII MEDIA WORKS